The Prophet's Trilogy: Book One

The Prophet's Shield

Sarah Dalziel

©Sarah Dalziel

Copyright Information:

Copyright © 2015 by Sarah Dalziel

All rights reserved.

Published 2015 by Sarah Dalziel Media

Duplication of this content is prohibited by copyright law. Permissible use is limited to small excerpts used in works of review or critique. For inquiries contact: sarah@sarahdalzielmedia.com

Disclaimer:

This is a work of fantasy fiction, any resemblance to real people, places, or events is accidental.

Dedication:

To all who supported and encouraged me to pursue the story and to not stop writing when it got difficult.

Acknowledgements:

Thank you to my parents who worked around my writing endeavors, beta-read my story, and were always encouraging.

Also thank you to all my friends, online and in real life, who asked about my writing and encouraged me to talk about it. And to all who said they were looking forward to when this story was published.

Thank you also to my friends in the game, Lord of the Rings Online, who listened when I needed to vent, and challenged me to writing sprints when my motivation was lagging.

Contents

Chapter 1: Beginnings 1
Chapter 2: Friends 5
Chapter 3: Rest for a time 10
Chapter 4: A time of learning 16
Chapter 5: Light Training 18
Chapter 6: Changes in the making 22
Chapter 7: The Giving 28
Chapter 8: Visions in the Night 36
Chapter 9: To School 43
Chapter 10: Raiders of the Bar Hills 47
Chapter 11: Decisions 52
Chapter 12: The First Fight 59
Chapter 13: A First Enemy 67
Chapter 14: On to the School 73
Chapter 15: Enemies or Friends 79
Chapter 16: Day One 87
Chapter 17: Magic Class 90
Chapter 18: Specialties 97
Chapter 19: Secret Learning 101
Chapter 20: Learning in Darkness 103
Chapter 21: Detection 108
Chapter 22: Hiding the Trail 120
Chapter 23: Revived and Strengthened 125
Chapter 24: Through the Swamps 134
Chapter 25: A New Light 138

Chapter 26: An Ambuscade 143
Chapter 27: The Party Grows 146
Chapter 28: Stories of the Former Time 150
Chapter 29: Friends in Need 154
Chapter 30: Friends Rediscovered 161
Chapter 31: Visions in the Night 167
Chapter 32: Training in the Swamp...173
Chapter 33: Undead Encounter 180
Chapter 34: Decisions in the Making 187
Chapter 35: March to the Forest 192
Chapter 36: A Challenging Encounter 199
Chapter 37: Into the Forest..205
Chapter 38: Preparing for Battle 209
Chapter 39: The Calm Before The Storm 213
Chapter 40: The Battle 217
Chapter 41: Endings 223

Chapter 1: Beginnings

I struggled into awareness. A headache pounding through my temples. It was cold, and something dug into the flesh on my back and shoulders. I tried to move, but my limbs would not respond. I tried again, panic welling as my right arm refused to move. The soft clank of chain hitting stone rose from my efforts.

Feeling like millstones weighted my eyes, I forced them open. Gazing up on a drear sky, grey with the first hint of dawn. I struggled again, adrenaline giving me strength and I felt a slight give from the chain that bound my left wrist.

Twisting my head I saw the chain was held by a simple wooden peg, slotted into a small ring within the stone on which I lay. The wood was weak, and a short struggle sufficed to snap the wood, freeing the end of the chain.

With my left side relatively free, I twisted to look at the fastening of my right wrist. It was the same as the left, and using the left hand it was a simple matter to wriggle free the fastening peg from the wrist shackle. A few more seconds sufficed to free both my wrists from the encumbering chains.

The leg fastenings were stronger, being fastened with metal bolts instead of wooden pegs. As I began wiggling the metal fasteners a faint sound whispered past. I paused, the sound was low and rhythmic. I did not recognise it, yet it added urgency to my struggle. I kept tugging. The fastener was partially rusted and resisted my efforts.

Suddenly the metal fastener gave, and the chain tumbled onto the stone with a rasping clang. I froze, feeling my heart pounding in my temples. The sound paused for a moment, and then continued, gradually growing louder in the still air.

The second pin was, if anything, harder than the first. But, finally it also gave way. I had changed position so the falling chain did not rasp against the stone. Slipping away from the spot I had been bound I saw I was on a low hill.

Lying flat, I crept to the edge of a ring of tall stones. A short distance away I saw a procession winding steadily toward the hill. Torches cast the walkers in a red glow, a wicked glow it seemed. Gazing upon the steadily approaching line, a sense of unease, and then fear grew.

It looked like the road wound up the hillside before me. Turning from the oncoming procession, I crouched and dashed to the far side of the hill. Creeping through the stones I slid slowly down against the hillside. A few low bushes provided temporary shelter from anyone one on the hilltop. I began to descend, utilizing the bushes as a screen. Half way down, I stumbled over a stone and skidded roughly down the rest of the hill.

Scrambling to my feet at the bottom of the hill I paused. The stones were now lit with light, likely from the procession's torches. I could see shadows of movement against the stones. Movement that was foreign to me yet drew me as mosquitos are drawn to the living.

Dread crept within me again, yet curiosity held me captive. Curiosity, as tight as the chains had held me a few minutes before. Crouching down, within the shelter of a cluster of leafy bushes, I watched the unfolding drama of shadows on stone.

Shadows moved in a circle, holding dishes or braziers of some type. They marched around and around the central flat stone, the same stone from which I had escaped. A confusion of shadows approached the stone, suddenly sharpening into the form of a girl in the center, being dragged forward by two men. She struggled desperately, and was forcibly fastened upon the stone.

Curiosity rising higher, I stole back up the hillside. Feeling an irresistible draw, I crept forward and soon crouched behind one of the standing stones. Close enough to listen and see, but far enough away to flee if I was detected.

The men wore long robes, ranging in tone from light to dark blue. All the robes were belted with a plain rope, some with one knot and others with seven knots. The girl, now chained on the central stone, wore a plain creamy white robe. The man in the darkest blue robe stepped to the head of the girl. The marching stopped as he raised his hand and began to speak:

"My brothers, we have long awaited this day. We stand here as the veil between the spirit realm and the mortal plain grows thin. It is the time to appease the Raphey and this maid was chosen as the sacrifice."

As he began speaking the maid stiffened, her slight trembling causing the chains to rustle. As the man declared her a sacrifice she cried out:

"In the time between times the veil grows thin.
Between world and world the twining doth dim.
From dark unto light the colors do weave. As the one enters in who this world would reave.
Yet even in darkness the light shineth still, as reaver doth enter his doom enters too.
To face unafraid mid darkness and blood a maiden of valor, of shield and sword, of magic and light like never before.
Enters she now this world of death."

The maid paused, gasping for breath. The priest gazed upon her, a sneer distorting his face as he said: "And what pray are the characteristics of this maiden of doom to the Reaver we gather to welcome this dawning day?"

The maid replied: "By these signs you shall know her:
Faith is her shield when all seems lost,
Truth is her sword in which she trusts.
Light is her garment, mercy her belt.

When all seems lost she never despairs, and the darkest storm her friend shall bear.
Of her deeds all will speak, from greatest to least.
But to you who so ask, she shall never be revealed for this very night her doom is unveiled.
When the Reaver falls her own doom will come. "

"Silence!" the priest exclaimed "The sun is about to rise, you witch, you would have us miss our only chance." Seizing an ornate dagger from somewhere within his robe's folds, he stepped to the bound maid's side. Falling silent, she ignored him, twisting her head to the right, and gazing into my eyes. A smile crept over her lips, and a voice like a summer's breeze whispered within my mind.

"You are our hope. When the tor is vacant flee to the east. You will be hunted"

The chanting of the head priest interrupted the voice. His eyes were fixed upon the westernmost stone pillar. As the sun's first ray struck the pillar, his knife fell.

The maiden's blood poured over the stone and the priests began dancing around. Leaping, shouting, and chanting their voices grew loud. Suddenly, the sun kissed stone shuddered. The ground before it split apart. Something, in form like a man, rose from the ground. It was taller than a normal man, and dread surrounded the being like a garment.

As the ground stopped trembling, the priests fell upon their faces, and worshiped what had come forth. Hailing it as "the Reaver, son of Raphey destroyer of nations"

The Reaver stood, slowly scanning the worshiping priests. "Who summons me?" he said, still watching.

Trembling, the head priest stepped forward, his hand grasping at the knots in his belt, "We summoned you, Great One, tell us your will"

The Reaver's stance softened, as if he relaxed, then he spoke "Lead me to the seat of power, it shall begin there."

Turning with surprising swiftness, the priests left the tor with the Reaver striding along in the center. If they were trying to be secretive they were failing. I grimaced, the Reaver stood head and shoulders above the surrounding priests.

Chapter 2: Friends

As I turned to leave the tor, as the priestess had called it, my eye caught the glint of metal coming from the ground. Turning I saw that her mantle, cast aside by the priests, had fallen open upon the ground with a golden brooch just catching the light. Although she said "flee," something within me could not leave the mantle there and I crept forward, into the light of forgotten torches.

Slipping over the stones, I lifted the mantle from the ground. The soft wool was comforting against my bare arms, and I realized that the air was chill. Slipping on the mantle, I adjusted the fabric to hide the brooch completely. Turning to leave, I paused again.

Something drew me closer to the altar. As I crouched alongside the girl's still body, I began to tremble.

A flood of light overwhelmed my senses. I could see nothing except the blazing brightness of pure light. Slowly the intensity dimmed, and a figure became visible through the light. Despite the brilliance and suddenness, a sense of peace pervaded my mind. A feeling of hope also rose, despite the horror which I had just witnessed, the horror of innocence being used to summon forth darkness and evil.

A voice spoke, perhaps from the figure, but seeming to come from everywhere at once.

"Fear not child of light, for as you have sought the light you shall never need to fear the darkness. Stretch forth your hand and take that which belonged to the prophetess. You stand now in her stead."

As the voice finished, I felt a liquid sensation, like oil, pouring over my head. Still confused I spoke. "Who am I? What should I do?"

The voice replied "you shall learn and grow. But remember this, at all times embrace the light, fear no darkness and do not embrace it. By light will you be guided when everything seems hopeless. You are anointed the prophetess for this hour."

I knelt, trembling as the light faded. Opening my eyes in astonishment, I gazed again upon the altar. A wind had shifted the prophetess' robe, and a golden dagger was now visible, strapped upon her leg. Having been told to take what was hers, I stretched out my hand. As I touched the dagger it loosened and fell into my grasp.

Swiftly, moved by an inner sense of urgency that had not been there previously, I strapped the dagger on my own leg. I noticed that I was clothed in a simple white robe, even as the prophetess had been. This was strange, but I could not grasp why. I sensed that though the robe would make me more visible in darkness, the forest could still provide cover.

Footsteps sounded nearby. A voice rose in anger.

"Fool, you knew she was the anointed prophetess yet you left her body unguarded. Do you not know that only the next prophet or prophetess can take the symbols from her? If we do not watch, how are we to know who our enemy has chosen this time?"

Turning I fled blindly down the eastern side of the tor. Hardly had I taken a dozen steps when I slipped on the dew wet grass and slid down the hill, tumbling roughly into the center of a thick patch of thorny shrubs.

The voice, which I now recognized as the Reaver's rang out again: "Twice a fool, the mantle and dagger are gone. A new prophet has arisen to wage war against me! Search the surrounding area and leave no bush or stone unsearched. This prophet must be destroyed before they learn the power within the light that they serve."

At that moment the prophetess' words rang into my ears "flee to the east for you will be hunted." Unfreezing from my crouch I turned from the bloodstained tor and fled. The light of dawn steadily increased as I raced through the forest.

The land was a combination of woods and fields spread over rolling hills with gentle valleys. It did not take long to get out of sight of the tor and through a few small woods. Steadily I walked on, often tripping and stumbling over the tangled grasses. It was a struggle to make my way through the bramble thicketed forests, where game trails are few and far between, and never lead in the right direction.

As the sun rose above the horizon, I stumbled out of a larger forested sector and found myself facing a large, and rapidly awakening farm. Half a dozen cows moo'd their way across the field, heading for a large, turf thatched building gated onto their field. To the south of the cows, two horses cantered their way over to a smaller building, also thatched with turf with walls of woven branches daubed with mud. Crouching in the low bushes at the very edge of the forest, I watched these animals and their curious looking home. Why it looked curious, I really do not know for it seemed normal in this place. All the same, it was strange to my eyes.

A man appeared, heading from a patch of trees in which his house resided. He headed to the north side, where the cows were. He began moving the cows around one at a time, into the barn then back to the field. As he was working, two young men came from the same direction. One appeared to be a child, while the other verged on adulthood. Both headed to the horses, and began brushing them down, then harnessing them. One was harnessed to a wagon, the other, larger horse, to a plow.

The older youth took the plow horse and headed to the east of the horse pasture. There was an open and barren field where he began plowing. The younger child led the wagon horse toward the barn and tethered it to a post of some type outside. He then entered, seeming to be helping the first man I had seen.

Their activity was peaceful, normal, and after the strange things and the horror of the previous hours I rested, watching them. Watching and resting, instead of moving on. As I watched the man appeared again, glancing around briskly as if looking for someone. Shaking his head, and glancing toward the steadily rising sun, he gestured and sent the child off toward the house.

A few moments later, the child returned running and gesturing. His father paused, and gestured while he talked. Suddenly he sent the child off to call the older son from plowing. Hardly had the two sons returned before the man's wife also appeared, walking briskly. She seemed agitated. Frequently the father gestured to the west, the direction of my hiding place, and I wondered what they were speaking of.

The older son gave an abrupt movement, and rapidly removing the wagon horse from its traces, he mounted and galloped away. He followed a path that ran north and west. After a few more moments talking, the other three family members dispersed in different directions. They seemed to be searching and calling for someone named Angusina.

Glancing around, as tiredness overwhelmed me, I noticed a snug looking hiding place. Hidden among the roots of an oak tree, covered over with holly bushes, there was a hollow thickly lined with moss. Creeping into it, I saw it was nearly impossible to see out of. As I relaxed on the mossy sward and drifted toward slumber, my right hand strayed up over my chest. Just above my right breast, a thin indentation, as of an old scar, met my searching fingers. Vaguely I wondered how a scar had come there even as exhaustion overcame me and I slipped into a dreamless slumber.

I woke with a start, a voice yelling nearby. "Father, there are tracks here of a person. Should we try and locate them?"

I froze, my trail at the edge of the forest was discovered. I moved to the edge of my hollow, and peered through the intertwined holly bushes. The lad and man, his father, from that morning were searching the woods, and were now following my trial to the oak. The lad spoke again, seemingly careless that the one they were tracking could be so near.

"Do you think that Finan has discovered anything? It seems impossible that we should find no sign of Angusina at any of her haunts."

"I do not know" the man said, pausing and glancing around. His eye rested on the oak and he paused, laying a hand on his son's shoulder. "I fear we will never see Angusina again. The priests have always despised and threatened her. It is for her successor we must worry. Whoever it is, they will be hunted, aye and hated even as she was."

The man seemed sad, yet his gaze was keen and never left the oak. Glancing at his son, he smiled and said. "You have good eyes to see a trial that was made at dawn this morning. Yet I think the maker of the trail is closer than you realized."

"What do you mean father?" The lad said, cocking his head and glancing at the trail curiously. "The trail is old, this morning as you said, so why should its maker still be near at evening tide?"

"We shall ask the maker of this trail when we find her. At least I think it is a her and I think she is quite near."

My heart froze at his words. The prophetess had said I would be hunted. If I were hunted who could I trust? and how would I know who to trust? I did not move as they approached. The man was tense, seeming excited or nervous.

There was no route out of the hiding place without revealing myself to those now approaching. No longer did the hollow appear to offer protection and secrecy. It had become a trap and a cage holding me in. When within a few yards the men paused, and the father glanced around. Inspecting my trial again it seemed.

He spoke "We know you are hiding under the oak. Your trail betrays you. You have nothing to fear from us."

The child added quickly, "and I'm sure you can join us for supper too, you must be hungry after being here all day."

There was nothing else to do. They knew my location. Even if there was no trail, the abrupt growling of my stomach would lead them in from a mile away. I rose slowly, stretching out the kinks from sleeping on the ground. Then slipped carefully through the holly and stood before them.

The man nodded, "I am Brenan Donoghue, and what you see is my farm. We are the farthest distant farmstead here so there is little fear of interruption. As my son mentioned, you are welcome to join us for a meal, or many. You seem worn and weary and a few days of safety may be needed."

My voice shook as I replied "you are kind, and I gratefully accept your kind offer."

Chapter 3: Rest for a time

When I tried to step forward, my legs gave way and I stumbled onto my knees. Brenan knelt down, and with a gentle hand on my elbow, aided me to rise. He supported me as we walked slowly across his fields.

Due to my weakness the sun had set by the time we reached Brenan's home. The house was tucked back from the barns and hidden within a grove of rowan and oak trees. Tired and sore as I was, the home appeared as a vision of peace and shelter within the darkening night.

As we arrived at the door, Brenan's wife appeared. Her eyes were red from weeping and worry crowded her features. Looking me over, her brow furrowed and she turned to her husband about to speak. He cut her off saying gently "our guest is weary, and it is right that we offer hospitality. I have extended it for as long as she needs to rest. While she is here she is my second cousin's sister-in-law's niece."

His wife raised her eyebrows at the distant relationship story. Then she said gently "You have arrived here during a time of great grief, but our hearth and home are thine for as long as is needed, I am Calawen."

My eyes filled with tears, as the light fell upon Calawen's face. The resemblance was clear. The maiden of the tor was her daughter. I spoke, my voice wavering "Thank you Calawen, and Brenan for extending your hospitality to a stranger." I paused, but could say no more as I choked with emotion.

Calawen smiled, gentleness rising over her earlier question "you're exhausted child, come we will talk about yourself later. For tonight, you shall eat with us and then rest. There is no rush to speak."

Taking my arm, she led me into the house. It was a small home, with only two rooms on the lower floor. One room forming a sitting and work area, the other room the kitchen and dining area. A ladder in the kitchen corner lead to the upstairs, where I guessed the sleeping area was. Calawen guided me to a chair by the dining table, close but not too close to the fire. The night had become quite chilly.

Glancing at her husband, she said "Finan has not yet returned from town. I am worried."

Brenan nodded, his jaw tightening perceptibly, "Sometimes I wonder at our eldest, Angusina was the only one who could talk with him with any success. Otherwise he would always be off on one of his harebrained schemes. One time he even tried to run away and join the raiders." He shook his head, "I will take the brown and check along the road, hopefully he is nearly home but if not" his voice trailed away. Turning he headed out, and Calawen turned back to her cooking.

"Calanan go and fetch some preserves from the cellar, we have a guest tonight." Calawen said, glancing to her youngest son with a sad smile. Nodding, the lad dashed out of the house.

The kitchen and dining area was comfortable, though simple. Two chairs and two benches framed the main table, clearly used for both meal preparation and eating. Calawen moved efficiently around the room, shifting food in the oven. The oven was set into the stone wall alongside the open fire. She also was boiling water, and what appeared to be a type of broth over the fire. Calanan returned swiftly, carrying a crock of fruit preserved in syrup. Calawen ladled a few cups of fruit into one of her pans and began mixing another concoction.

About an hour after Brenan left, the canter of galloping hooves approached. Shortly Finan, the eldest son, and Brenan came to the kitchen. Brenan did not smile when he entered.

Glancing briefly at me, he nodded, and turned to the rest of the family.

"Some news can wait till after we have eaten, but one item cannot."

Calawen and Calanan exchanged glances, even as Brenan and Finan exchanged grim looks. Finan spoke "Angusina is dead, slain last night as a sacrifice on the Blood Tor. There is a rumor within the village that an apparition of darkness was summoned. Of course, no one knows for sure except the priests."

"And I guess they ain't speaking" Calawen snapped, turning briskly back to the fire hiding her tears. "We guessed they got ahold of Angusina, but who would ha thought they'd kill'er so fast?" she hiccupped.

"There is also some good news dear" Brenan said gently, "When the body was found by our friends, her ornaments, the mark of a prophetess, were already gone." Calawen stopped crying. Spinning around, she stared at her husband, seeming afraid that he was lying.

"You aren't just saying that to get me ta stop crying?" Calawen hesitated "for if that is true, then the new prophet is in greater danger for their presence is already known."

"It is true, and already the priests have called for people to watch for someone wearing the mantle and ornaments of a prophet. However, no one knows what happened to the one who took the ornaments. Most think they would have fled westward. I suspect however that the new prophetess fled to the east, toward us."

Calanan broke in, "Angusina had the ability to mindspeak, if she could see her successor she would have told them which direction to go!"

I froze, fingering the mantle I wore. None of them seem to have noticed it. Yet I knew it was one of the emblems of which they spoke.

Finan spoke, bitterness raging in his voice "surrounded by chanting druids gives no opportunity to speak, mentally or otherwise, to another. It would be illogical for anyone to flee into the wilderness here! It is too easy to be discovered. More likely the individual will be found in the cities or villages along the coast."

Calanan cringed and stared at the table as his brother criticized him.

Calawen broke into Finan's tirade gently "we have a guest, Finan, and she is weary from travel. Let us to meat, and we can continue this conversation when the meal is over. Grief is no excuse for ire." Finan fell silent and slowly took his seat.

A smile darted between Brenan and Calawen, as together they served the meal. I shifted to the bench closest to the fire, to the right of Brenan. Finan sat alongside me, with Calanan and Calawen on the other side.

The meal was eaten in silence. Indeed, I had not realized the extent of my hunger until I began eating. Nothing could have induced me to talk until that hunger was satisfied. Of meat there was little, but plenty of bread and boiled, baked, and fresh vegetables. However, the fruit pudding was the highlight of the meal, drawing surprised gasps from the two men and eager bouncing from Calanan.

After the meal and dishes were completed, we withdrew to the other room. It was set up as a work room. It contained spindles, a spinning wheel, bags of wool, wool cards, and a section of distaffs filled with combed flax fibres. Seating was relegated to three chairs and a few stools scattered around the small hearth.

Once we were all settled comfortably Brenan turned to me and said, "Now stranger, you have eaten with us, and the night draws on. We know nothing about you except that you came here tired, and hungry and from the west. What is your name?"

"My name is..." I started, and froze. I had no name within my memory. Indeed, no memory beyond the darkened tor of the night before. Questions whirled through my mind. Who was I? From whence had I come and how? What was I to tell them since I could not answer honestly?

Finan spoke, breaking through the whirl of my thoughts. "She is a nothing without a name or family" he sneered, "obviously a person who doesn't want us to know that she deserves only to be kicked out into the wilderness."

"Silence!" Calawen snapped, "It used to be that no questions were asked of a guest until the second day. We have asked on the first." She glanced over to Brenan, who was nodding quietly.

"Your mother is right, and it is not right for you to speak thus of a guest Finan. I am ashamed of your lack of manners. Even in grief and bitterness hospitality is mandated for our people. Impolite statements are not in line with hospitality. It is your bitterness speaking rather than yourself Finan. It were better you remain silent till it is mastered."

Brenan turned to face me fully and said gently "It seems that you desire to answer stranger, yet cannot. I do not wish to pry. But is it that you cannot remember or that you desire to remain silent?"

Brenan's compassion broke through my fear. Nearly crying I spoke, my voice barely above a whisper. "I do desire to answer your questions, yet I have no memory of my name, or indeed anything beyond yesterday's dawn."

Suddenly interested, Finan leaned forward, all traces of bitterness and angst vanishing as Brenan asked the one question I dreaded the most.

"Were you on the Blood Tor?"

"I do not know. In the dawn of yesterday I awoke on the tor west of this place" I said, glancing at Calawen for reassurance as I spoke.

Rising to his feet, Finan stepped forward and knelt before me. "First" he spoke swiftly "I ask your forgiveness for my harsh words. Grief is no excuse, as my father mentioned, for ill words and ill deeds. Do you forgive me?"

His voice was quick and his gaze intense. Tremors shook his shoulders as he knelt facing me. I hesitated, wondering at the sudden change in his demeanour.

Finally, I nodded, "I forgive you" I said, keeping my voice low.

Finan smiled slightly, "second, I have a gift, the gift of discerning memories from those who will permit me. As it seems you remember the tor with grief and some fear, I request your permission to probe your memories. That way you do not have to verbalize what you remember." He smiled gently, leaning forward a little.

I glanced at Brenan making eye contact. Brenan nodded almost imperceptibly and said "I think it would be a good idea. However Finan, you are not fully skilled or trained, for indeed there are none now who train the gifts of the Light. Do not seek to dig beyond the tor, touch only known memories."

Chapter 4: A time of learning

Finan nodded. His jaw tightening as he turned his eyes to mine. His gaze was intense, and seemed to burn into my very soul. As he gazed, the room slipped away and I found myself revisiting the Blood Tor. Gazing again upon all I remembered.

Time slide away and it seemed hours before my memory came to this place again. It was but a few moments in reality. Finan slowly turned his gaze away, and met his parent's eyes grimly.

"Our guest is indeed the foretold one, and the Reaver has indeed come forth. Alas that it was my sister's blood that paved his way."

Calawen's face paled at the mention of the Reaver. She glanced between Brenan and myself. Why she should glance toward me, as if seeking reassurance, I do not know. Yet somehow my presence brought a measure of comfort to her heart.

Brenan spoke slowly "so Angusina died upon the Blood Tor last night, and we did nothing. Yet even from that apparent benefit to our enemy, his greatest fear is unleashed upon him." Grim as his voice and words were, a slight smile formed as he continued. "Guest, since your name is unknown to you and to us I give you the name Mayim - which means water, for you move as smoothly as water in its gliding and as insidiously you will one day undermine the evil that entered our peaceful land."

Silence fell around the fire, as the glittering flame attracted the gazes of the family. They did not weep as Finan described the scene he had gleaned from my memory. Starting from when I had woken to the realization of being a captive, to the very moment of my discovery the tale was told. Finally, Brenan spoke, glancing at me "you have the ornaments upon you?"

I nodded, reaching to my throat I turned the folded mantle outward, exposing the hidden brooch. "The dagger is fastened upon my leg, at mid-thigh."

Finan smiled, "it is well hidden, and well thought of. If they cannot find anyone bearing the icons of the prophet what will they do instead? Father?"

"They will likely attempt to corrupt all the youth and with them the land, though how that would work I have no idea. Some of our families have strong beliefs and will not take kindly to interference. How great the Reaver's power will be, or is, we do not now know."

Calawen spoke, her tone quiet "the fire falls low, and Mayim needs rest if you men do not. Indeed I think we should all rest. Grief and sorrow will sap our strength if we rest not while we may."

Taking my hand, Calwen guided me up the ladder to the upper floor. It was more like a loft, with thin dividing walls and simple doors, than proper rooms. At the back, under the peak of the roof was a small room, set aside for a single occupant.

"This was Angusina's room, she will be glad that it is used again so soon." A tear slipped down Calawen's face. She turned to hide it and I touched her arm, stopping her from leaving.

"Thank you for your kindness. I only hope I can indeed become what you seem to think I am. I have no idea what being a prophetess means. I shall do my best to learn. I hate that which I beheld upon the tor. If there is a way, perhaps I can help end the darkness I felt when that creature appeared."

She nodded and a sad smile tugged at her mouth as she spoke. "Angusina spoke rightly that you were to come to us. You shall have all the training we can give you. Such training is little valued any longer. Light we have and skill in the sword. We shall train you in both as much as we can. For now, sleep well and rest, fear not the darkness. Light has always rested upon this home."

Nodding again, she closed the door and left me alone with my thoughts.

Chapter 5: Light Training

I woke with the dawn, birds sang in the trees and the comforting sound of the cows reached my ears. It had been a week since I arrived here, bedraggled, tired, hungry, and confused. Although I was still confused, I was no longer as out of place as I had been. Calawen had kindly refashioned Angusina's no longer needed garments to fit me, and so that they would not be quite as recognizable. Finan and Brenan encouraged me to get out of the house and join them in physically demanding labour, planting the fields and caring for the new calves.

But of all the things we did, perhaps the last few hours of the day were most important. After darkness fell we trained. Apparently there is a gift in this land that few know how to use. It is called simply "The Light" for its manifestation is light, among a rare scattering of other gifts. What it does uses light, and it is used only against the darkness of evil. Finan has some skill with it, being able to form globes that can either give light, or be hurled to deter a dark foe, as well as his mind skill. Brenan can coat his sword blade with light, making the lightest touch lethal to some of the dark foes. This technique is particularly lethal to the dark foes that are manifestations of hatred and fear.

The daily training had begun hardening my muscles, though they still ached in the evening. However learning to parry and attack with the sword or slowly gaining enough understanding to use the Light is worth the struggle.

I rose, dressing in a plain brown gown, and fastening the mantle as a sash across my chest, the brooch hidden against my waist in the folded fabric. I descended the ladder silently. I smiled remembering the first morning. I had forgotten the ladder and nearly fell through the loft opening. I would have fallen had not Finan been coming up the ladder and scared the sleep right out of me. Today it was still early indeed it was earlier than I had ever risen. The first blush of dawn was barely hinted at on the horizon and as I descended the ladder I asked myself "why did I wake so early, what is the purpose when I could have had an extra hour's sleep?"

Sitting at the table, I leaned my head in my hands, wondering. My thoughts turned toward the skill of using Light. Light was the anomaly within a world of anomalies. It was not magic, for magic was dark. Light operated on faith, trusting that the Light Giver would continue to reign, greatest of all. Despite the verbalized greatness of the Light Giver Brenan's family still feared the darkness, warriors though they were.

A voice intruded into my reflections:

"Faith alone will be enough
Even when the going's tough
Despair not in the dark or gloom
Remember what the light has won
When the hour darkest grows
Then the light has bright repose
Darker as the darkness gets
Light will shine the brighter yet
Trust and faith alone can seal
The Prophetess through the Reaver's fall"

The voice ended as abruptly as it had begun. Silence alone pervaded the house. No one was there, that was obvious or the two dogs would have barked. Rising and checking the windows and door confirmed that no one was here to speak. But then, who's was the voice? I shook my head. I would ask Calawen about it later. We would be preparing dinner together tonight.

The day was a normal day, at least for my understanding of normal. It began with caring for the animals and farm. After dinner we adjourned with jugs of cooled water to a small glade. The glade was about a mile from the farmstead. It took about fifteen minutes brisk walking or jogging to reach. We usually ran it, as Brenan always said "there is nothing that gives endurance like a good brisk run, provided you do not overdo it. A mile is a good start, and when you get to running it in one go you can start trying to run home at the end of the training too."

At the glade, the grass was soft, deep, and padded with moss. Besides being well sheltered, the trees were close and interwoven with brambles so there was no chance of our being spied upon. It was within the glade that we trained.

Training began with archery, as it required a cool hand unshaken from other exertions. After twenty shafts each were loosed, we collected the arrows and compared the day's score to previous days. After a full week of training, my archery was so far improved that every arrow hit the target, compared to the first day when only half my shafts flew remotely close to it.

After archery, it was sword drill. Perhaps my second most preferred weapon. Today I was matched with Finan and after securing our simple padded vests and helms we began to circle.

I fixed my eyes on Finan's, for eye movement was a clearer indicator of intention than the sword's movement. Our swords rasped together, and after a few seconds of light parries we were at it. I ducked his blade, jabbing a feint at his leg. He jumped back, thrusting his blade at my shoulder. I rolled, just missing the thrust. Kneeling I parried a downward strike, and slapped the flat of my blade against his shin. He jumped, but not fast enough, and gave a surprised gasp as the flat of the blade connected. I rolled, to evade his retort, and scrambling to my feet I parried again.

Advancing swiftly he dropped a barrage of blows, faster than I could parry and I rapidly retreated around the glade. Suddenly, my foot caught in a bramble and I went down on my back. My sword flying out of my grasp, and reach. Finan smiled, and holding his blade at my throat said "do you yield?"

I grinned slightly "Never!"

A brilliant flash of light caused Finan to stumble backwards. I scrambled to retrieve my blade. Finan shook his head, then turned to me with a grin.

"You are improving nicely, though I did not expect you to combine the use of Light in the use of the sword, the two are normally considered exclusives."

"Perhaps next time you could inform me when mixing techniques is inappropriate, though it seems a pity to not combine, it makes one's weapons far more lethal and confusing to dark forces."

"True" Brenan broke in "but even in our glade, far from other people, the forces of darkness can sense the Light which is why we only use it as our last exercises."

At that moment a horn sounded, "Calawen calls" Brenan's brow furled "Stay here Calanan, Finan and Mayim accompany me. We shall see what visitors we have, but Mayim use not the Light no matter what!"

I nodded and ran alongside them, back along the path to the farm. There was little time wasted along that run, for Finan and Brenan sped as if the legions of darkness where both behind and ahead. Just before we reached the clearing, we slowed down and walked easily out of the woods. Indeed, no matter how fast we raced the path homeward, we always walked out of the woods to disguise how far away we had been.

Calawen stood at the front of the house, two men clothed in medium blue robes stood alongside their horses beside her. Nodding to Brenan,

Calawen turned and entered the house, closing the door with greater care than normal. Almost exaggerated care, indicating that she would probably have rather slammed it.

Chapter 6: Changes in the making

The leader, who bore a silver torque upon his throat, spoke "Greetings and favor to you Brenan farmsteader. It has come to our attention that you are uninformed of the changes current in the kingdom."

Brenan inclined his head slightly and said, "we hear little of outside goings on here in the woods. And but little gossip reaches the villages near."

The man curled his lip, sneering slightly at the perceived ignorance of farmers, and continued. "From this year forward all children born are to go to school, arranged by the priests. The children will begin at twelve years and continue till they are twenty. If, as will happen at the beginning, the children are older they shall only continue till reaching the age of twenty."

Brenan and Finan exchanged sidewise glances, and I felt doubt creeping over me. These men were too smooth spoken to be up to good, let alone our good.

Brenan spoke calmly, though from the way his body tensed it took some effort to do so. "What will the children be taught in your schools? For it seems to me that school will little prepare a child for any trade, still less for battle or war."

The priest sighed audibly and said "All children will receive basic instruction in all necessary skills, girls in herbology, the making of clothing and preparing of fibers, and of course cooking. Boys will receive training in farming for the school must have food, animal husbandry, and forestry. This is what they will be taught separately. However, math, religion, weapon training, horse riding, heraldry, and hunting will be taught to all."

"That is a lot for anyone to learn, even given eight years to do it in." Finan said, pausing then added "and from the start some will not have the full eight years either."

"We have already given that thought" the priest replied "and so with the first classes, for the first eight years, each student will be evaluated and placed in a program which highlights their strengths. For example a person skilled in the religious practices would not be placed in arms training."

"That makes sense" Brenan responded "however farms do not tend themselves. When does this school start, and how long does it run?"

"It begins when the first snow flies and will extend till spring planting" the priest responded "and your son and the girl staying with you are expected to attend."

Without waiting for reply, the priests mounted their horses and galloped up the road toward the village. Glancing at the sky Brenan said "in a hurry to get to town before the moon sets I doubt not, well it is time for us to be about our evenings work." Glancing at Finan's fuming face and my bewilderment he added "we will discuss this development after finishing practice, and Mayim it is well that we should spend more time in training. You and Finan will need it."

The night's work passed slowly. Finan seemed distracted, while Brenan and Calawen never spoke, and never smiled. Even Calanan was subdued and I did not dare say a word. Finally, when the late evening meal was cleared away and the day's work was over, we assembled in the main room. After a few minutes of silence as we gathered our occupations, I was making yarn on a spindle. Brenan spoke over his carving.

"It is clear that these priests of the Reavers aim to corrupt the youth to prevent the foretold prophet from arising. However, as this is their intent those entering the school must be prepared to be under constant bombardment from the darkness."

Brenan glanced over Finan and I, before continuing. "Therefore, it is imperative that both Finan and Mayim increase their training in regular combat and the Light. Thankfully no one in the village knows of Calanan, for we did not know if he would survive his first year. For that reason we told no one, as all sickly babes were murdered at the priest's command."

"also known as sacrificed" Finan muttered.

Calawen shot him a sharp glance as Brenan, taking no notice of the outburst continued.

"Therefore, as Mayim noticed they mentioned only her and Finan for enrollment. Therefore, we must take extra care that Calanan's presence is not discovered, otherwise they could demand his life." Brenan paused, letting the implications of his words sink in.

I shifted, grabbing more wool to continue spinning. Not only was more care needed, but Finan had also begun focusing far more on the Light. I suspected he desired to know my past, and was therefore constantly practicing his gifts.

More care was taken in the coming weeks as spring turned to a golden summer. But although we laboured cheerfully together, there was an undercurrent of gloom and dread for the coming harvest. Indeed, it was the most abundant summer in record for this farm. But not every farm shared our prosperity.

Each day passed in a blur of steady work. Weeding gardens and fields had to be done. The flax was a high priority as the weeds had to be pulled before the flax was six inches high. Many days passed solely in the mind numbing occupation of weeding, or hauling water for the house gardens. Farther from the house were hay fields, which as summer drew on also required harvesting, drying, turning, and raking to be ready for the lean days of winter.

Despite the heavy work in field, kitchen, and forest that the summer brought. A full hour every evening, and sometimes two or three when the moon was near full, were spent in weapons training. As I mastered all they could teach of the sword, I focused more on archery and gained a fair degree of proficiency. Frequently we were visited by the two darkly clad priests, who seemed far more watchful of me than of any other young person in the area.

One evening they arrived, just as we came in from the field. Finan, who was in the lead, let loose a surprised whoop "Company!" Instantly Calanan dashed into the bush, laying down in the slowly deepening shadows. Hardly had he gained shelter, before the two priests reined their horses around the front of the house and saw the three of us walking forward.

The main priest scanned us grimly "it has come to our attention" he began coldly "that there is a third child in this vicinity. Whose child is it and where did it come from?" His eyes focused on Brenan who met his cold gaze unflinching.

"I know of no other child than these two before you. But even if there was a tramp in these parts, which would not be surprising, I would know nothing."

The priest snorted "we will catch you yet and when we find him, you will regret it." He turned away, his laughter harsh in the still evening. The other priest glanced at us, as he turned his horse, and our eyes met. He gave a slight shake of his head, his eyes sad. Then turned and followed the other priest at a hand-gallop.

After they were out of sight, and all trace of their presence had faded, Brenan spoke.

"So it comes to this. Those we thought were friends have betrayed us, and those who are enemies may be friends in disguise." He shook his head, and glanced toward the window where Calawen was visible gazing out at us, likely looking for Calanan. "I little thought to see these days, let alone to live through the demise of my own daughter."

For the first time since I had arrived, the weight of grief threatened to cause Brenan to break. But, the moment past, and we entered the house for dinner. It was a more sombre meal than any we had yet partaken of. At the end of the meal, Brenan spoke again.

"It is no longer safe for Calanan to remain on the farmstead, there are those who know too much and would love to see us fall. There are those within the wilds who would take him in, and you as well Calawen. Nay" he said as Calawen moved to object "one hand is enough to run this farmstead. And besides, I have seen how that pompous priest behaves around you. I fear they are working on the people to denounce us, and you know what will happen then."

Calawen paled but her voice remained calm "I know the fate that would await us both were we discovered to be wielders of the Light of the Light Giver. Though I fear not for myself, I will go with Calanan if it is indeed what you think best."

"It is" Brenan stated shortly, before leaning forward to embrace her.

Turning to face Finan and me, Calawen spoke. "It is a week till you must leave for the school." Glancing sidewise at Brenan's surprise she continued, "the priest informed me of that this afternoon, they shortened the time frame as the fields are barren in much of the land. Around here our farmstead is the only one which has produced in abundance."

"Which is likely to be why our lovely neighbors have been speaking maliciously of Calanan's presence, and why there are so many nasty looks when I go to town" Finan said, a wry smile on his face.

"If we are to thrive and not just survive the coming storm, we must be prepared to act like lightning." Brenan said slowly, "we will start with Calanan and you leaving, Dear. Once Finan and Mayim have left I will bring the majority of the produce within the forest, and hide what we value within its protection."

The storm gathered around us. The week past swifter than those previous, but slower compared to the gathering storm.

For the final week of farming we pushed ourselves into the night, every night. Fields needed harvesting, hay storing, and apples, pears, plums, and all other manner of veggies and fruit needed curing and storing before we left. But, despite the almost desperate attempts to preserve the whole harvest, we still took a few minutes to an hour a day to train, though we no longer went to the isolated glen. Training instead along the path itself, and remaining close to the house.

Walking back one evening with Finan I asked a question that had been bothering me. "Finan," I began "how will conjuring a light, or a bright flash, do anything against the darkness? We know they can conjure dark spirits, fogs, and even chains to immobilize their victims."

Finan's face darkened, but his voice remained steady "Most of the skills of Light were lost generations ago, and even the prophets have the same skills as a lay Light wielder does. Alas" his voice broke, then steadied as he continued "if we still had the ancient Light skills there is nothing the darkness could do, indeed if my sister had had even a tenth of the ancient skills they could never have seized her."

"But how could they be lost? It seems if they were being practiced it would be impossible?" I asked, finding it difficult to restrain my confusion and curiosity.

Finan smiled slightly "your curiosity will be the death of all of us if you do not take care. But, I heard once that the skills were lost through neglect and because they were not used and were not passed on. Those who should have guarded the skills and kept them going were tempted and fell to the lure of dark powers and skills which seemed greater than their already lessening skills in light. Forgotten, the skills passed beyond memory and recall, except for a few families that retained only a remnant of their former abilities."

Drawing near to the house, I watched Calawen moving about in front of the door. She was carefully harvesting the herbs which had grown there through the summer, and were now prime for drying for winter needs. She kept her face turned away from us, and the one glance she shot toward us showed her eyes red and swollen from weeping.

Due to the random visits of the priests, Calanan had taken to spending his time in, or near the woods. Even at night we dared not let down our guard, for twice the priests came just at dawn or dusk to see if there was indeed another resident.

That evening passed too swiftly for our liking, for the next morning would see Calawen and Calanan leaving to enter the wilderness, while the dawn after would see Finan and myself leaving for the unknown as well.

Chapter 7: The Giving

Sitting around the table after dinner, Brenan broke the silence. "It was the custom in ages past for the father to give gifts to his children before they left. Although Mayim is not the child of my body, yet she has become a daughter to Calawen and myself over these last months. It is right that we should do as our ancestors did, though they faced not what we face today."

As Brenan paused, I glanced around the room at the others. Friends they were, but more than friends they had become my family. Finan with his brisk and nearly harsh manner yet hid kindness within. Calanan young and impressionable, yet skilled in all the farm practices and able to calm the wildest animal with ease. Calawen, careful mother and joyful friend, she had taught me much of how to survive in this still untamed land. Brenan, father first and farmer second, his skill in fighting was still unmatched, though Finan drew a close second. But now the joy of our evenings was gone and grim determination replaced the smiles and laughter which had graced our over dinner conversations.

Rising to his feet Brenan strode around the table, and placed his hands upon Finan's shoulders. "To you Finan, my eldest, I give my father's sword and dagger. Wear and wield them well. In all things uphold what is right and true." Brenan leaned over Finan's shoulder, placing the weapons before Finan, upon the table.

Brenan then stepped to Calanan, again placing his hands upon the shoulders of his son. "To you Calanan, my youngest I give the bow I fashioned in the winter months. It is thine to keep and wield within the forest to which you head. Remember at all times to wield it for what is right and true. Use it in honor, to provide for those who cannot provide for themselves, and to protect those who have no protector." Leaning forward, Brenan placed the five foot longbow on the table before his son.

Brenan exchanged a nod with Calawen and she now arose and stood behind me. "Mayim" she said her voice clear and calm "to you there was no single gift that would fit." I noticed broad smiles creeping over the faces of the men on the other side of the table, as Calawen paused then continued. "Instead, we have prepared gifts for you as our beloved daughter, and as our sons' beloved sister.

Calawen leaned forward, placing a small bundle upon the table before me. Her voice was steady as she said "from myself is a gift, the gift of tools such as you have learned to use. Use them well, and remember the skills your hands have learned here. In dark times they will provide comfort, and when you are troubled or in need they will provide a way to survive."

Calawen returned to her seat as Brenan stepped forward. "As a daughter you have been to me, even for this short time. For you I have prepared a bow such as you know well how to use, and a second dagger which will be less conspicuous than that you already carry. Wield them well for what is right and true, and, my daughter, remember the skills you have learned in the Light even when the darkness deepens."

As Brenan returned to his seat, Finan rose the blood creeping into his cheeks as he spoke with effort. "Mayim, as my father and mother have stated, you have become as a sister to me. Take then this cloak, fashioned after the manner of the forest cloaks. May it keep you well in cold and damp, and hide you from unfriendly eyes if perchance the day comes when all who hold to truth and justice must fly." Leaning across the table, Finan gently laid the fabric bundle down before me, alongside the gifts of his parents.

Calanan then rose, almost before Finan could sit down. Calanan's face was composed, even serious, and he spoke calmly. "You have indeed become a sister to me, and my grief was lessened for your presence. For you I have prepared a kit containing dried forest herbs whose uses my mother has taught you. It also contains linen for bandages. May it keep you well in sickness, or injury and prove useful in the days ahead."

I broke down and began weeping as Calanan finished his presentation. After a few moments, I managed to speak "Thank you all. I have tried to learn from you, to adapt and grow here. I do not know what waits beyond this evening."

My voice strengthened and I felt a strange sense of calm come over me "Whatever the dawn may or may not bring. I will treasure your gifts, and seek to use them wisely. However" I smiled even as the tears again filled my eyes "you did not mention the greatest gift that you have given me. You gave me your love and acceptance, even when I was bewildered, and knew nothing, you still took the time to love and teach me. Even in the midst of your own grief you found the ability to love a stranger."

Leaning forward, I took Finan's and Brenan's hands in my own, nodding at Calawen and Calanan to also join hands. A feeling was rising in me, seeming like a mixture of excitement and terror. The feeling built till I raised my voice and spoke:

"Giver of Light, hear us this day. Only you know what tomorrow will bring, or even our next breath. You hold all things in Your hands, to You alone belongs praise and glory, wisdom and power. Grant to those assembled here your protection in the days ahead. Within the forest grant protection for Calawen and Calanan, from predators, and foes more cruel and cunning than wolves in winter, those predators in human form who hunt our steps and days. For Finan and myself, traveling to a school to be instructed in ways contrary to Yours I ask wisdom, to learn without being bound. And to see the darkness for what it truly is, and the ability to remain free from its slimy grasp. Last but not least I ask that you would provide abundantly in strength and courage for Brenan, who will be separated from his family and running the farmstead on his own. Finally I ask that if anyone intends harm to those present You would warn the one threatened so that they can escape, or take shelter in Your presence if the threat is of the dark powers. Amen." All echoed the amen, then leaned back and watched.

Calmness now pervaded the room.

After a few minutes Brenan nodded "It is well said, and worth more than all our gifts. The protection of the One, prayed down by His prophetess, is worth far more than all the gold of all the petty leaders within this sad country. But we will not talk politics now" A chuckle sounded around the table, for our evening discussions had frequently centered on the avarice and capriciousness of the leaders. Indeed it was the greed and shadowed dealings of the leaders which had given the priests strength and the ability to summon forth the Reaver.

Still gazing at the gifts I had been given, a new question formed in my mind. "Do you think the priests suspect you of wielding the Light? or me of being the new prophetess?"

Brenan shook his head "They may suspect, but provided neither you nor Finan use the Light when around them they should not receive any confirmation. As for your prophetess status, that is still in question for them. They have no idea, and if you continue to hide the brooch, mantle, and dagger, then they will never know that their enemy is in their midst."

Many thoughts had puzzled me in the last weeks, and as this was our last night together for some time I spoke. "Although these items came to me, I have felt no change since I arrived. How can I know for sure I am the prophetess, not just an impostor?"

Finan spoke "If you remember I doubted you that first night and have not been easy upon you in our training in the Light either. However, the dagger and brooch are the symbols or emblems of the second in command prophet, or prophetess. The highest prophet always wears a golden torque, set with blue gems, and of which one braided strand is silver. The high prophet also bears a golden sword, with the pommel set with a green gem and three blue gems set along the hilt crosspiece."

"What happened to the high prophet then? Since I have but come as the second prophet?" I winced even as I asked the question, knowing this type of question often stirred a cauldron of emotions that was best left untouched. But, I could hold my tongue no longer, if I did not learn now, how could I ever learn?

Brenan's face darkened, and a hint of steel crept into his tone "The high prophet saw these days coming, and though he spoke a message of warning he did nothing to prevent what has now happened from happening. Seeing the darkness drawing ever closer, he fled crossing the seas, a coward who should never have borne the prophetic mantle."

Nodding slightly Calawen spoke up "The night yet passes swiftly, and Calanan and I have a long journey on the morrow. Within the next day Mayim and Finan will also be on their journey. Let us close this night, therefore, in fellowship together."

Brenan nodded "well spoken wife, and indeed we know not what the morrow may bring. Let us stand together, and strengthen each other for the days ahead."

The remainder of the evening sped past. After the long conversation and gift presentation we adjourned to the front room, where each of us took our handwork, from fibre preparation to woodcarving. With our hands occupied, our tongues found equal occupation in talking of the everyday together. Many memories of the previous months were brought forward, from my first attempt at riding horses to Finan's unfortunate experience with a giant catfish when fishing in the river. Finally, as we prepared to adjourn to our beds, Brenan spoke.

"It is well to tell you, Finan and Mayim, of where you can find Calawen and Calanan if anything should happen to me. They are going to dwell with the Brachite Foresters, a group of roamers in the Brachite forest. They are often termed outlaws, and among them are many who "polite society" has rejected. However, our family has always had a good relationship with the band, and we know that many of the outcasts and outlaws within it are there because they believe even as we do. If anything should happen to me, or you should require succour or aid of any type fly to the Brachite forest."

Finan nodded and then said, "Just so that I remember. If trouble threatens or aid is needed fly to the Brachite forest. That will be a long flight from the school."

Brenan nodded with a smile "you have remembered, from the direction of the school, you would have to head toward the center of the forest, which is north for you. There are mountains within the forest depths, and it is at these that the Brachite band prefers to hide. If I remember my wanderings rightly, there is a river flowing near the school which leads toward the forest, and water is good for hiding scent."

Having now established some type of escape plan, if needed, we headed to bed. The tiny room, over the northern gable of the house had truly become my home. Upon the tiny side table, I placed the gifts I was given and then turned to survey once again the place I called home. The bed was simple, covered with a pretty quilt made from scraps and stuffed with wool that had accidentally felted or was clean but too matted or coarse for other items. On the wall by the door hung my spare dress, another of

Angusina's actually, that had been altered. Alongside it was the cloak Calawen had helped me create, of heavy fulled wool for the coming winter, it was lined with a fine, soft wool fabric as the coarse, heavy outer fabric would not be comfortable. I lifted the hooded cloak with a slight smile. Double layers were also warmer than single, and the extra batting added upon the shoulders and quilted in place, made triple layers of warm, water repelling wool.

I would wear the spare dress and cloak when Finan and I joined the city's caravan headed for the school. The cloak Finan had gifted me would remain a spare until needed. Why we were all traveling together I did not understand, perhaps to make sure no children said they were going and then slipped away into Brachite forest or back home.

Stretching out on the bed, my gaze fell one more time upon the bow and dagger and I tensed. Finan had mentioned that the plains to the south of the road held raiders. Mounted on swift horses, they would attack travelers and steal women and children away. Taking them to the southern coast, they would sell them to coastal slave traders. Suddenly restless, I rose and again inspected the dagger and bow, though both were in perfect order. Then, I smiled for the prophetess dagger was still on my leg. I grasped it and pulled it forward. It was still in perfect condition, its point as sharp as a winter honed icicle, and it's blade as keen as a north gale.

I stepped to the window, gazing upon the simple pebbled road that led to the farmstead's front door. This simple farmstead was the only home I could remember knowing, the only place I had ever belonged in my memory. Something however, was wrong. I was tense. For the first time since I had come here, a sense of impending doom shrouded me, cloaking my heart in its suffocating folds. I grasped the dagger, even as a thought spread through my mind.

"Infants who die are listed by name and parentage, Calanan is upon that list though he lives. Go to him."

Stepping to the door, I paused "should I go?" I wondered. I had never left my room in the night before, let alone gone into Finan's and Calanans' room. I eased the door open, trembling slightly as it creaked, seeming to protest my night intrusion louder than normal. No sound came from the other rooms, and I crept softly to the ajar door of Finan's room. Calanan lay calmly on his bed, appearing to be sleeping peacefully.

But within that peacefulness a sense of evil flooded my being. Grasping the doorpost with my left hand, my right still holding the prophetess' dagger, I beheld a vision.

Thirteen men danced and leapt around a fire on the Blood Tor. The alter was empty. At the side was a slaughtered, male lamb. The Reaver stood, looking on at the ceremony. In an instant I realized that it was a ceremony to bring the dead to life as a permanent, mindless and disposable, servant. The priests were chanting through a list of names, and upon that list was Calanan's name. Even as the priests began the chant to summon Calanan's soul, supposedly in the otherworld, the live Calanan jerked awake with a scream of anguish. His cry instantly waking the whole house.

Calanan began thrashing as the priests, seen clearly in my mind's eye, continued their fell chant. Calawen pushed past me, as Finan strove to calm his brother, but nothing they did helped.

Suddenly I saw a dark line, extend from Calanan's chest out through the window toward the Blood Tor. Clarity descended upon me. The line was the priest's attempt to physically steal Calanan. To literally rip the soul from his body, as they tried to pull souls from beyond the grave.

Without thinking I reached for the Light, my free left hand turned the brooch within so that it touched my side. Stepping forward I watched as my hands moved on their own. My left grasped the black line, and my right the prophet's dagger. Words came and I spoke them

"By the Light within me, and the Light within this home, I bind all powers of darkness from working within this place. I claim Calanan for the land of the living and repudiate all claims of darkness and death over his soul. By the authority invested in me as Prophetess I break every blood bond that was fastened upon him. By my own blood do I say he belongs to the Light alone"

Driving the point of the dagger into my finger, the blood struck the line of darkness. Then, where the blood marked the line, I struck slicing clean through the line with the dagger. A flash of light filled the room, shooting down the black thread as well. Instantly Calanan stopped thrashing, and his breathing calmed.

On the Tor, still visible to my mental eye, a blinding ball of light flashed along the black thread, hurling the priests backward and even causing the Reaver to flinch, and then bellow in rage "Find that boy and Find the one who has saved him from my grasp!" With those words ringing in my ears, the Tor faded from view. I opened my eyes on Finan and Calanan's room, with the whole family staring at me.

Chapter 8: Visions in the Night

"What?" I asked, feeling uncomfortable at their stares, "did I suddenly sprout horns or something?"

"No Mayim" Brenan said, his voice bordering on reverent. "You have not grown an extra appendage, you saved Calanan's life, and broke the bond the darkness would otherwise have exploited. If you still had doubts about your call, it seems this night has proven that they are false. No one other than a full prophet or prophetess of the Light could break one of the soul pulling spells, particularly after it had already seized hold of the child. And only the very highest could prevent lasting damage from the attempt either."

Calawen and Finan nodded grimly, and Finan added "Also, your use of light was amazing, it was as if the whole room was filled with cleansing and purifying fire. How did you do that?"

Brenan raised his eyebrows "I felt that as well, Finan, and I too wondered how it was that such a display of Light skill could happen when us, your teachers Mayim, did not know it."

"I do not know how it happened," I admitted, "nor how I knew what to do to stop the spell from working. All I know is that a feeling of deep unease prevented my falling asleep, and encouraged me to check all my weapons. This dagger was the last I checked, and then worry for Calanan overcame me. Reaching the door, I sensed the evil loosed against him, and actually saw the Blood Tor in my mind. When I beheld the darkness, I sought and surrendered to the Light. You all saw what happened then."

The last words I heard flashed through my mind, "However, it is not safe for Calanan to remain in the vicinity. The Reaver was present and saw the display of power, he has sent guards to search for both of us. However, I do not think I will be expected, but Calanan and Calawen should start at or before first light."

Brenan nodded grimly "grab a few hours' sleep, it is gray by four and by then they both shall be upon the road. But, Mayim" his voice turned gentle "you can hardly carry the brooch and dagger to the school, at least not without disguising them. After Calawen and Calanan leave we shall address that issue, hopefully before any blue robed cowards show up to annoy us."

Returning to my room, I sat upon the bed gazing out of the small window. The night was dark and the new moon, the perfect time for black acts. Darkness is their time, for their deeds are dark and light would expose them. No wonder priests all hate the light, for it shows how black and putrid they have become. My reflections wandered, then focused back on the brooch and dagger. What was I to do with them?

The brooch, four inches across, solid gold with a two inch inset gem, designed to hold a heavy cloak and the mantle no matter the weather. Its very size prohibited most disguises. While the intricate design of intertwined knots around the edge, unique to the items given to prophets, would reveal it to any who saw it. Unfastening the brooch from the mantle, I laid it upon the bed to inspect. Slipping my hand down to my thigh, I also unfastened the dagger sheath. Even the dagger's strap bore the knot work design, and the slightly curved dagger hilt also clearly displayed it. There was no way these could be easily disguised. The one other item present was a fine golden chain, actually sewn along the length of the strap. As I ran my finger along the gold chain, attached to the leather, a picture came into my mind.

A priest, in a white robe, stood before an assembly. In his hand he held a sword, blazing with Light. Upon his throat also rested a golden torque, with one strand of the many stranded braid being silver. The torque also gleamed with light. But, what caught my attention was a fine gold and leather chain that hung around his throat below the torque, upon the chain rested two tiny pendants which looked like a dagger and a tiny golden circle set with a gem.

The vision broke, and I looked again at the items before me. I sighed, the dawn was coming swiftly and if this did not work no harm would be done. Taking the brooch and dagger, I carefully threaded them onto the leather strap. Lifting it, I placed and fastened it about my neck.

For a second the weight of the items was felt, then nothing and reaching within my dress' neckline I found a miniature dagger and brooch adorning a fine leather and gold chain. The chain was long enough to hide what it carried, and fine enough to not attract undue attention.

Now that the emblems of my position were hidden, I also lifted the mantle and placed it around my neck. The same phenomena happened with the mantle. It shrunk from a large rectangle of cloth, large enough for a full cloak, to a small but supremely finally woven scarf, exactly the thing to keep one's neck warm, and to hide the presence of a certain leather and gold chain. I smiled despite the doubts I still had, it seemed that things were being taken care of.

Stretching upon the bed, I relished the lumpy and slightly coarse consistency of the straw stuffed mattress. Who knows when I would feel this comfort again? Just before sleep claimed me, a thought streaked through my mind. "Why had I received a vision of how to hide the prophetic emblems? How had I known what to do to prevent the priests from stealing Calanan? Who gave the power of the light? How do I know I am a prophetess as was foretold when I do not even know who I am?" Wide awake again I lay and struggled mentally with these questions finally speaking the only answer I had out-loud to the stillness of the pre-dawn air.

"I do not know why I received two visions this night. All I know is that it was not by my own strength. Both visions were a gift. I do not know who I was born, nor the identity of my father or mother, therefore I am what I have been called. I am Mayim, who is as a daughter to Brenan and Calawen. Whether I am a prophetess or not remains to be seen. Visions tonight, and emblems that change with position and need, seem to indicate that I am. But, what that will mean in the end, I have no idea."

Calm settled upon me, yet doubt still nagged at the back of my mind. I know who I am now, but who was I before? Am I worthy? Questions nattered through my mind like a woodpecker at an ant infested hollow tree, and there was about as much chance of sleeping with one as with the other.

I did not sleep. Instead I rose and headed down to the main room and kitchen. Moving quietly I collected the travel food, prepared over the previous days, and settled it comfortably into rucksacks. Taking two of the leather water bottles I filled them with water and added a handful of oats, which increase the thirst quenching power of the water.

After preparing the rucksacks and bottles for the journey, I also prepared two bows, checking the arrows and waxing the strings. I laboured steadily until dawn broke, at which time the family descended. Calawen looked slightly surprised and said "it appears you have not slept this night, Mayim, it is not good for ye to be without rest."

"I am well, Calawen, but my mind would not permit me the luxury of rest. Instead I made the best use of my time, so that you and Calanan can leave early, and that Finan and I can disguise or hide your trail lest search be made for you."

"It is well thought" Brenan broke in, before Calawen could reply "I see you have a sack of food for each of us. Therefore, let us away ere the dawn fully breaks. Finan, I expect you shall be able to muddle the trail after doing the necessary morning care."

Finan responded with a slight bow, and after swift hugs and farewells all round, Finan and I headed to the barns and corral. Glancing over my shoulder, I watched Brenan lead his wife and youngest child into the forest. They did not look back.

After completing the animal care Finan and I headed into the cool, early morning darkness of the forest. Slipping easily along the path, we soon came to the first of many side trails, where Brenan had carefully brushed their tracks away, in such a manner however that the leaves remained mostly undisturbed and undented. Turning on the forked path, Finan and I stomped our way down the trail, making as big a trail as we could. I scuffed leaves like a young child who does not want to walk, while Finan alternated between treading as delicately as his six foot, broad shouldered, and well-muscled frame could, and stomping like he was trying to stove in a wolf's head with just his heel.

Ducking under low hanging branches, we soon came to a well-worn game trail. Finan spoke "perfect spot to completely lose the trail. It is also about time you and I headed back to work in the fields. If any nosy blue robbed interloper came through it would be suspicious to have the farmstead untended.

"How are we to lose the trail?" possibly one of my dumber questions, but with no water in sight and only a forest for company I could not help but ask.

Finan smiled "It is simple really, we take a short hike along the game trail, then take to the trees and clamber for a mile or so and drop back down on another game trail. That leaves a large enough gap to throw all scent or tracker off our trail. If we dropped down too close our trail could be picked up again."

I nodded, and followed him up the game trail, this time seeking to walk where the ground was hardest and leave as little sign as possible.

We traveled for half a mile up the game trail, then Finan did a quick leap and grabbed an oak branch which hung lower than all others we had passed. Leaning down, and bracing himself, Finan grabbed my arm as I jumped, pulling me none too gently onto the branch. Rising after I had caught my breath, he lead the way through the canopy, stepping easily from limb to limb. Though always careful to not disturb any moss, or leave other signs which could betray our presence.

After a mile of tree travel, we dropped down onto a well-worn and hard packed road. Heading onward at a jog we soon arrived back at the farmstead.

We arrived home none too soon, for hardly had we replaced our supplies, and changed to regular farm garments, then a band of eight priests cantered up to the door. All wore the darkest shade of blue. Their leader, a thin man with no redeeming feature, dismounted and stepped up to us. "Where is Brenan?" He demanded, his voice hard. "There is suspicion that he is dabbling in no-good superstition. It is also suspected that he deliberately interfered in an important and vital ritual last night. Both of these crimes are worthy of death, though we are of a mind to question first."

Finan spoke calmly, "My father and mother are away this day, on their own. I do not know where they have gone, though this is not the first time for such a journey. We are told that they go away to reconnect, away from the stress of farm life."

The little priest flared his nostrils, and growled "Perhaps then, since you are his eldest, you can answer our questions. First, do you know of any stranger in the area, women or man, who acts strangely and can" his voice dropped to a whisper "move their hand to light up a room, or hurl a lightning bolt at something in their way?"

"I have seen no stranger for over six months, and before that it was but an itinerant peddler. As for someone with the magic you describe, I have seen no one like that. Nor have I heard anything of a person with such abilities. So far out of the ordinary do they appear, however, that whoever possessed them would be the talk of the region, not to mention the towns."

"Do you have a brother" the priest snapped, seeming to ignore the ease with which Finan had answered.

"My only brother died in infancy sir, I would ask you not stir up the memories of my siblings. I am libel to forget your distinguished position in my grief." Finan stretched, flexing his arms and cracking his fists softly. Finan's gaze roved over the priests dismissively before settling again upon their leader.

The priest drew back a pace, and glanced toward me, seeming to notice for the first time that a girl bordering on womanhood stood alongside the young man.

"Is he often like this" the priest asked me, shooting a second nervous glance toward Finan.

"Only when strong emotions are stirred, unfortunately grief has been stirred much in his life of late and I would rather not be present if such a line of inquiry were to be continued." I smiled slightly, and shifted away from Finan for emphasis.

The priest drew back, and had a swift parlay with his companions. Stepping back he spoke, wringing his hands in a very distracting manner.

"We are satisfied with your answers, and consider your family to have done nothing in the past night. It was merely a mistake in our calculations which we attributed to outside factors. Remember you will be picked up for schooling tomorrow, be ready as close to this time as possible. And" he paused, as already scurrying for his horse he was reminded by a whispered injunction "come armed, bow, sword, shield, and dagger if you have the skills. We do not know what may be met upon the road. "

Brenan returned that evening, tired, dusty, but happy. "They are safe, and I defy the keenest and bravest false priest to penetrate deep enough into the forest to discover them. There is little chance even if they could survive, however." He smiled grimly, "the Brachite foresters bear no love toward those blue robes. Nor will the Foresters wait around to be hunted like animals."

Chapter 9: To School

On learning the route Finan guessed they would take to the school, Brenan shook his head. "It is one thing to drag children from their homes for "educational purposes" though what education darkness can give I do not know. But what is worse is dragging a bundle of children for days along the Bar Hills, where they boarder Brachite forest. It is one thing to travel the forest with priests, quite another to tempt the raiders of the hills with a band of unprotected children."

"Yes father, it seems folly itself to tempt it right at prime raiding time." Finan said, grimly perusing the map "but other than heading straight into the Bar hills themselves, I see no other logical route to the school. At least the route I've plotted has the marginal protection of the forest available, though the priests are unlikely to permit us to fly within it."

I spoke "will there be any protection worth having, or are we sunk before we start?"

"The priests will provide some measure of defense, how well they will do so I don't know. Both you and Finan must carry swords. Yours should be hidden if possible, though your bow can be visible Mayim. It is not unusual for a woman to use the bow, though a woman knowing the sword is rare."

I nodded, still staring at the map. For a journey in the sultry days of harvest it would be long and dusty. Thankfully it was not a full winter or spring journey, where the dampness, cold, and mud would have made it more difficult. The road was long, and it would take four or five days with the number of children traveling. Though, I smiled again, at a brisk pace Finan and I could probably hike the trail in two days. Fully half the time it would take the larger assemblage with ponderous wagons.

The last few hours went past in a flurry of preparation on my part. There was still some food to preserve, and storage areas needed organizing. Finan and I would each carry a small bag of provisions, which would last for most of the trip. The simple cakes, and some dried meat would last even if we didn't eat it.

The dawn of our departure was cool and dreary, damp mist covered the fields and forest. I shrugged into the warm woolen cloak Calawen had provided, and triple checked the small bag I carried. Within the bag lay the tools, along with some wool, the scarf mantle of the prophetess, Finan's gift cloak, and a change of garments. Over my shoulder, I slung the shafts and the unstrung bow, and at my side hung the light sword Brenan had prepared. I adjusted my cloak to disguise the sword, then swung the satchel upon my shoulder. Finan looked formidable with his sword and bow slung upon his back, a small bag held a change of garments, small knife, tinderbox, and sundry other articles. At his side hung a long dagger, half hidden by the gray cloak he wore.

Just past dawn, a rumble approached, and along the road trundled 6 wagons. Two of which were full of young youth, the youngest being ten and the eldest looked to be thirteen. The other four wagons appeared to hold provisions and tents, likely for the ten priests who were accompanying us, mounted on fine horses. Behind the priests came a second band of youth all well mounted, and acting like it was a party, wealthy children of wealthy parents by all appearances. They mocked at the youth in the wagons as inexperienced whelps. I glanced at Finan as we walked easily down to the wagons. The lead priest glanced at us, then at the full wagons.

"There's no room for you in the wagons, and clearly" he sneered "you do not have horses. You can walk alongside the wagons, or behind the mounted party. Two of our priests bring up the rear so there is no fear you would be lost."

Without comment Finan fell into step alongside one of the laden provision wagons, and I walked easily alongside him. It did not take long for the mounted youth to notice our position, and barbs soon began to fly.

"Hey yokel, don't you know how to ride." shouted one.

His comrade replied "Na they can't ride cause the horses won't let their clumsy behinds on em"

Brutal laughter came, despite the fact that the jokes completely lacked originality or wit for that matter. Leaning slightly toward Finan I whispered "they may be armed, but I would sooner trust in a single dagger in my hand against a bear, then the lot of them against a dead fish."

Finan struggled to keep a straight face. Failing miserably, he burst into a hearty laugh. He quipped back "aye, or trust a squirrel to defeat a wolf." I grinned, and with spirits restored continued effortlessly alongside the wagon.

All morning we tramped, the wagons rolled and the horses trotted. Soon the barbed banter from the mounted nobility dissolved into complaints of sore behinds, cramping legs, and exhaustion. I shook my head, it was not yet noon and the gay party of strong nobility was already failing. Pausing mid-stride I stretched my back, flexing the muscles in my shoulders and shifting the weight of the bag.

The walk was not hard, but around eleven a steady downpour began. There was no wind, but the steady rain began to gradually soak through cloaks. If it kept up, we would be one miserable party when evening fell.

Around noon, we paused under the dripping trees. Without easily accessible dry wood, the priests refused to let us attempt a quick fire. Insisting that we eat and then move on. Glancing frequently into the forest, and then out toward the plains, the priest's never paused in their movements. Small loaves of bread, nearly stale, were handed out to everyone. The young nobles turned their noses up at it, and turning proceeded to eat from small satchels upon their horses. Smells drifted over from their location, of fresh bread, jam, and meat either lamb or cow. Finan and I ate the loaves given to us, or at least the first bite.

It was herbed bread, and after the first bite we both stopped. Glancing at the priests, with the bread still in our mouths, we paused. It was clear, from the taste, that they were focused on giving everyone some type of herbal mixture.

"What type of herbs do you think they used?" Finan said, as he leaned carefully back behind me, so it would not be obvious that he was speaking.

"I do not rightly know, but I do not think we should eat it. There is nothing in the flavour that I recognise."

Taking a bit, I tossed it down alongside a mouse that had crept out of its hole. Staring at the morsel for a few seconds, the mouse sniffed it, then nibbled it. Spitting out the bite it had taken it scampered back into its tunnel. Finan and I exchanged glances, as we carefully hid our bread in the leaf-mold, brushing crumbs off as if we had finished eating, we rose and returned to our wagon-side position. As the march continued, we snacked on some meat from our provision bag, being careful to keep the priests from noticing.

At the end of the day, tiredness and exhaustion warred with frustration at the verbal barbs of the mounted youth. However, despite the exhaustion, I could not rest. Both Finan and I carried satchels of travel bread in our bags. But, even going as steadily as we had, we had covered scarce 10 miles that day, and had left the moderate shelter of the forest to camp in the open. The tents from the other four wagons had been set up as soon as we stopped, one of the tents was the priests and the other nine tents were the property of the young mounted nobles, except for two. The final two tents were filled to overflowing with the youth who rode in the wagons. These had not spoken during the day likely depressed at being taken from their homes. After glancing at the overfull tents, Finan and I had rolled ourselves into our cloaks under one of the wagons, after taking care to place an empty sack under us to prevent ground water from the earlier rain seeping up.

But, I could not sleep. After vain attempts, I rose, slipping out from under the wagon. Keeping low, I slid over the ground to the edge of the encampment. Lying in the shadow of the tents I scanned the open ground. Despite the danger of the area no guard had been set. Stillness reigned, yet a vague uneasiness had forced me to move. Hardly had I settled before a gray figure rose against the skyline. It scanned the sleeping and unguarded encampment, then turned and dashed away into the open plain.

Chapter 10: Raiders of the Bar Hills

Rising to a crouch, I dashed over the open ground until I reached the spot the scout had stood. Looking around, and feeling the ground with my hand, I detected tracks deeply imprinted in the ground, tracks from a riding boot. Bellying up to the top of the ridge, I lay still while scanning the surrounding country. Just on the horizon there was an encampment of low profile tents surrounded by moving men and horses.

Rising I dashed back down to our encampment. Reaching the wagon, I ducked under and roughly shook Finan awake. "Arise Finan; there is an encampment to the east of us, men and horses. They are coming this way shortly, their scout has already returned to them."

"Enemies?" Finan asked, still fighting off sleep.

"I suspect so, for if they were friends why do they prepare to meet us in battle?"

"Awake the priests and the other youth" Finan said, wriggling out from under the wagon. "It may be a false alarm, but I doubt it. We know the Raiders are in these plains, and we are camped in a deucedly open location. If I didn't know better I would have said the head priest did it deliberately."

The temptation to slip away alone rose in me, but instead I crept to the tents. Creeping inside one of the crowded tents I shook the sleepers roughly hissing out "awake, get up" but no one stirred from their slumber.

Suddenly the herbs in the bread made sense. The strange flavor came back to my mind. It was from a yellow flowered plant that induced sleep and deadened pain. I dashed back to Finan who was emerging from the nobilities' tent shaking his head. "They will not awaken, I do not know what we can do."

"They are all drugged, and we would have been as well since the bread and evening tea was drugged but we did not eat or drink of it."

Finan glanced at the wagons, then at me with a smile. "How strong are you?" He asked "I think we could safely place everyone in a wagon or so and get them to the forest's edge without being detected."

I nodded, "I was wondering if we could do something, let's get to it."

Working fast, and starting with the most crowded tents Finan and I carefully lifted and carried each youth to the wagons, laying them down on the sacks of provisions and some covered bolts of cloth in two of the wagons. In the other four wagons we placed them down on sacking. We had just enough room for all the youth. We did not bother the priests.

Instead of taking the wagon horses, we grabbed the highest value horses of the nobles. Carefully yoking them together, in teams of six and leading the wagon horses behind. We silently, with minimal creaking and rumbling, moved the full wagons away, into the shelter of the trees.

As soon as they were sheltered, Finan and I dashed back to the encampment. Keeping low we hid behind one of the now empty tents.

Within minutes a band of mounted and armed men galloped up. Holding blazing brands, the leader rode strait to the priest's tent. "Come out, Excellen" the leader called "Where are those you promised us?"

The head priest scrambled out, looking bewildered. "They are within the tents, and their horses are hobbled over to the right of the wagons."

With a wave, the leader indicated that his men should search. After a few seconds the men returned

"The tents are empty." "There are no horses" were the reports. The men who reported shifted slightly, moving from foot to foot.

The leader, a grim-faced, dark-haired man, turned back to the priest "you have betrayed your bargain, priest, and overstepped your bounds. You promised us thirty strong youth as slaves, and not a one is here."

Even as the man finished speaking, his men turned the terrified priests out of their tents. Trembling the ten priests stood, staring at the raiders surrounding them.

Riding along the line, the raider's leader indicated a young, weak looking priest. "Leave him behind, the other nine bring, since there leader reneged on his agreement he shall fulfill it himself. Take down the tents, leaving the cooking tent with its provisions only. It is clear that there are some who are alert among the priest's convoy." A slight smile crossed his lips "we shall see if they can bring the others safely to the school. This will be an interesting game."

As Finan and I were hidden behind the cooking tent, we were not disturbed or detected as the raiders dismantled and stole the camp. Leaving the youngest and weakest priest behind, likely to attempt to guide us, the raiders soon departed leading nine terrified priests into slavery.

"Tis not really fair that the priests should be taken for their leader's dishonesty." Finan whispered in my ear "do you think we could rescue them?"

"I do not think it would be feasible, we have thirty plus youth that likely do not know the first thing about war. On top of that, the only possible way to defeat the raiders would likely involve extensive use of Light, not the thing we want to advertise knowledge of before going to a school of darkness."

"True, but it still seems hard. The little priest seems quite cut up about it, then again he thinks he's alone." With a shrug Finan slid out from under the tent skirt, and I followed. The priest left behind and basically alone, stared into the darkness without moving. Stepping near, Finan said "how long do you think the drug will make the others sleep for?"

The priest jumped, spinning around and staring at us, mouth agape. Recovering himself with an effort "I do not know, I... I didn't know anyone was drugged. Where are the others anyway, and the horses. And what are we to do? Our leader is gone..." His voice trailed away.

Finan spoke "we moved the others to the forest's edge, it is sheltered there and safer as our outlines are not visible against the tree's darkness. We will head there now, and come back with the wagons to claim the cooking tent at dawn."

Still shaken, the priest followed Finan and together we jogged back to the forest's edge. The others still slept soundly, and without saying a word Finan and I headed to opposite ends of the wagon line. Wrapping myself in my cloak, I settled against the bole of a nearby oak. Watching the forest and plain for movement, nothing moved. And soon, I dropped into a rhythm of sleep and watchfulness that lasted through the night.

Just as dawn broke, the others stirred, waking abruptly from dreams filled with darkness and terror. Evean, the most vocal of the mounted youth, struggled awake with a cry of fear. Starting up he gazed around then shouted "where are we? Where are the tents and where the hell is my horse?" Scrambling out of the wagon, he turned and saw that his precious horse was harnessed to it. "What fool harnessed the riding horses to the wagons, and where are the priests?"

Trembling the priest came forward "The other priests were taken by the raiders. If you had remained there you would also have been taken along with your horses."

"How were we moved? Who did it?" The slight edge of panic had returned to his voice, as he realized that his comrades were still drugged. I rose, and after a cursory scan of the open plains jogged into camp. "Finan and I moved you and the others. Two horses alone could not drag the loaded wagons, and we assumed you would prefer horses to walking." Finan arrived at the same time, and gave a slight nod as he heard the conclusion of my words.

Pausing for an instant Evean spoke gravely "I am Evean of the house of Brachide, I thank you for preserving all youth from capture and our horses from slavery. To who do I owe this gratitude?"

Struggling to keep my face strait, I was surprised as Finan responded in similar terms. "I am Finan Donoghue and this is my sister Mayim. It was our pleasure and joy to have been of service to the whole group. Yet, we are not in safety and will likely not be for many days. As such perhaps we should take council for our next step."

"Tis well thought, Finan Donoghue, we shall take council and Mayim shall join us. As my friends have not yet awoken, it appears that with the priest a four person counsel will be best."

Chapter 11: Decisions

Settling down around the small fire the priest had lit, I watched Evean closely. He seemed ill at ease, frequently glancing toward the wagons still crowded with sleeping youth, who tossed and turned in dark dreams.

"It appears," Evean spoke first "that the wagons will be but a hassle, as will the individual horses. In total the horses' number 42 and the youth number between fifty and sixty. As such it is conceivable that we could double mount, though I am not sure if that will be beneficial to distance." Evean paused, chewing lightly on his lip as he watched Finan and the priest, avoiding looking toward me.

Finan spoke "Abandoning the wagons is a given, but those who can walk must for we cannot abandon the provisions. However, though I approve not the head priest's decision to hand us all over to the Raiders I cannot leave the other priests in their hands."

"But, Finan we do not know where the priests may be taken and surely the youth deserve first priority. After we all are safe, the priests can worry about reclaiming their own." The briskness in Evean's words, and carelessness of others grated harshly and the priest spoke out.

"We are early, and will hardly be expected for another two weeks. I would suggest that the youngest youth go with a selection of the eldest for protectors and continue to the school. The others then can see what they can do to retrieve the other priests from captivity."

Evean shook his head but I broke in before he could speak. "It is known that the Raiders do not care for priests as slaves. I will not have the consciousness that they died a cruel death because we preferred our own safety to the risk of a rescue." I barely noticed how my voice rose as I spoke. Breathing heavily I continued. "I for one will search and see what I can do, if you want to join you are welcome to. But no one will accompany me who is not willing and ready to risk their own life for others, whether priest, noble, or peasant."

Evean looked chagrined and responded gravely, directing his words to Finan. "The young woman is clearly distraught over imagined dangers. Even to the most optimistic it has always appeared impossible to rescue those who the Raiders have once seized. It is best if we continue to the school in the manner I have already explained."

"I will go with Mayim for what she says is truth. When the others are awake I will place it before them. Those who choose to go with us may come, those who choose to head to the school can go. I will stand in the way of no man."

Evean's mouth slowly dropped open, as Finan took my part. Exchanging a quick glance, Finan and I rose at the same moment and headed for the wagons. A nearby stream provided buckets of water and soon the distressed sleepers spluttered awake under a deluge of icy stream water.

After everyone was awake, and fed with non-herbed bread. Finan and Evean called an assembly. We assembled around the morning's campfire, built up so that those wakened with water could dry off.

Finan spoke, his voice carrying easily in the enclosed glade.

"Last night you were saved from captivity through alertness and caution. Today we must choose between caution and recklessness. The priests, nine in number, who accompanied us were seized by the Raiders in your stead. You are aware that no love is lost between Raiders and Priests. Therefore, it is the decision of myself and Mayim to search for and rescue if possible those who were seized. Evean here has decided that safety is more important and intends to lead whoever does not join Mayim and myself to the school. To show your decision, those willing to take the risk can go to my right were Mayim is standing, those for caution and safety can go to the left where Evean is standing."

Three of the older commoners immediately headed to my side, one of them a young woman the other two young men. Two of the eldest horse riding youth also joined us immediately, both lads who looked to have taken a fair number of knocks in life already. The rest moved as one body to Evean's side.

"The choice is made" Finan declared. "with seven, eight, we shall seek." For even as Finan spoke the little priest scurried from the left side to stand alongside me. Leaning toward me he whispered "I won't leave them behind, though they do not trust me one whit." He grinned slightly "secrets are ill among priest or peasant, but I hope to help somewhat."

Why priests did not trust one of their own was something I would have to find out. As it was, eight walking individuals against two score mounted Raiders was long odds.

Moving quickly we aided the other party to pack food onto the horses, taking for ourselves haversacks full of travel provisions, and two water bottles apiece. We did not take horses as we did not have enough for all of us, and the only two with horses preferred that the horses should reach the school. After the hard work was done Evean showed up to take his place in the lead, I suspected he had been speaking of the route with the priest for the priest had re-appeared five minutes earlier and pitched in to help.

After the other group left, Finan turned to our little party. "So my friends, we have eight against two score. Rather high odds, about five to one, and with horses thrown in, it is a rather dismal perspective. However, I do not intend to fight openly if I can help it, but to infiltrate by stealth to rescue the priests who had nothing to do with our betrayal. It is likely that the Raiders will slay the traitor priest first, as they hold him responsible for our earlier escape." The others nodded, then the young woman who had joined spoke up.

"Who is leading us, Finan, and do they already have a plan?"

"Mayim and myself will both lead." Finan replied "as for a plan, our first stop is the Raider's camp from last night. From that we shall see what direction they traveled. I fear that they may plan to cut off our friends from the school. That is what I would plan if I were in their place."

"Aye," one of the former mounted youth said, "that is well spoken. I am glad it will be a joint leadership though I know nothing of you and Mayim, yet I am willing to follow whatever you command as our leaders." Bowing slightly the youth stepped back.

"Thank you," Finan said a queer look creeping momentarily over his face. "We will do our best to be worthy of your estimation and confidence."

Smiling slightly the youth responded, "that is the best that anyone can do, and I for one have more confidence since I know that you are not overconfident."

With little more than a nod we turned and headed over the plain. After covering a short distance, Finan nodded to me and said "you remember where you saw the Raider encampment, dash ahead and see if you can find a trail."

Without a word, I lengthened my stride and was soon running easily toward the low hill over which the enemy's movement had been visible. Despite the lack of sleep I felt fresh and ready for anything, possibly the excitement of the hunt, or my months of farm training kicking in. I dropped flat as I reached the top of the hill, bellied up to the crest and peered over.

The plain stretched before me, empty and desolate. Just below the brow of the hill was an area of trampled grass, and charred circles. To the south and east a trail led away, made by both wagon and horses. Rising lightly, I walked down to the encampment. Little else was evident that my earlier scan had not shown. Searching carefully, I moved alongside the outward bound trail and soon discovered a scrap of dark blue cloth, along with a long drag mark in the trail. Jogging back, I met the party just as they crested the hill.

"Looks like they've headed south and east, likely to try and cut our comrades off from the school."

"Then we must follow fast, how long do you think they have gone for?" Finan asked, glancing over the site.

"The ashes are but slightly warm, at least eight hours since fuel was applied, likely but two or three hours since it was banked down."

After a second, Finan nodded and turning to the group said "we will follow. Is anyone here skilled in tracking? it were best that two should scout ahead."

The youth who had spoken earlier stepped forward "I have some skill in hunting and trailing game, likely it could be applied here."

"You can join Mayim in scouting then, follow alongside the trail my friends and never over it."

Turning, I led the way down the trail. Running as before at a pace I knew I could hold easily. After a few miles, the youth spoke. "You run well Mayim, unfortunately I do not run as well, can we slow the pace for a mile?"

Slackening the pace, I glanced at the youth. Breathing hard he spoke again "I am called Jaywen of the house of Heratia, though I prefer to be called Jay."

I inclined my head to acknowledge the introduction "greetings to you as well Jaywen of the house of Heratia, you run well over the plain."

"I do my best, yet you run with greater ease than I." I smiled at the complement, and then paused.

Turning I inspected the trail, it was fresher than before and the grass damper seemingly freshly broken. A few small hills rose ahead, and the trial lead around them. We ran on, slightly faster as I sought to identify the smells coming near.

I raised my hand, coming to a stop below the brow of a small hill, around which the trail led. Dropping flat we crawled to the top and peered over. Just below the hill lay a small encampment of Raiders, but ten or so in number. They were standing guard over the priests. But, of the rest of the band there was no sign, nor were there horses near.

Creeping back down the hill, I glanced over the route we had already covered. Our comrades were not in-sight. "Jay, head back and stay low. When you get to the others have them advance with caution. I will scout around this encampment and see what I can pick up. I will meet you at the hollow just over a mile back along the trail, hold the others there until I come."

Jay nodded before running back along the path.

I rose, having to pause as strange tremors seized my limbs. Creeping back to the top of the hill, I saw the men take the head priest and bind him to a pole in the center of the encampment. The other priests were staked out nearby, forced to watch, helpless.

Turning to the side, I spied a low hollow running down the side of the hill, filled with mid-sized bushes. Lying flat I was able to creep through them without disturbing the branches, and I was soon sneaking along the edge of the encampment. Two guards stood near the hollow.

The red bearded guard spoke suddenly "Do you think the others will catch the young scholars easily?"

"Aye" the brown headed guard said "don't think there will be an issue. They ain't likely to set a guard. Once we get the younguns here we'll have some fun with the priest, see how their darkness stands against that of our leader." Both laughed harshly then Redbeard spoke.

"The only thing that could spoil the party is someone who can use light skills, and has enough courage to challenge our dear leader to a duel."

"Which is impossible" snorted Browny.

Creeping backward, I made my way back up the indent. Once out of sight, hidden behind the hill, I ran back to our little rescue band as fast as I could pelt.

Arriving before them, I waited. The raiders would succeed in seizing the other youth. Hopefully that would simply be all, and not that the weaker ones would be instantly killed. Even with all seized the raiders would be likely to make some examples, so anyone who resisted could expect to be brutally slain as a warning. Bondage to fear is what the darkness loves.

The others arrived, jogging into the hollow. I did not wait for Finan to address me, but spoke out.

"The raiders have encamped a mile from here, within a larger hollow. There are but ten men there now, guarding the captive priests. The other fifteen are away to the south and east hiding in wait for the other party."

Murmurs of dismay came from two of the band, and Finan looked grim. I continued, making deliberate eye contact with Finan.

"I overheard two guards talking. They plan to make an example of the head priest, to see if his darkness is greater than their leaders. They are confidant. There is however, one chink in their plans. If a wielder of light challenged their leader, he could be defeated. The rulership of the band would then go to the victor."

Silence filled the rescue party, then the young woman spoke. "A light wielder when all our youth are going to be trained in darkness?" She snorted harshly "They are right to be confidant for I know nothing that could help."

The others nodded agreement.

"It appears then, that we must rely on stealth and attacking when they least expect it. Perhaps we can free the priests before the rest of the band gets back." Finan said, yet even as he spoke, cold dread settled upon me. If Light was indeed the only hope, then one of us had to show their skill, for myself it would reveal a prophetess. For Finan, how could he return? What would I do without him to guide me?

"We should rest for a few minutes before we act." Finan said, "I will reconnoitre and return shortly."

Chapter 12: The First Fight

I lay back on the grass, course fully grown stems heralding the soon approaching fall. I watched Finan slip out of the hollow, barely stirring the long grass as he crept along. The others had settled in the shaded section of the hollow and appeared content. I appeared relaxed, but the butterflies in my stomach told me I was faking it.

Finan soon returned, and called us together for a decision. "I do not feel right taking our whole band into the encampment, something is fishy about it. There are now no guards posted at all, but two tents now stand behind the place where the priests are bound." Scanning over the band, Finan nodded as if making a decision. "Mayim, you and Jay shall remain without. Watch what transpires and if we be taken then do you do what seems best to you."

"I would rather risk it with you all," I said, without thinking, "But, why should only two stay without?"

"Two does not weaken our force severely, and six can take on ten without too much hassle I hope. However, if we become the ambushees instead of the ambushers I would rest better knowing two at least could still carry the news, and perhaps bring help."

Finan's logic was undeniable and with a sigh, Jay and I watched the others creep out of the hollow. Hardly had they gone, before I said to Jay "Let us sneak up to the top of the hill, we can lie hidden there and observe what takes place."

Jay nodded, and accordingly we first ran, and then snuck to the top of the hill overlooking the Raider camp.

Hardly had we taken positions, before I spotted a nearly invisible, cautiously crawling figure creeping up to the first priest. A glint from the knife shot across the vale, as the crawling figure started to cut at the rope. An unearthly scream rang across the plain. The figure rolled away from the rope, which kept screaming.

The guards on the far side spun around. They moved fast, dashing forward to prevent a renewed attempt at rescue. The tent sides behind the bound priests crashed down and the rest of the Raider band burst forth. Within moments of the first attempt, all escape was cut off. The raiders had cut off the rescue party, without even half trying.

A short struggle commenced, with our friends trying to run away or fight. The only one who stood was Finan. Who, drawing his sword faced off with three of the raiders. He held his own well, inflicting several slight injuries. But, just as it looked like he could run. The Raider chieftain walked behind him, and with a club bashed him senseless.

I grabbed Jay as he started to rise, pulling him back and pinning him below the brow of the hill. "Let me go" he hissed "I have to help them" He struggled wildly, trying to get away and run down the hill.

"Stop it Jay" there is nothing you nor I can do, not against enchanted rope. They have all our friends, if you didn't notice the other band bound within the tents the raiders came from. Our only hope is that they do not know we are here."

"What will that matter, I'd rather go with them." Jay continued struggling, straining to escape my weight pinning him down.

"It matters because we can do no good running down and giving ourselves up, there is one bit of hope and that is that they will do the usual trial by battle for our groups' leader."

Calming slightly, Jay shook his head "only Light can defeat the raider, and no one wields light. Today it is a forbidden practice. Anyone who wielded light would be unable to return to their home, let alone continue to the school."

"That as it may be" I whispered back, fearing that our raised tones could have carried beyond the little hill. "It is raider law that the one who defeats their chieftain will be chieftain in his stead, so if one triumphed they would be unlikely to return anyway."

Jay nodded, and I rolled off him. With my ear to the ground, I froze. "Quick" I whispered, crawling rapidly over into a tiny cluster of bushes and long grass. Jay followed. We had barely reached shelter, when four men strode over the hill top. Standing still they scanned the land in the distance, and then close to hand.

"I don't see anyone, you must have been hearing things." The one to the right said, snorting at the middle man. Who's slight build, and uneasy demeanor did not comport well with a band of fierce raiders.

"I heard voices, I know I did." He said, frowning at the landscape as if by will he could make us appear.

"I don't know why the boss is taken with you" the third man sneered "yesterday it was footsteps through the ground, today its voices on the air. What will it be next time, the foretold prophet of the Light Giver showing up in camp?" The two men laughed harshly at the slight youngster, and pushing him roughly returned to camp.

Jay leaned against my shoulder, "how did you know they were coming?" he whispered, a hint of awe in his tone.

Turning I wriggled through the bushes, and headed for the opposite side of the raiders camp. The side with the Raider's tents. "I heard the vibrations through the ground when I rolled off you, it is a simple skill." Chancing a glance over my shoulder I could tell that he did not think I was telling the truth.

After an hour and a half worth of creeping and crawling, combined with many stops as dark thunder rumbled over the camp, and shocks shook the ground. We finally, without being detected, crept under the edges of the newly set up side tents, and then forward under the tent flap to see what was happening.

Within the center of a makeshift arena was the chief priest, who had betrayed us. He was bound, thrashing, to a post. The ground was scorched with signs of blackness, the dark magic. Inhaling carefully, I detected a bitter and metallic tang, like rusty iron, in the air. Jay breathed in my ear "the raider boss just cast a transformative spell, that priest is going to transform into a Verat!"

"What is a Verat?"

"It looks like a giant winged and scaled rat, it can take the head off a man in one swipe. Destroy a grainfield in a night, and even cast spells of its own, depending on the strength of the individual it came from. Some say they can even breath fire."

Even as I started to question the description, the raiders brought forward a large cage. Solid iron bars, floor, and roof left little doubt of the intention. Even less when the flailing, screaming, and still bound priest was thrust into it.

All present, for the other priests, those who sought the school, and our band of would-be rescuers were tied up, watched in horror as the transformation became complete. What had once been a priest was now a beast dedicated to serve the same darkness as the priest had been.

The Verat was five feet tall, with a wingspan topping fifteen feet. The body was covered in dirty brown scales, and the wings were covered in fine downy fur. Two canine teeth protruded over its slobbering lips, and its feet and wingtips were armed with five inch long claws.

Jay gulped audibly, and crept backwards deeper under the tent's pegged edge. My eye was drawn from the Verat to the Raider chieftain. Dashing in his own right, he swaggered in front of the captives.

"Well slaves, as we took three groups of ye who's going to face me next. I'm still prime for fighting that wasna even a warm-up." His eye roved over the youngsters who had sought the school. Scanning them myself I realized that Evean was not among them. Nor, I realized with a start was his horse among the captured horses. It appeared the foppish noble had mounted and left, perhaps seeking aid, or simply trying to save his own skin.

Finan had twisted his head around, and after a few seconds he spoke. "The one who was left to lead them is no longer present. They have no leader to face you."

"Silence" yelled one of the raiders to the side, stepping forward to strike Finan with a whip. The Chieftain whirled, glaring at the interference. The raider stepped backward slowly, "I didn't mean anything by it captain, I swear" he swallowed hard.

"Of course ye didn't, how could ye. But I'd remind ye laddie that I'm in charge here and as I asked for a leader to step forward. Ye should na interfere, one more out of line from you lad and it'll be your last."

The man turned and fled into the shadows of the other watching raiders. The chief raider then turned to Finan. "Why would ye tell me the second group was leaderless? It doesna seem a wise thing to say as it draws attention to ye."

"Sir" Finan said, always respectful, "it appeared just to me to speak, as I was for a time counted as leader of the whole group. It was not until we had decided to split into two parties that there were two leaders. As such, I am willing to take responsibility as leader of both parties."

Leaning forward, till his nose almost touched Finan's the Raider chieftain hissed "Does that mean you'll fight me little man. A cockerel like you fighting Raider Zar!" He nearly tumbled backwards laughing. "Twill not be a fight but a slaughter." He shouted to his men, who readily joined in the laugh against Finan.

Suddenly Finan's ropes dropped off, as Zar stalked to the center of the ring. "Give him back his weapons lads," he ordered "then let him face me."

Two raiders returned Finan's sword, dagger, and a shield to him. He immediately dropped the shield, and drawing sword and dagger checked that both were sound. Then he turned and entered the area of trampled grass that formed the arena.

Fear filled me. Fear like I had never known. Darkness swirled around me, blinding and choking at the Light within. Struggling against it, I breathed aloud "The Giver of Light is my Light and my justification, why should I fear you servant of darkness? My hope is founded on an eternal foundation, you cannot steal it from me."

Suddenly the darkness lifted, and I beheld a man before me. Clothed in radiant raiment, his belt and sword were of gold. His shield, armour and helmet gleamed with unearthly radiance. His voice rang within. "The One is my shield" he said "focus on the One, for faith in Him is your shield in every battle and can shield those whom you love." The light blazed around him, forming a six pointed star of solid light, then he faded away.

Swords clashed and grated. Finan ducked and dodged away, barely evading a deadly thrust. Suddenly Zar raised his sword, uttering a few words in a language I did not know, his sword lit with black flames. Leaping back, Finan stood on guard. Then a panicked look crossed his face as no answering flame of Light appeared on his sword. He vainly struggled to repel the powerful attacks. Staring at his sword, I whispered "the Light of the One is our sword, His word our mighty weapon." Hardly had I finished before white flame sprang up on Finan's blade. Zar stumbled back as the Light temporarily bewildered him.

Finan advanced swinging steadily. Then, suddenly he stumble back. His sword flew from his hand. The light disappeared, and ropes rose to bind him.

"A pretty display, and if you had not used light you might have lived as a brave foe. But anyone who wields light is my deadly foe and from me receives death." Zar said, stalking forward. "But for you, you have a choice of what I shall transform you into. A horse, to carry us willingly to different places on raids where your spirit will yet fly free in battle. Or, a Verat as the other, to do our bidding and never be free till the darkness consumes you."

Pushing himself to his knees despite the ropes, Finan gasped out "I will die rather than serve you in any form. The Light is my strength and by it I will fall"

The words of the blazing man returned to my mind, and I breathed "the One is my shield, and my strong tower. He protects those who love Him and His light guides and protects them no matter what."

Zar sneered, "you have no choice, fool, a Varat you shall become." A stream of darkness shot from his hand, streaking straight for Finan's chest. Within a foot of his chest, a blast of white light shot from the ground. Absorbing the darkness and scattering it around the Light Shield. A solid six pointed star formed around Finan. The ropes, magic as they were, dissolved as the shield formed. Finan rose, reaching out to grasp his sword and coat it in Light, even as we had been trained. Stepping forward the shield moved with him, still blazing.

Zar stumbled back, tripping on a rabbit hole and falling flat on his rear. "Mercy" he whined "I did not know you were a knight, protected by the prophet's promise. Have mercy..." his voice cracked as Finan did not slow his advance.

Stepping in front of Zar, Finan spoke "When the priest cried for mercy, did he receive it? When women and children begged for mercy, did you grant it? When men quailed before you, begging to die as men and not as beasts, did you have mercy?" Finan's voice rose steadily, till he shouted "Having no mercy, should you receive mercy? If even one" his voice dropped "could tell me you showed them mercy. I would grant it to you."

Finan's eyes roved over the band, but no one moved. Not one captive moved either. "No one speaks for Zar dreaded captain of the Raiders?" Finan asked, "then by their silence your men have condemned you."

Raising the sword, still coated in Light, Finan stepped back and struck. The blade did not touch Zar, but the Light did. Strengthened by the shield, the sword shot a beam of pure light over Zar. A single scream, and Zar disappeared in a flash of Darkness. Never to be seen again.

Turning, Finan spoke "I have heard it said that when the Raider's leader is beaten the one who is victorious is given the leadership of your band. Is this true?"

The biggest and nastiest looking of the Raiders stepped forward trembling, kneeling down he spoke. "It is true Lord Finan, and we are your servants to do with as you please."

"What is your name?" Finan asked, looking slightly startled at the man's actions. For when he kneeled all other raiders also knelt before him.

"It is Zypher my lord."

"Then Zypher rise, for I will have no one kneel before me. Your adoration belongs to the Light Giver alone, I am but a man as you are."

Shocked looks were exchanged by the raiders, but they rose even as Zypher rose. Zypher hesitated and then said "what of the captives Sir Finan, they are thine now."

Chapter 13: A First Enemy

With a smile Finan responded, "First, Finan will do fine I need no fancy title. Second, we shall escort these youth to their destination. At which time, when they are safe, we will decide where the band shall roam and what the band shall do next."

As the decision was declared, a cheer came from the men and the captives. Indeed the captives were hardly captive for when Zar died the magic ropes had disappeared. The only thing that remained of Zar's activity was the Varat, unfortunately. How it was to be dealt with I had no idea.

Glancing around Finan smiled and called "Mayim, I know you are hiding around here somewhere... you and Jay" before he could finish we both scrambled out from under the tent flap. Cueing astonished looks from all present. "I did not realize you were that close" Finan smiled. "How long do you think your journey will take now that we have enough horses for all?"

"Not long" Jay replied "a day and a half at most."

Finan nodded, turning to the raiders, "two men shall ride and scout around the school. I suspect that one of the second party tried to ride there to give warning. If he can be intercepted all the better for the rest of us. But if not, we must have warning if the school launches a full scale re-gain attack."

Two of the raiders jogged over to the hobbled horses, whistling lightly. Within a few seconds they had retrieved their horses and were mounted and galloping off toward the school.

Food was prepared, and that night was spent in feasting, resting, and tall tales of the adventures of the raiders.

After the others were settled Finan and I withdrew to Zar's tent. "It needs some serious cleaning" Finan commented. I nodded, taking in the blood red walls decked with pentagrams, intertwined circles, never ending knots, and other and sundry symbols of darkness. Reaching for the Light Finan gathered it into himself, then let it go with a bang. Instantly, everything related to darkness was dissolved in overwhelming light.

"That works" I said, settling down on the one stool that had not been dissolved.

"It took more than I expected, but I guess that is no surprise." Finan frowned, then flopped down onto the floor. "What I want to know is what you and Jay were doing in the middle of the raider encampment, particularly after the rest of us got captured. That was not in your orders."

"It may not have been in the order you gave, but it was in the orders I received." I responded, "I doubt you'd have lived if we had not been present."

"That is true, but what if you were discovered and slain? Using the Prophet's Shield did help, but it was a foolish risk."

I shrugged and, avoiding the question, changed the subject. "It does not help that you are staying free while I must go to the school. Anyway, I doubt anyone suspects, except perhaps Jay since he was so close to me and I have no idea if any visible sign appeared on me."

Finan rolled his eyes, "If Jay guesses it does not matter, but if he tells then it matters a great deal. What do you think we should do, I could keep Jay with the band?"

"I'd rather not, let us talk to him first. If he did notice, perhaps he will agree to not say anything. If he didn't notice anything then we are fine. He is likely to be suspicious of our questioning, so how will that work?"

A knock sounded outside the tent, coupled with a low cough. "Can I enter Finan?"

"Come in Jay"

Stepping through the tent flap, Jay hesitated when he saw that Finan was not alone. "If you are busy I can come back later."

"It is no problem" I broke in, "if you need to talk to Finan alone I can leave." I rose from the stool, glancing at Finan as I did so.

"Well," Jay replied "I was actually hoping to talk to both of you. The priests and encampment are in a furor over what Finan did. But I for one am not so sure it was all Finan's doing." Jay dropped his voice and quickly sat down between Finan and myself. "I was next to you Mayim, and the ground around you was blazing with light. If you had not been under the tent it would have blinded all."

"Does anyone else suspect anything?" I asked, noticing that Jay still seemed amazingly calm for someone who was in the presence of two accursed light wielders.

"Not that I have heard." Jay said "few can understand how it happened, particularly among the priests as they claim to be able to detect skills in the Light. However, you two are not the only ones among our party who bear the Light." Jay hesitated, glancing between us. Then without saying another word, he raised his right hand. A small ball of light formed on the palm of his raised hand, illuminating the tent.

"A light in the darkness" Jay said softly "the only skill my family knew, and the one that was passed down. I was amazed when you coated your blade with Light, Finan, for I had only heard of it being done in the ancient tales."

Finan smiled "It is not a difficult feat though apparently fear makes it more difficult, Mayim coated my blade the first time and I only succeeded the second time. In truth I am glad that you have some skill in Light as well. Mayim is continuing on to the school, as you both bear the burden of Light perhaps you can watch out for her as I would?"

"I would be honored" Jay replied, his eyes widening perceptibly. "Yet I do not feel worthy, or able to do such a" he hesitated an instant "responsible and joyfilled task."

"Joyfilled? More like 'likely to be terror filled' task" I quipped, glancing sharply toward Finan. "Besides , I doubt protection will avail if discovered."

"That is true" Finan said, "protection would not avail once discovered, however a friend can aid in keeping that discovery from happening. Now, if we remain closeted in here too long the others will suspect that something is up."

However, we need not have worried about others missing us. All and sundry, except the sentries, were sound asleep despite the fact that the sun was just setting. I settled myself down near the edge of one of the fires, far enough away to avoid spontaneous combustions. But still close enough for warmth.

Dawn came soon, and with at the scouts to the school with a very angry Evean in tow.

"Looks like you caught the right fish" one of the sentries quipped as the scouts with the prisoner entered camp. The scout gave a broad smile, glancing sidewise at the mortified look on Evean's face.

"Greetings commander" The scout said, saluting Finan as he reigned up "apprehended the individual you requested before the school could be informed. The youngens should meet with a normal welcome, instead of a warm welcome, now."

"Thank you for your service sir," Finan responded politely "I will take charge of the lad now and you can go and refresh yourseves and your horses"

With a nod of thanks the scouts rode away. Finan turned to find Evean glaring daggers at him. "So," Evean hissed "you are in charge of this little band of brigands; I might have known that your false sense of ability was but a cloak to hide your pride. And your deception."

"Silence" Jay snapped, stepping forward into Evean's field of vision "Finan won the command of this particular band of brigands in fair combat. Ask anyone present here, whether brigand, priest, or student what happened. As for you, you have no reason for ire as you would have brought out the school to annihilate a band of brigands and instead annihilated us."

"You are not my equal to rebuke me like that, little noble" Evean nearly shouted, not noticing or caring that all eyes nearby were now on him. "I have been unjustly apprehended, confined, and dragged halfway across the plains and" he stopped abruptly, as my fist slammed into his chest, knocking him flat on his backside.

"And," I said calmly flexing my right hand "if you do not shut up I am likely to decide you need to walk for the remainder of our trip to the school. These brigands will be our escort to make sure no other bands of rovers look at us as easy prey. Furthermore if you speak one more word of what you do not know, I will make you eat it, you," I paused deliberately "you dusty bottomed, lame legged, excuse for brigand target practice."

Leaving him sitting on the ground, where I had knocked him, I stalked over to the opposite side of the camp. Sitting down on the crest of the hill, where I had first spied out the encampment, I watched the steady stream of activity down below. Jay soon joined me.

"It is not good to make enemies Mayim. Evean has many friends, and a loose tongue unfortunately, I call him not my friend but tis ill you should make him a foe."

"He deserved it" I shrugged.

"That as it may be, we must be on our guard. Although the insult was well crafted, it is all the more stinging for the directness of its strike." Jay chuckled slightly "Brigands target practice is insulting to anyone, though it seems more insulting to the brigand since the target is still alive."

"Perhaps, but since the brigand's goal was a live capture, it still seems relevant" I smiled slightly. "I will remain on guard."

Jay nodded "I am sure you will, but can personal guardedness guard against a vile tongue, or a stab in the back?"

Rising without waiting for my reply, Jay jogged back down into the camp, which was steadily being broken up.

Laying back on the ground, I stared up at the sky. A brilliant shade of aquamarine blue with scarcely a white cloud to mar its perfection, even the sun itself blazing brilliantly did not detract from the piercing blueness.

Perhaps Jay was right and I had gotten carried away. Yet at the same time the son of a stuck up prig needed to be put in his place. There was no reason or purpose, except spite, for speaking the way he had, without even knowing what was going on. He deserved it.

Chapter 14: On to the School

The more I lay and thought the angrier I became. After a time, I realized that laying there thinking was not going to accomplish anything. Rising I jogged back down into the camp, and threw myself into packing, and organizing for the two, six hour jaunts, that would bring us to the school.

Nothing exciting happened, and as the sun began to set on the second day from leaving the encampment. Finan called me to his side. "The school is just beyond the next hill. From here to there you must travel alone. Watch Evean closely, and do you and Jay make the first report if possible. I do not trust Evean one whit, for he carries a grudge as a tree carries the effects of an insect attack."

Turning Finan placed one hand on my shoulder "take care, and if ever you are suspected do not hesitate to flee. I learned yesterday that the band normally roams along the path we planned to take, and down from there about ten miles. It is a large area, yet still small enough to find us if you have need."

I nodded and then walked to the front of the youth. They were unsuspecting really, for most this was simply a big adventure, yet for Jay and I it had become life or death. Glancing around I spied the priests and waved them to the forefront.

"It would be best for you to lead" I said, addressing the senior priest present "there is less likelihood of a mistake being made of who approaches then. If anyone needs to be questioned concerning what happened when you and your brothers were absent myself, Jay, and the priest who was with us would be happy to answer them."

The priest nodded gravely "I understand" a half smile formed and leaning slightly forward he whispered "at least you don't want Evean to have the first shot. I was watching and he was just asking to be knocked down. You did it wonderfully though he doesn't think so." I grinned as the priest winked, and went to rejoin the other priests.

Without looking back toward the plains we proceeded in procession toward the school. The raiders had managed to position us exactly as we would have approached had our course remained unaltered the previous days. Thus their goal was that it would not be suspected that there were raiders, nor could we be suspected as being raiders.

No stir was occasioned as we drew near, and soon we were welcomed into the safety of the school walls. It was called the "Priestly School for Divine Enlightenment" and many priests were in evidence, bustling around to take the horses to the stables and help the new arrivals get into the shared rooms. That is shared between girl and girl, or guy and guy.

Two priests led the guys away, and soon some priestesses came to lead the girls to their dorm. Hefting my bag back up to my shoulder, I dropped into the rear of the group. A younger girl from a different area that had also just arrived dropped into step beside me, without saying anything. As we arrived at the dormitory the lead priestess turned around and said.

"You will learn the rules. There is to be no books in the dorm, no boys permitted in the girl's dorm, and no food permitted here either. Anyone caught fighting, bullying, or being obnoxious to a teacher will be punished by being docked a meal. Anyone who breaks a rule will be severely punished, either by enforced fasting or temporary imprisonment for correctional teaching. Is this understood?"

Dumb nods followed the pronouncement. The priestess continued "If you have a friend, stay alongside them as rooms will be assigned in order of arrival at their doors." Without waiting for a reply, the priestess led the way within the building.

Dark and narrow hallways assailed our line, preventing easy access to the building. Trailing deliberately, myself and the younger girl entered last. Swiftly stepping down the hall we could hear the priestess saying "Next three in this room, Four in this room. Hurry up at the back there." We wound rapidly through the floors, until we reached the top story.

Finally I was just behind the priestess, when she turned and glanced behind "Just two of you? That's perfect this last room is just large enough for you. Do you know each other?"

I shook my head slightly, even as the younger girl did the same. She piped up softly "I didn't know anyone, and I'd prefer someone I completely didn't know to someone who I recognized but who didn't know me."

The priestess hesitated, a slight smile graced her lips and she said "then I hope you two can get along well, for we do not usually place two people so diverse in age together." With a nod, she turned and left us at the door to the room.

We stepped into the narrow room, barely wide enough for the two straw pallets that were on the floor. Bumped against the end of the pallets was a low table, stuck tight against the wall under a narrow window. Over the beds were hooks for clothing, and upon the bed a single thin wool blanket.

"It is good the window is glass" the girl said "otherwise we would be far too cold come winter. Do you have a preference for side?"

"They look the same to me, so whichever side is fine. My name is Mayim"

The girl turned with a smile, "I am Frost, though why my parent's called me that they never explained. I am happy to meet you Mayim, and I hope we will get along well together."

Frost settled down on the left hand side, and I settled down on the right. It was still early afternoon, but even with the sun setting on that side of the house, little light came through the window.

"I hope we can have candles. At least they were not on the short forbidden list we were given." Frost said, shifting to start unpacking her bag.

"Aye, though since we do not need to read here as we cannot bring books, I am not sure what use a candle would be. They probably expect us to master how to conjure a non-burning light of some type first."

Watching her as closely as I was, it was hard to miss Frost's slight jump of surprise and shiver of distaste at the mention of a non-burning light.

Changing the subject Frost said "I think we have an orientation, or whatever they called it, session or something in half an hour. We'd better finish getting settled in first. It is likely our room will be among the warmest since we are on the top floor."

Hanging up my spare casual dress, and light cloak, I stretched and then folded the sack I had packed them in, placing the sack over the thin blanket, at the foot of the pallet. I placed the herb pouch and equipment pouch above the door lintel, hidden from sight unless you knew their presence.

Frost's nervousness at the mention of conjuring a non-burning light surprised me. Most were eager to learn the dark skills, unless they were like Jay and myself who already wielded the light. Making a snap decision, I broke the silence.

"I hope so, but as I am already finished, perhaps you can tell me why you shuddered at the suggestion of learning to conjure something."

Frost spun round, staring at me. Barely masking the shock in her gaze she finally said. "I do not desire to speak of that, it is…"

I did not let her finish, but raised my right hand carefully. "Hush" I said, carefully summoning a tiny gleam of Light. Frost's face paled.

"How can you do that, those skills were lost long ago." she whispered "yet they are the reason I will never chance the dark powers. Once my family held those skills, yet long ago the memory of them was lost." Suddenly she glanced around, "you should not do that here it can be detected!"

I had already released the light, as soon as I had her attention, and I smiled slightly. "I learned on the way here that this place was once a school for the study of Light. It was even said that some rooms were built with a field that hide the presence of the Light within them. If the story is true, then some places in the heart of this darkness can have Light practiced without detection."

Frost shook her head, "foolishness" she whispered.

I smiled "At least until we learn if there are still safe spots, or if they have all been destroyed. I doubt it was detected. It was quite brief."

The bell clanged outside in the courtyard. "Time for assembly" I quipped, scrambling out the door as Frost dashed off. As our room was on the third floor, our quick scramble down was impeded by those on lower floors also scrambling. As it was, we were the last into the courtyard for assembly.

The head priest and priestess stood together in the center of the courtyard. "Welcome, I am pleased that some of you could tear yourself away from your rooms to attend here." The priest said, his eyes never leaving Frost or myself. "As this is your first day we shall be lenient, but from henceforward tardiness will be punished, and the last comer disciplined." The priestess leaned forward and whispered in his ear, with a nod the priest continued. "For those of you on the upper floors, some allowance will be made, though not waiting for the bell will be best."

With a nod the priest stepped aside and the priestess spoke.

"The schedule will be as follows for the first month. Mornings start at six with breakfast, after you are finished eating you can go and tidy your rooms. At seven the lowest floor and the second floor will go to magic class, the third floor will go to archery. At ten the second floor will go to archery, the third floor to sword practice. At noon is lunch. At one the first floor will start archery and the third magic, while the second goes to sword play. At three the first will go to sword, while the second goes to horses. At six is supper. At seven the second floor will have three hours of magic practice, while the first and third floors have two hours of horse. At either nine or ten you will convene at the library for an hour and a half, half an hour if you just came from magic. At half past you will go to your rooms and sleep till six. Understood?"

"Aye" we chorused, though I realized that we would scarce have time to study anything until our specialties were revealed due to this insane amount of practice. They probably designed the first month to tire out the students so there would be less resistance.

The priestess' voice broke through my thoughts, "If that is understood, dismissed! I expect you to be prompt to dinner, for now you may explore."

We stood waiting in ranks until the priest and priestess had gone inside. Glancing at Frost, I said "Let's check out the perimeter and see what we can see."

Leaving the others to their own devices, we headed around the building. The girl's dormitory was on the Western side of the school precincts, just across from the guys' dorm on the eastern side. To the north was a huge building, which we soon discovered held many classrooms and the library. Farther north of that was the dining hall, and beyond that was the horse fields. I could recognize some of the horses out in the fields alongside many more horses that I did not recognize. Over at the side of the fields, exactly opposite the stables, was a large circular building. Its purpose was not evident, it reminded me of something but the word evaded me. Walking along the fence we came to the archery and sword play areas. Some men, perhaps priests or older students already skilled, were standing around looking over weapons, guards, and other paraphernalia.

"Hey gals," one of the guys called "You planning on deliberate specialization, or you going to try and do your best with everything?"

"I did not realize you could deliberately specialize" I replied, "Why do you ask?"

"Cause if you were going to try and specialize in weaponry I'd tell ya don't bother" the guy said, shaking his red hair "No woman can ever wield a blade let alone compete with Ian McBregnal"

"Well Ian," I smiled slightly "I have not been a woman to back down from a challenge, and as my brother is not here to hear your comments I will reserve the right to challenge you. If indeed you aid in sword practice."

"Well" Ian said, shaking his head so that his hair flew across his eyes "if ye can defeat me tomorrow, before ye receive training, I will admit a woman can fight. But if not, I'd say stick to womanly arts and leave the fighting ta the men."

I blinked so that he could not see me roll my eyes. Frost whispered "Let's look at the archery area, I know I can do that." She smiled, and we continued walking. After the archery we passed by the start of the farm fields attached to the school, already harvested.

"We still have an hour till supper, let's head back to our room" Jogging lightly we swiftly covered the distance, and walking up the stairs entered the room. It was a disaster zone. The ticking was shredded, our clothing ripped apart, and the window smashed. Even the heavy table had been hacked, though not much damaged.

Chapter 15: Enemies or Friends

Frost stepped back, her mouth hanging open. "Who would do such a thing?"

"I have my suspicions, or at least my suspicions of who instigated it though the instrument could have been found within this dorm. Do you go and find one of the priestesses and report what has happened, I will make sure no one comes back here." With a nod, Frost dashed off down the stairs, her footsteps nearly silent.

Stepping inside, I crouched carefully behind the door, to remain invisible if anyone approached. Glancing up I confirmed that my small bags were still safe. A few seconds of silence came, and then I heard soft footsteps creeping down the hall.

"Do you think they both left?" A girl's voice whispered

"Yeah, probably to report it but we'll make it far worse ere they get back" the second girl giggled maliciously. "I have the pitch and mud mixture, we'll teach that upstart to lip to a noble."

Standing up I stepped in front of them, "Hold right there" I said, meeting there gaze calmly. "It seems you have a grudge against me, and I would know why it is that you'd make another suffer to suffice your spite."

The one carrying the pitch stepped backward in surprise, and tripped on the hem of her dress. Even as she fell, I stepped forward lifting the pitch and mud bucket out of her hands with my left while grabbing her wrist with my right, to prevent her fall. The eldest startled just as much, finally said softly "Evean told us to because you'd lipped him off. And he said that you'd steal the respect we deserve as nobles."

"If you act in a manner worthy of respect then you shall receive it." I said, shaking my head. "But if you act in a manner unworthy of your station any respect you had will be removed and replaced with scorn. Respect must be earned. It can never remain with one who does not deserve it."

Placing the pail on the floor I added "you had better retreat quick, as Frost is coming with a priestess and they are nearly at the door. As your room is on the second floor you can reach it if you are quick."

With a nod, the two girls dashed down the stairs, surprisingly silent for their haste. A few minutes later Frost and the head priestess arrived to the scene.

"This is unprecedented" The priestess said staring at the destroyed room. "It would appear you have made some enemies here. Do you have any ideas?"

"I have an idea" I admitted, "but would rather not say anything."

She raised an eyebrow "it would be better if you could, however we will install a lock on your door. Some new straw ticks will be brought up and you can stuff them with the straw here. A workman will be here soon to put a board over the window. I will make sure you are taught how to conjure a light tomorrow, but for now you must remain in the dark."

"I think that the table can be adjusted to work." I said, inspecting the hacked legs. Taking some of the larger hackings from the floor I soon had balanced the table comfortably.

The priestess nodded "It is good that you are innovative, perhaps some of the fabric of your clothing can also be salvaged, I will send needles and thread up to you by a servant."

After the priestess left, as regally as she had come, I turned and began sorting through the scattered fabric hackings to see what was mine, and what belonged to Frost.

After a few minutes, I noticed that Frost was crouching by the door in a state of melancholy. "Why are you so upset Frost? We can salvage some, and I am sure the school will provide another blanket apiece."

"Two things contribute" Frost sighed "my cloak was special for the winter, created by my mother from the last of our wool. Now that it is gone, I do not know what I will do for winter. That we shall lose our regular light to darkness is the other thing. I do not desire darkness, and there will be no other way to illumine our nights unless we risk all."

"Even so, sadness should not prevail. There are enough scraps of these blankets, and of both our cloaks that we can craft a warm cloak for you, or at least a warm covering for the beds."

A knock sounded at the door, and a servant stepped in and handed us two needles and two spools of thread. "From the chief priestess, you can use any fabric scrap you desire, whether blanket or ticking."

I nodded my thanks, and we began piecing and sewing the scraps together.

All too soon the dinner bell rang, and we hurried downstairs and north to the dining hall. Assembling into lines outside, we were ushered in. One line per table. To my surprise we ended up seated alongside the two who had destroyed our room. The younger one smiled slightly and leaning forward whispered "both of us have some extra clothing, if you and Frost are willing meet us tonight and we shall replace what we wrecked."

I nodded, but before I could say a word the priest stepped to the front. "Many things, my students, can be done using magic. Some may think it darkness, but it is skills, power, and ability to those who embrace it." Smiling craftily he added "dinner is served"

Almost before "served" was out of his mouth, full plates appeared from nowhere floating down the tables and settling before everyone. As we ate, a man came to the center of the hall. Sitting down on a stool, he took out a harp and began to strum it. Soon the sounds of a ballade rang through the hall, an ancient one I had been taught by Brenan. However, it was not the same story, for at the critical point of the battle the Light side summoned the Terror, and the Dark side destroyed it, history rewritten.

After he finished the head priest stepped again to the front. "I hope you enjoyed our guest tonight, he shall remain here for your first week and teach you of the ancient battles between deception and truth. You are now dismissed to bed."

Rising in an orderly fashion, we headed back to the dorm. Stepping swiftly along Frost and I soon arrived at our room. The window had been boarded up during dinner, and the straw ticks replaced. Our sewing however, was still on the table and had remained untouched.

Hardly had we settled down when a soft knock sounded on the door. Rising I opened it and observed it was the two sisters, back again.

The eldest spoke softly "I am sorry for what we did, and I ask your forgiveness Mayim, and you as well Frost. For our injustice was against you both, though our quarrel was with one of you, and not even personal."

"I, as well seek forgiveness, and to make restitution" the younger girl whispered, "will you accept"

Frost nodded staring at the two girls. Glancing at me for a second she spoke "I did not know you were responsible. How? What changed?"

"Mayim caught us coming to do more nastiness" the eldest admitted "I am ashamed to even admit our plan. However, we would make restitution if you would forgive and permit us."

"I forgive you freely" I responded

"I also forgive" Frost said smiling at the other younger girl.

"Perfect" they exclaimed together, relaxing visible. Shifting slightly they brought bundles out from under their cloaks. Each bundle contained two heavy dresses, and a heavy cloak, which amazingly were perfect fits.

"Thank you. We only had one spare dress each" I said, smiling.

"As it may be, we were sent with four winter dresses each" the elder girl said smiling "by the way I am Zey and this is my sister Zoe. We are from one of the coastal towns to the West of where Mayim lived."

"I am pleased to finally make your formal acquaintance." I smiled "I hope we shall be friends hereafter, or at least not enemies"

"In all seriousness" Zey said laughing "most of our group has shunned me since I told them I thought I saw a unicorn on our last day out."

"A unicorn? I thought those were mythical." Frost exclaimed, clearly surprised and perhaps a little impressed.

"As did I, at first, but it was so like a horse that I thought it was one, until I saw the horn. It was unlike the mythical ones in the stories though."

"That is interesting, Zay. What do you think of the other supposedly mythical beasts, like the Verat and the Dragon?" Frost asked.

"Well according to that harp player the light wielders summoned a dragon, which was vile and evil and was destroyed by darkness' side. As for the Verat, until last week I would have thought it was also mythical. However," she glanced at Frost, who had asked the question. "I watched as a raider captain turned the priest leading our group to the school into a Verat. I also watched as the one who challenged him was protected by Light, a shield such as I had never seen. So I personally doubt that the light wielders actually summoned a dragon."

"Aye," I agreed "that Verat looked nasty, far nastier than anything I thought of facing. I was glad that the raiders knew how to deal with it. However," My voice dropped to a whisper "I take it from your words that you do not mind Light working or those who wield it, is that correct."

"I guess" Zay responded glancing at Zoe, who was nodding. "Yeah we don't mind the Light, but we know nothing of it really. Our family has always hated the Light, but after what we saw." She shook her head.

"I really want to have a look in that library. There may still be some books about Light within its precincts, for this school used to be a stronghold of training in the Light." I said, watching the others carefully.

Frost nodded "We can help you ferret out the information" she grinned and added "I just hope that weasel of an Evean doesn't show up when we are doing it. I think we'll have a one hour session there for the first month. Though I doubt we will be able to search anything out till later, but after we are assigned our specialties there should be more time."

I laughed softly and glancing at the others said "yet we should be going to bed soon. We can renew our secret talks each night for a short time."

Morning dawned too soon for Frost and I. Dawn came cold, and we scrambled out of bed pulling on our dresses and cloaks. Slipping softly down the stairs, we arrived at the dining hall just as the breakfast bell rang out. Glancing around, as we settled down alongside Zay and Zoe I could not spy Evean anywhere.

"I wonder where Evean is, I would hate to be late. The priests are likely to be looking for an example." Zoe whispered, glancing around.

Shortly thereafter the priest stepped forward. "It seems not all of you were sufficiently impressed with the order to be on time. Let this be a reminder to you all, as well as a reminder that no males are to enter the female quarters at any time, for any reason."

Two under priests dragged Evean roughly forward. Glancing around he spied me and shouted out "Don't blame me, that prissy Mayim put a drug in my water last night. It's her fault, she hates me." He struggled wildly between the two priests.

The head priest raised an eyebrow at the accusation. "Mayim was here on-time. Come forward young lady."

Trembling started in my knees, but with an outward facade of calmness I rose and walked to the front. Inclining my head, I waited.

"Look me in the eye" he ordered.

Raising my head I paused, light filling my vision then dissipating as a voice said. "What should not be read, let it be blocked." As the words faded, I breathed them out, and looked without fear into the priest's eyes.

Flame leapt within his gaze, seeming to leap out and penetrate into my mind. As the fire intensified, burning pain lancing through my mind, suddenly it soothed, the fiery heat withdrawing as the priest looked away.

"The accusation is false, you may return to your seat Mayim."

As I walked unsteadily back, the priest spoke. "Bringing false witness is another forbidden practice within the school." He faced Evean "and as you can see we have ways of getting the truth, unless they can block. A feat which is impossible, for even the trained cannot block one who is more skilled in darkness."

Sitting now, my legs trembling, I could see that Evean was desperately searching for another accusation. But before he could speak the priest did.

"As a lesson today, you shall feel what it is like to face the fire of our lord's wrath. The fire you shall face forever if you fail him, or if you turn from him to follow the accursed path of" he spat the final words like poison "the Prophet's Shield."

Gazing into Evean's eyes, he immobilized him as the two guards released him and stepped back. Holding Evean helpless, the priest twitched his left hand and the lad caught fire. Flame leapt around him, and he screamed in terror and pain.

Anger flashed through me. Jerking to face the table, I leaned my forehead against it, blocking my ears. It took all my strength to remain seated as anger and fear warred within me.

Five seconds were all that passed, but it seemed like an eternity before the flame disappeared as suddenly as it had come. Evean collapsed upon the ground when the priest's gaze released him.

"Let that be a lesson to you all. Whoever does what is forbidden shall receive far worse punishment."

Chapter 16: Day One

We said nothing as we split up, Zay and Zoe heading to magic class while Frost and I headed toward the archery field. After the instructors finished their verbal instructions, I stepped forward to accept one of the bows. Frost was also handed a bow and a quiver of arrows.

"It is recommended that one shoots at least a score of arrows, that is twenty arrows, per session. As we have a three hour session two or three score of arrows can easily be shot." The instructor said, smiling maliciously at us all.

"Mayim, I canna string this bow at all, it is too heavy a weight." Frost whispered.

"Try mine, it is too light for me." I lifted Frost's bow and found it similar to the bow I had used at Brenan's. Frost nodded, signifying that the other bow would work for her.

Lining up, we each had a straw stuffed target in front of us.

"When ready, fire the full twenty arrows into your target. Once all the arrows are fired you are to go and retrieve your arrows, all of 'em, and return here. Then go sit in the shade while the other half shoots, and take turns till the end."

"Turn your bow arm out a bit, so you will not have the string hit your arm" I whispered to Frost.

We fired together, both shafts hitting the target. Within ten minutes all twenty shafts were embedded within each of our targets. Though some of the other girls were not so lucky as their shafts flew wide, high, or even low and missed the target completely.

Retrieval was quick on our part, and we soon settled comfortably down under the trees. The lads shot next, and instead of calling the girls forward to take their turn, the lads kept shooting for the full three hour archery session.

"I hope sword practice doesn't have the same thing happen" I whispered to Frost "I have a score to settle with that Ian McBregnal."

Frost shrugged "no one thinks gals can fight, I guess they think all gals enter the priestess-hood or something."

Ian was handing out blunted swords as we arrived. "Greetings lassies, are ye planning on challenging me today gal? I'd be happy to have a pre-volunteered sparring partner for the introduction."

Inclining my head I replied "I would be happy to oblige you, though it may not have the impact you desire."

He shrugged "that is a chance I am willing to take, for indeed I spied on the archery match and none of the lads shot as well as you two did. Twenty shafts a day will be plenty to keep your eye in shape." He smiled and whispered "though as for sword and shield, or dagger, we shall see for I still think no lassie can take on a man."

Assembling around the arena, each of the trainees was armed with only a sword. Ian stepped into the middle.

"Some have expressed doubt in learning the sword and if it would be of any use against magic. Well, against magic it is useless, but against beasts created by magic it can be of some slight use - or against brigands, robbers, and others who fight with dagger, sword, or spear, but not magic. Today I already have a volunteer for the first demonstration. Mayim would you come and demonstrate how to attack and defend with only a sword" Ian said, smiling grimly.

Walking into the center, I faced him calmly. Feet spread in a relaxed neutral stance, and sword raised ready to attack or defend at will.

Stepping slightly forward we began circling. Our eyes locked. The circling became faster. Ian lunged striking low. My parry rang across the circle. Talk ceased and eyes fixed upon us, the still circling combatants. Lunging again, with a thrust and feint combination Ian attacked, I turned it easily. I then advanced with a simple feint, lunge, parry, lunge combination, nearly making it past his guard. Ian jumped back with a brief look of surprise. Then rallying he attacked fiercely. Yet for all his speed and ferocity there were many openings. Far too many openings, I smiled.

After fifteen minutes intensive play, I lunged lightly forward. Catching his blade on mine, I slid my blade down his to get power near my hilt. With a quick twist, his sword flew through the air and a moment later my blade tip rested lightly on his throat.

"Do you yield?" I smiled, breathing as lightly as when I had begun the fight.

"Whist lassie" he exclaimed wringing his stinging hand "What was that last move? for ne're did I see the like afor. I yield aright, neva have I seen a lassie so skilled with the blade. Like an extension of your arm it seemed, and as deadly as yer bonny um..." he blushed suddenly, darting a sharp glance at my face, and stumbled off to retrieve his sword.

"If ye had finished that comparison, I may have been forced to doubt your yield. That would not be a good idea" I said.

Splitting us up, the three instructors soon matched students together. I was placed back with Frost, for as Ian said "your skills are better to train the youngsters, you can train in the last hour or so."

Sword play was brisk and we rarely stopped. The fresh alertness that came from being active, using every muscle to jump, parry, attack, and dodge was invigorating, even for the laziest present.

Lunch was normal, and afterward we convened to the stables. After cleaning out the stalls, we were given a mere thirty minutes of riding. When that was over we were ushered off to the magic classes.

Chapter 17: Magic Class

As we headed into the central building for magic class, I glanced at the other students. Most seemed tired, likely from mucking out the horse stables, but some were fuming. Frost, jogging lightly, caught up to me and said "What do those instructor's think, that we'll sit around and do nothing just cause we're commoners and women?"

"I do not know what they are thinking Frost, though I highly suspect that this month is simply to tire us out so we will not fight or argue."

"If that's the case" Frost paused, "then we'd better be alert" she winked.

"Aye, alert and ready for anything. Did you hear that the youngest priest, John I think his name was, is now the school janitor and no longer a priest? I wonder why they kicked him from the priesthood, maybe for being left behind by the raiders."

We headed through the dim door, and turning followed the other students up the stairwell.

"I don't rightly know" Frost replied, "there were some rumors about him refusing to tell who had light in your party."

Shaking my head, I fell silent. Jogging rapidly up the stairs to the top floor, we followed the other students into a single large room. The room had a sharply pitched ceiling, likely due to being under the roof. Rows of chairs and narrow tables spanned the room, leaving little space for walking. A larger lane ran down the center of the room lengthwise and the exact middle of the room widthwise.

Most students had already taken seats near the front. Frost and I grabbed two seats, close to the middle of the room and slightly back from everyone else.

An older priest, in the darkest blue robes, advanced to the front. "Welcome, students, to introductory magic class. Today you will learn of the history of this esteemed and useful practice." He smiled, and a chill went through me, for the smile was only skin deep. It did not reach his eyes.

He began expounding on how the magic they used was first discovered, and how vital it had been in the "war against the terror." Said "terror" had, as the bard had proclaimed the night before, been summoned by the "accursed Light Wielders."

As the priest droned on, my mind wandered. Cautiously I scanned the room, while apparently keeping my attention fixed on the priest. The room was lined with shelves of books, though one book near the priest caught my attention. It had a green and gold cover, unique since the other books either had red or dark blue bindings in this room. It was a narrow book, and nearly obscured by a thick layer of dust and grime.

My attention snapped back to the priest as he said "you may each choose two books from this room to look at for the rest of class. The right hand wall has history, the left basic magic skills. The back wall, by the entrance has combat magic and the wall behind me has defense magic. Any questions?"

No one answered.

He nodded "good, grab two books, return to your seats and read them."

He left the room, and everyone rushed for the back and left walls. I glanced at Frost "Let's get the front wall, with the defense skills." She nodded, and we quickly made our way to the front.

I headed for the book that had caught my attention. It was obscured between "Basic Defense Magic" and "Basic Shadow Magic Defense" I grabbed both titles, sliding them out with the green book between them. Frost had grabbed two smaller books, both on mitigating magic.

It took a few moments to navigate back to our seats, and once seated we began looking over the books. "How about we each brief the other on important points?" Frost said "It seems we'll get more covered that way."

"That sounds good" I nodded, Frost glanced at my books and froze. "I thought he said two books, why do you have three?"

I opened the thicker volumes and used them to obscure the smaller one. Turning it over I stared at the cover. "Light wielding: Basic defense, offense, and cloaking." It was the very book I needed. Thinking quickly, I shifted the mantle/scarf I was wearing so that it obscured the book even more. Then I slipped the book down into my dress, and wrapped the scarf as a belt around my waist and the book.

Glancing at Frost, who appeared to be very engrossed in her reading, though she kept glancing at me, I winked and began reading.

The Basic Defense Magic was actually surprisingly interesting. For a shadow or darkness magic attack one defended with a flame shield. Against flame, water or earth were used. Along with the descriptions was the methodology of casting. It was clear that only those fully into the darkness could cast the strongest defense or attacks. The dark magic's source of strength was the wielder's own depth of evil.

I turned to the other book, having finished a full scan in an hour. Defending against shadow magic appeared, from the first book, to be the hardest. It was shadows that had transformed the priest to a Verat, and once the shadow took hold there was no reverse. At the end of the shadow attack descriptions, I paused, for within the page was a note.

"Only light can truly defend against shadow and darkness. And only those who know the light can read this. Three places there are, made of Light infused wood, where Light can be trained undetected. In the dormitory, the final room on the top floor of the eastern dorm, the top floor of the main hall, and the tack room of the stable. Be aware, Take Care, and Learn well."

I leaned back, scanning the room as if in thought. So that is why they had not detected my foolish flash of light yesterday. For our room was one of the "Light infused" and therefore undetectable rooms. This room we were in now was also protected, likely because it had the smallest floor space and the roof was also infused. I grinned slightly, it was worth testing with care.

Hiding my hand under the table and closing it carefully, I leaned over the books again. I summoned a tiny light, keeping it fully hidden. No student seemed to notice. I waited, holding it for fifteen minutes, and then releasing it. The Light had remained undetected; I would try the tack room tomorrow. I grinned again, leaning back away from the books as if finishing reading.

Frost stretched, "Hefty reading" she shook her head. "Apparently the only way to successfully mitigate shadow or darkness is through using fire magic, and even then it doesn't always work. Earth can be marginalized with water or darkness, and water and fire mitigate one another. What did you learn?"

I grinned again "Shadow and darkness skills are the hardest to fight against, and shadow is the transformative one. Only the most powerful, and evil, of shadow wielders can cause shape change, but it is irreversible. Some temporary changes can be caused with earth, water, or fire elements though."

Frost nodded and stretched, "Guess it's time for supper, what are we to do with the books?"

Before I could reply, the priest entered the room. "If you are finished with the book, close it and place it in front of you. If you are not yet finished, leave the book open at your place. This room is for your study times, when they begin, and also for your magic training. The other classes have rooms below these. Once you are finished adjusting your books you are dismissed."

Frost and I rose immediately, and headed down to the dining hall. The timing had been adjusted so our group ate later than the others so that we'd have an uninterrupted three hour training stretch. After eating, since we still had time, Frost and I jogged back to our room.

Closing the door, we were plunged into darkness. With a flick, I summoned an orb of light. Frost gasped "That's dangerous Mayim, why would you do such a thing?"

"In here it is not dangerous, and there are three places where it is not dangerous. Our room, our training room, and the tack room at the stable. I summoned a light for fifteen minutes in class, and it was not detected."

Frost stared at me, and then shook her head again. "That is still risky. How did you know it was safe?"

"The last book I read, the final page was only half filled. But, the last half of that page was filled for those with eyes to see. It told me where the safe places were."

Frost grinned "Tips against the darkness I guess, but what are we to do with that" she inclined her head toward my waist.

"We will keep it hidden, if they knew it was here it would be destroyed. I doubt they will miss it, though it could have been detected while we were walking." I bit my lip "We will just have to watch."

"Aye, and hurry or we'll be late for library." Frost dashed out the door, as I quickly hid the book within my herb bag, above the door frame.

Library time was quiet, far too quiet. The lower floors, and higher ranking students, had settled in the comfortable areas. Cushioned armchairs and the like, Frost and I found a dim corner, and began inspecting the books near us.

A faint tingle drew me toward the darkest corner of the library, deep shadows hid the shelves and no one was nearby since it was too dark to read titles. I ran my hands over the book, and paused. A thick book vibrated slightly in the very darkest corner. Slipping it out, I turned and caught the title - "Skills of the Knights of Light" Studying the book carefully, I realized it had a protection upon it so that no one without light skills could locate it. It would remain invisible, or look like a normal book on darkness to ordinary browsers.

"Greetings Mayim, how was your day?" A light masculine voice whispered nearby. Glancing sidewise I saw Jay, leaning easily against the bookshelves.

"It was alright, except for mucking out the horse stalls instead of riding. How was yours?" I winked and grinned.

"It was alright, Evean is determined to make your life miserable though. He's claiming that you" he made quote marks with his hands "dabbled in light and are unworthy to live." Jay shook his head. "Other than that, the only class that was interesting was magic class. I noticed that everyone seems to want to know how to fight, and not how to defend."

I nodded, and turned back to the shelves, scanning for a second book to browse. "You might be interested in this one" Frost said, handing me a volume that tingled as the first had. "A volume on shadow weapons" Frost winked, "it looks interesting at the least."

Jay glanced closely at the books, and then grinned "I have a small table near. There is no one else close to it, so let's get studying."

Two books awaited us on Jay's table, both vibrating as the other books had. Reading steadily we waded through the three smaller texts rapidly. Within an hour we had each finished one book, and then preceded to read the other books as well. I slipped the thicker book back on the shelves in the back, once we had more study time there would be time to read it. The other three narrower books I placed on a low shelf beside the study cubby, where we could retrieve them the next day.

We headed out of the library last of all the students, the priests running the library smiled slightly as we passed. One of them commented "It is good to study hard while you have the strength. Do you know why we have the open study time?"

I shook my head, "No idea, though I would guess it is to see where the student's interest lies to help facilitate their specialty."

The priest nodded, "You are a smart one lass, you are the first to correctly guess the reason." He glanced at me again before heading back into the library.

"That was strange" Jay remarked, accompanying us to the spot where the path divided. "I guess we need to make sure we study widely while we have the chance."

"Aye" I agreed, "Learn lots while we can, and keep the knowledge secure." Jay bowed slightly and jogged rapidly down to his dorm. Frost and I turned the other direction, and ran lightly to reach our room. Arriving there just before the curfew bell, we collapsed on the bed chuckling.

"For not having any light in your rooms you two are sure cheerful." Zoe said, stepping through the unlocked door. "Zey and I want to know how you intend to specialize."

"I am not sure yet, I plan on looking for weapons technique books tomorrow, and possibly some history the day after. It seems best to get a full knowledge and then see how they specialize me."

"Same for me" Frost agreed. Zey and Zoe smiled in the dim hall-light. "We were thinking the same thing." Zey said with a smile. "We just wanted to make sure as we really would like to train with you eventually" Zoe added.

"We'd better get to bed" Frost whispered nervous suddenly "before they realize we're breaking curfew."

The sisters nodded, and slipped silently down the stairs. After they left, I closed the door and lit the room with a tiny sphere of light. Collapsing on the bed, Frost was asleep before I managed to remove my outer dress. With a smile I lay back, reviewing what I had learned that day.

Chapter 18: Specialties

The first month passed in a blur of activity. Weapon's practice became harder every day. Ian seemed to delight in training with Frost and I, even helping us perfect facing multiple opponents. Archery remained the same, with the girls only getting one quiver of arrows to fire a day. Barely enough to keep our eye's in shape let alone improve. Eventually we were given more time riding horses, and the last few days of the month even saw some horse combat training. Although that training was unlikely to continue after the specialties were unveiled.

Magic was the least eventful class, starting with a one hour lecture and ending with two hours of reading time. Frost and I nearly always managed two books apiece in that time, and varied it between technique, attack, defense, and restoration. Though indeed there were very few books on restoration and none of them involved the shadow, fire, or darkness magic only water and earth. During library Jay joined us for study, and over time we detected ten different books on Light skills within the library, all cloaked to hide them from detection.

The specialties were to be announced at breakfast today. As Frost and I headed for the dining hall, Zey and Zoe joined us with Zoe skipping uncontrollably.

Frost smiled, though they were the same age their temperaments were completely different. "What's got you so excited today Zoe? I doubt there is anything to be super cheerful about."

"We get our specialties today" she grinned "which means no more hugely long days, I hope."

I laughed, "Perhaps no long days, though I heard that they are going to shift roommates if their specialties are not the same." Frost froze, glancing at me sharply.

"I hope we don't get moved."

I shrugged, "We will see what happens."

With that we ducked into the dining hall, which was louder and more disorganized than any previous day.

Fast as we ate, it was still almost an hour before the head priest appeared. Frost wriggled nervously beside me, and suddenly Jay sat down on my other side. The priest began with the least desirable posts. Farmers and Craftsmen were called, first in general and then by profession and areas of interest. Farmers were broken down into crop and animal, and still farther into types of crops and types of animals. Craftsmen were divided into professions, such as weavers, potters, tailors, tanners, smiths, bowyers and the like.

Neither of us three were called during this section, though I caught the head priestess watching us closely during this time. Leaning closer Jay whispered.

"We're likely to be either arms-men or what they are now terming mages. Though since we have divided our studies fairly evenly there is no assurance until they call."

"Aye, even our studies makes us unsure of our specialty." I just resisted rolling my eyes. To fight for them mindlessly or become a willing servant, some specialty we were being given.

The newly chosen farmers and craftsmen were ushered out. I heard a whisper that they were to move to different floors of the dorms.

Next were called the arms-men, or warriors, those who were skilled with the blade and bow. Only men were called in this section, despite women having been trained as well.

After they were ushered out both the head priest and priestess stepped to the fore.
"Those of you who remain are our mage class, and have shown an aptitude and interest in the pursuance of magic. For this class alone you have a secondary choice as well. Mage classes will take the majority of your time, but for one hour of each day you may choose another area of study. This extra area may simply be the library, or it may be training with the sword and bow. This area may also be changed every week."

With a slight nod the priest and priestess exited the building. At the same time under-priests came and lead us back to the dorm. Our dorm was the same, though now the boys were down the left corridors and the girls were down the right hand corridors. The former all guys dorm was now the dorm of the craftsmen and farmer apprentices. The warrior apprentices were moved to a third dorm, which had been built during the month we were here.

Turning one of the light-blue robed priests beckoned me over.

"You and your roommate are both mages, do you desire to remain in thy room or move to a lower and more comfortable floor?"

"We will be happy to remain, it is less hassle to remain instead of moving around."

"Thank you" he smiled slightly, "your two friends" he nodded toward Zay and Zoe who were also mage apprentices, "have asked to move upstairs to the room next to yours. Your male friend over there has also asked to be moved to the top floor. You do know that male and female apprentices are not permitted into each other's rooms?"

I nodded, then beckoned Frost over.

"We are remaining in our room. Let's help Zay and Zoe move. Jay is also going to be upstairs." The grin I'd hitherto resisted broke through, and Frost laughed out loud.

It took less than an hour to help Zay and Zoe move upstairs, and by the time we finished helping them get comfortable it was time for lunch.

The dining hall was divided into sections according to profession. Mages were at one end, warriors at the other, and the farmers and craftsmen were down the center. Once everyone was seated, food was served in order of training. The food was blander than normal, consisting of boiled vegetables, plain bread, and a small serving of boiled meat. Jay raised an eyebrow at the food, and glanced over to see that the warriors had large servings of meat, while the farmers and craftsmen had more bread.

"What is it" he whispered into my ear "they want us to become vegetarians? I thought that was slang for a lousy hunter."

A slight smile flickered over my face, "supposedly the meat prevents focus, though I highly doubt the truth of that presupposition." I rolled my eyes. Then turned and applied my attention, and mouth, to the business of food.

Chapter 19: Secret Learning

After lunch we were taken to our introductory classes. Farmers and Craftsmen went to the fields and a low building near the stables. Warriors headed to the practice fields. While the mages headed to the top floor of the study building. We settled in on the benches. Our new teacher, an older mid-level priest, stepped forward.

"Today you are going to learn the basics of making a fireball, for the purpose of a non-burning light. This is the simplest skill, and should be the easiest to master. A fireball for light does not need the same strength of will, as a fireball which must be hot enough to burn."

Stretching his hand forward, a two inch ball of flame formed effortlessly. He passed it around the room. I lifted it cautiously, and felt an almost overwhelming urge to extinguish it with the Light. The ball of flame itself was barely warm, but vibrated strangely. I hurriedly passed it on.

The class dragged on as the priest droned on about the technical aspects of forming a fireball. My mind was in a blaze, without needing a fire.

How was I to form anything using darkness? Even the tiny fireball contained malice, anger, and evil intent. As one who professed to follow the Light, how could I possibly do anything to wield darkness? But, if I do not somehow manage it, they will learn that the Light remains strong. All the books we, I glanced at the other four alongside me, had studied in secret dealt with the Light and not with darkness.

It was growing dusk by the time the priest finished speaking. Glancing out the window he sighed and said. "It is too late to practice tonight, tomorrow morning we will assemble and practice." With a smile he headed through the priest's entrance, and the other students filed out in a hurry, all hungry for supper.

Supper was the same disappointment as lunch, vegetables and bread and only a vague hint of meat. Jay grumbled as he rapidly ate everything served. "Almost makes me want to be chosen as a warrior. These vegetables are tiring." Frost glanced at him, and chuckled.

After supper we headed, once again, to the library. However, this time we were split into different rooms based on profession. Once we were settled in the "mage's library" room I headed to the side wall. Since we began reading nightly in the library, Jay, Frost, and I had discovered ten books on Light. This area was one we had not been permitted to explore, and I hoped to find more hidden books.

It did not take long. Having headed to the dimmest corner of the room, I began scanning the shelves by feel, running my hands over the books. One vibrated slightly. Pulling it out, I found it was a thin book far thinner than was normal. Perhaps only a dozen pages in total and, flipping it open, written in a crabbed and chalky script. It looked as if it had been written in a hurry.

Picking up a thicker book from nearby, about fire lights of all things, I headed back to our study corner. Zay and Zoe had found books on the different branches of fire magic, and Jay and Frost had both discovered books on defence against fire magic.

Opening the thicker book first, I tipped it up and opened the smaller hidden book within it. The small book was titled "Of Light and Dark" not too promising, but still worth reading. I was soon completely absorbed. This tiny book detailed the process by which a Light bearer could fabricate Dark magic. Not by drawing on their own inner darkness as the priests did, but by drawing on the darkness of their opponent, or the people in their surroundings.

I elbowed Jay and Frost abruptly. "This book has good info. Our room tonight, we need to practice before class."

Jay nodded imperceptibly, and then pointed to a passage in his book, as if comparing the information. Glancing up I noticed the young priest who had been with us on the journey. He had a broom and dustpan and was slowly cleaning his way in our direction. Almost as if he was trying to spy on us. Our eyes met, and he cringed, glancing around rapidly. No other priests were in-sight, and he rose and scuttled over. Keeping as if cleaning he whispered "I am suspected, take care for yourselves." Then scuttled away, leaving upon the floor a tiny gleam of light that winked out within a second.

Chapter 20: Learning in Darkness

As soon as we were dismissed, we dashed back to the dorm. Indeed, we ran so fast that we were the first student's back. Once safely ensconced within Frost's and my room, we opened the small book. I read it out loud, so that the other four could learn the information, without taking the time for all of us to read it.

Once I had finished, we leaned back. Jay was perched on the table, while Frost and I shared my bed. Zay and Zoe sprawled on Frost's pallet and leaned against the wall.

Jay gave a brisk nod as I finished reading. "If we can figure out what the writer means we will be safe. but what does it mean that 'darkness creeps like a serpent and it's sensation is coldness.' How does that explanation help us?"

"I suspect it means that the darkness is opposite the light. For the 'light is bright dancing through the senses and bringing peace, warmth, and joy,'" Zay responded.

Zoe nodded "Most of us can wield some Light, so perhaps we should try sensing that first."

Zoe had a point and I joined in the collective nod of agreement.

Despite that curfew was rapidly approaching, we lay back focusing on the Light. Almost before I began focusing I sensed brightness around me. Focusing closer a sense of calmness, peace, and perhaps even a hint of joy filtered around me. I opened my eyes, still sensing the Light's presence. The others were still focusing, with looks of intent concentration. Suddenly Jay relaxed, a slight smile forming. Soon Frost, Zay and Zoe also relaxed, clearly sensing the presence of the Light.

I lay back again, and this time focused searching for the opposite of the Light. It was as close as the light had been. Cold and dark, slimly and twisted. I sensed it writhing outside the door. Held at bay by the Light infused wood around us. I reached out, forming the malevolence into a ball in my hand. Opening my eyes I beheld a small ball of flame, cool to the touch. Closing my hand I summoned a touch of Light. The ball vanished, consumed.

Jay opened his eyes. "I can sense the Light, but cannot seem to find the darkness. What about you guys, any luck?"

Murmurs of "same" came from the other three. Jay's shoulder's slumped "will we be unable to use darkness if we cannot sense it?"

"You did not ask me whether I was successful." I smiled slightly as the others turned eagerly. "I sensed the Light before you did, and can still sense it without focusing. Now that I know it is present I can feel it all around. This room is fashioned of Light infused wood, thus I do not think that Darkness can penetrate it. I also suspect only the strongest could summon outer Darkness within this room, and only the strongest Light bearer could sense Darkness outside the room."

Holding up my hand I again focused and pulled the malevolence into my hand. A second time the ball of flame formed. This time I held it motionless.

"That is clear, how then can the rest of us form it?" Zay said, frowning.

I destroyed the ball with a flash of light before responding. "I do not know. We have all studied and reviewed the Light information." I leaned back with a sigh.

It was clear that only the strongest could outwardly manipulate the darkness without being personally touched and tainted by it. However, Light had become weak and few indeed could use the skills still. Indeed before I had come hither and read the books I knew only how to infuse a weapon, illumine a path, and to use Light as a shield, though the second was taught in a vision not by those who already knew.

Zoe, possibly the one who struggled most with the Light through our studies, had again closed her eyes. Focusing steadily she held up her hand. A tiny flame, just one tongue of flame, formed in her palm. Opening her eyes, Zoe smiled as flash of Light consumed the flame.

Jay jumped off the table. "Well done Zoe." He grinned, "it seems with practice we will be able to master this skill. We should work to master our Light skills at the same time too."

"Aye" Zay said smiling as she also succeeded in manipulating a flame. "it is dangerous to use the darkness, even from without, unless we can remain strong in the Light."

Frost and Jay exchanged glances, then began trying again to form flame by drawing from the darkness outside the room. They did not succeed.

"It is but two minutes to curfew, we should adjourn till dawn."

Jay nodded, his jaw tight. Slipping to the door, he peered out. Seeing the corridor was clear, he scampered silently down the hall to his room. Zay and Zoe slipped softly into their room. The door shut, leaving Frost and I together.

"How come Zay and Zoe could succeed while Jay and I couldn't" Frost snapped. Throwing herself down on the bed. "At least we had some practical training with Light before we came here. They had none, it's not fair."

"Many things in life are unfair, Frost. It is not Zay or Zoe's fault that they succeeded, and indeed it was not the ball of flame we will be taught to make tomorrow, but merely a single flame. Anyway, if we are unsuccessful in the morning, you and Jay can sit on either side of me. If it is necessary that all produce a flame, then I can slip you and Jay a ball and you can pretend it is yours."

Frost snorted, rolling over with her back to the wall. This conversation was clearly finished.

I focused again, as Frost drifted to sleep, and soon sensed a thread of darkness within the room. Reaching for it, I grasped it, willing it to become visible in my hand, which as a precaution I had already covered with a shield of Light. A single flame appeared, hotter than a furnace. If I had not had the Light over my hand I it would have burned through the flesh in seconds.

I sent a thin thread of light into the flame, and as the flame withered I knew what darkness had given it birth. The darkness of jealousy.

I woke before dawn, as had become my habit. Rising carefully, trying to not disturb Frost. I donned my outer robe, and slipped out the door. I headed downstairs at a brisk, though silent, pace and soon arrived at the tack room of the stable. One of the three rooms we were able to practice Light within without being detected.

Settling onto a saddle I began my morning practice. As I practiced, I found I was sensing both Light and Darkness without trying. Even after I left the tack room and headed back to the dorm my senses were keen. Entering with as much care as I had left with, I found Frost still sleeping. However, the darkness I had sensed last night remained, drifting on the edge of being present. Not yet having taken root but striving to supplant the Light.

"Frost, the day dawns and darkness threatens the Light, it is time to arise and prepare for the daily struggle." Frost yawned struggling up from the realm of sleep.

"I had the strangest dream Mayim. I stood upon a battle field and all around me Light shone brighter than I had ever seen it. Figures in radiant armour surrounded me, battling foes in black. I looked down, and beheld my armour. It had once been radiant but was now tarnished and stained. Looking up I beheld a bolt of darkness shooting down upon me, when it was intercepted by a beam of light so radiant it blinded me temporarily. I looked to the one who had cast it, and it was you. A man stood alongside you, who I didn't know, he was dark haired, and tall, his eyes were brown and seemed to pierce my soul. I felt as if he was reading my memory." Frost paused and glanced at me. "In his eyes I saw the reason my armour was tarnished and I could not fight." She paused again and then whispered "teach me the Light so that darkness can never supplant it."

We faced that day's mage class with trepidation. The first half of class was filled with a repeat of the theory behind fire magic. The second half was filled with students attempting to form balls of fire, with varying degrees of success. The teacher did have to conjure some quick water, and was grumbling about the foolishness of teaching fire magic in a room full of combustibles.

When it came to my turn to attempt the fire. I hesitated, pretending to focus as the other students had. In reality I had, for most of the class, been practicing sensing the Light and the Dark around me. Reaching for a hint of lesser Darkness, I formed it within my hand. A tiny ball of flame sat there, just the size of a chicken egg. Glowing just brightly enough to read by, but not even hot enough to ignite tinder.

"Well done, at least we have one person who can follow directions." the priest said, chuckling as he turned to Frost next in-line. Frost shot me a glance, shifting slightly. Raising her hand she appeared to be focusing, but no matter how she focused there was no hint of flame. Suddenly she smiled, almost sadly, and a tiny flame flared briefly on her palm. Then there was nothing.

The priest nodded "you'll get it after awhile lass" and turned to those next in line.

Zay and Zoe passed easily, each forming a ball of flame similar to the one I had formed. Jay formed a single flame, similar to Frost's. The priest appeared contented with our performance, and soon permitted us to go to our chosen time of other study.

I headed for the practice field. There was no point in learning the sword for over six months only to let the skills rust away. Magic would be useless, while the Light could be more danger than protection. This left only the sword and bow as safe weapons, at least safe from a detection standpoint.

Ian was there, and to my surprise, the other four had already arrived and were girding on practice blades and bucklers.

"I figured you'd alternate between sword and bow" Jay said with a slight smile "and possibly equestrian practice. So we decided to head down and begin, it's no fun to practice with the sword against only one person." He smiled grimly, remembering our little escapade with the brigands on the way here.

If brigands, such as those, were all I had to worry about life would be much simpler. I smiled, accepting the practice sword from Ian. "I think we should have a challenge today. Ian and I against the four of you, what do you think?"

Chapter 21: Detection

The weeks passed swiftly. No one suspected us of being other than five aspiring and skilled dark mages. Each week we shifted the after mage training classes between hand to hand combat, archery, and equestrian combat training.

Sword training was the most enjoyable, since Ian was always there and never ceased to pretend amazement that "them lassies can sure swing a blade nately." Yet the successes, studies, and organized days drifted by. With only a thin screen, a deception, keeping us separate from the darkness and from detection.

The tenuous existence was shattered three months after we arrived at the school. Frost burst into the dorm before breakfast, "Mayim, the young janitor priest, John I think. He's been arrested for practicing Light in secret, his trial starts in less than an hour."

"That is not good" I glanced up sharply, "are all summoned to attend, or is it private?" I rose shoving the Light books aside onto the floor.

"All are summoned, and there is little time. The trial will happen after breakfast."

"We cannot help before the trial then. But, if he is sentenced to death we cannot abandon him." I snapped, glancing around sharply. Footsteps in the hall drew rapidly near.

Jay strode into the room, his face grim. He paused, as we glanced at him, a slight smile reached his eyes. "One look at you two and the Varat would be out of its cage. They could label you three miles away with that panic. We need to be calm. Mayim, you can do un-traceable protections?"

"I can, but it is risky since they may decide to insult the Light by having students do the execution with magic, instead of priests."

Zay and Zoe, having just arrived nodded in unison. "That would be a good mode for insulting someone, but what if they turned it into a training exercise. You know a 'protect the traitor from your teachers and see how impossible it is to resist us' kind of thing" Zoe said, shaking her head.

I stopped re-stacking the books I had knocked onto the floor, and turned to pace the room. A few moments later, I turned to face the others.

"There is really only one thing we can do. Wait and see. When we see the opportunity, we blast it." I summoned a sharp flash of Light to emphasis my point, and my frustration.

Silent nods greeted my declaration, and turning we jogged to the dining hall, arriving first.

Hardly had everyone arrived when the head priest stepped to the front. Clearing his throat, he waited for the room to quiet. Once every eye was fixed upon him, he smiled. A sly, snakelike smile.

"It has come to our attention that someone within these sacred and protected precincts was engaging in that dastardly and lowlife craft known as 'Light.'"

The sneer in his voice was evident, and a deeper silence fell over the assembled students. Shock at the thought of light being practiced in a school that glorified darkness. I smiled slightly, if only they knew the truth. My reflections were interrupted by the priest continuing.

"The culprit has been apprehended and will be punished today. As such there will be no regular classes. As soon as you have finished breaking your fast, adjourn to the practice field to witness judgement on the traitor."

The priest stalked off, leaving a confusion of chatter over who the traitor was, and what the punishment would be. My spirits fell, with the whole school watching there was little hope of doing secret Light, still less of spiriting John away without notice. I rolled my eyes, if Finan had been near it would be easy to have the brigands attack and carry off the priest. But without knowing Finan's location it was hopeless to attempt contact. Particularly since brigands had a reputation of not enjoying being called upon. Tidying up our dishes before the others had finished, the five of us headed to the training ground.

Upon the larger training field a series of stands had been set up for seating. I selected a comfortable edge location, easy enough to get out of quickly and not too obvious. Having been first of our five, I waved the others to join me as they came over. Slowly the stands filled, students crowding into the stands acting like they were at a fair, rather than a life and death trial. Cheerful chatter filled the air, mostly centered on how the execution would happen and whether or not the "traitor priest" would be permitted to fight.

The stands were arranged in a semicircle, facing a raised platform. Upon the platform was a table, and before the table was a simple chair. Behind the table were five chairs, the centermost chair being raised above the others. Inhaling deeply, the scent of crushed grass teased my nose. Nearly tempting a sneeze, it was clear the stands had been constructed in a hurry. The soft aroma of freshly sawn wood drifted into my nose with the breeze. I shifted, pulling a piece of sticky sap off the stand.

"It seems they used pine wood for the benches, there will be some complaint from the laundry detail about that." I said, speaking for the sake of speaking, rather than being conspicuous through silence.

"Aye, good thing we got the top edge of the tree, there are not as many knots and less sap." Jay said his voice quiet.

"They come" the cry was raised by those in the top seats of the stand. And three overdressed priests and two priestesses came forward. The priests took the three center chairs, and the priestesses flanked them, sitting on the outermost chairs. After scanning the assembled students, the central priest spoke:

"Bring out the traitor."

John was dragged out by two guards, neither of whom I recognized. His face was bruised, and heavy chains bound his arms and legs. He could barely walk, stumbling helplessly as he was dragged to the judgement chair. Roughly the guards shoved him into the chair. They then moved to the side and stood watching the students.

"John, considered by many to be a priest of the medium blue, what do you have to say to this charge of being a traitor, and following that deception called 'Light?'"

John raised his head slowly, and gazed at those seated in judgement. "I have nothing to say, let those who claim to have caught me bring their evidence forward." The clarity and strength of his voice caused a few surprised murmurs.

"As you wish" the main judge sneered, and waved forward two young priests, robed in the lightest possible shade of blue. "Tell your story Acolytes."

The youngest lad began. "I was a walkin' to the stable sir, as I have charge of them horses. And I noticed this flash of light from the practice field, like a spark of white. I slipped closer, being curious, and saw this fellow with his eyes closed in the center of the field. A second later this weird bubble of whiteness surrounded him, and I took off scared, to the stable where I saw another person..."

The head priest interrupted him smoothly, "that is enough, and what did the other see?"

"Similar sir," the second acolyte seemed older and also calmer "but instead of it being a bubble it was a bolt. It took a good chunk of turf out. I went out afterward and even found the loose sod, twas over three feet square."

"Thank you both." The judge nodded, dismissing the two acolytes. Who, freed from scrutiny, scrambled out of sight behind the other assembled priests.

The judge ignored their hasty departure and glared at John. "What more evidence do we need, Traitorous Worm? The only question that now needs answering is the mode of your death."

One of the priestesses leaned forward then, whispering into the judge priest's ear. A few seconds later a grim smile formed on his lips. He laughed harshly and turned to face the accused.

"We will give you a chance at life."

John started slightly at those words, and then waited without expression. The judge did not make him, or us, wait long.

"Five students will be chosen, those most up on their work. As a learning exercise they will protect you from our magic for as long as they can. If they are successful" a low snicker came from one of the other priests at the table, "then you live. If not..." he let the thought trail off with a sickly smile.

"But how will you choose those who are most up on their studies?" John asked surprisingly calmly, "or is it not their studies but their enthusiasm that you will choose?"

"Enthusiasm works for me" snipped the priestess on the right. "The first five who arrived here today, they shall be the defenders. Let us adjourn to the arena." The other four priests nodded in agreement before rising to lead the way to the arena.

As the other students rapidly scrambled from their seats to follow the prisoner to the arena, I remained glued to my seat. It was probably the pine pitch. Turning I faced the other four. "What can we do?" Frost whispered, leaning in toward me. I glanced sharply at the approaching priests, who all bore the same nasty smiles. Smiles that anticipated taking enjoyment from the suffering of another.

"Leave the counter magic to me, but stand as close as possible to John." I whispered rapidly.

At that moment the two priests arrived, "you were the first five. Congratulations on being part of bringing justice here. We'll prepare you below the arena. Do you want weapons?"

"I believe it will be a magic contest" I stated calmly, belying the nerves springing to life in my stomach "so nothing is needed since we already have what we need."

He nodded, seeming satisfied, and we headed to the arena.

I had never thought of facing death or detection in this manner. Fear tingled through my system, preventing any coherent idea from forming. The others looked to be in as much shock as I was. But what was worse was that John knew, and likely remembered that I had knowledge of the Light. After all, he was there when the Prophet's shield bloomed around Finan. Only Jay or myself, both now entering the arena, could have given it life. Thus John would likely expect some light, though if I showed the Light it would be far worse for all six of us.

I scanned the arena. John was chained to a post in the center by a single chain around his waist to which his wrists were also manacled. To the side, the six who had sat in judgement now sat waiting for the "defenders" to take positions. I inhaled deeply, trying unsuccessfully to settle my nerves. A slight earthy taste filled my mouth, dust, from the hard packed dirt of the arena floor.

The five of us lined up before the five priests and priestesses. "If you would like to confer or strategize you have freedom to do so." The head priest said, "for five minutes" he added almost as an afterthought. The other four chuckled.

Quickly we formed a huddle close to John, but not so close as for him to overhear.

"I'll take the first attack" I whispered, "We'll see what they throw at us. If I have trouble each of you will join me in turn, Jay, Zay, Frost, and Zoe in that order. If cloaked, the stables are safe" I added.

The others nodded, knowing I named them in order of Light skill not Dark skill. Also knowing we could mention nothing remotely hinting at light, since even distance was no preventative for eavesdropping via spells.

The four positioned themselves at the four compass points, around John. "Compass points?" I shook my head, a thought that I did not recognize, but made sense. I positioned myself in the center, between Jay and Zay, closest to the six and also closest in proximity to John.

I glanced at him now, a look of helpless resignation rested on his face. The chain that bound his arms down, and him to the post, was heavy iron. He glance up, meeting my gaze and gave a nearly imperceptible shake of his head. I knew the message, to not try and save him but simply to protect ourselves. Glancing back to the self-satisfied, and eager for blood priests I felt my jaw tighten. I made eye contact again, and gave a slight smile. I was not about to let the darkness win, not today and not ever if I could help it.

"Are you ready?" The head priest inquired, glancing curiously at our protection arrangement.

"We are ready" I replied, placing at the same instant an invisible Prophet's Shield. Provided it was not struck by magic, it would remain an invisible barrier. If struck it would blaze brighter than a thousand torches.

I opened my senses feeling the darkness creep and swirl around the five priests and priestesses. They were the strongest in darkness that I had yet met, a darkness blacker than pitch. I forced myself to be still, and drew upon their strength. Feeling the darkness swirl and squirm under my control. I controlled it with an effort. Though it still writhed to control me, it could not succeed due to the light that burned within me.

A blast of black lightning struck strait down upon us. A black shield sprang to life, absorbing and using the energy of the strike. Two of the priests exchanged sharp glances. The shield was an advanced move, and one that was likely unexpected. John lifted his head, suddenly taking an interest in the dance for his life, or death. I smiled again. He probably hadn't known that darkness could be manipulated without giving in to its power.

Twin black twisters spiralled toward us. I sent black blade winds, slicing through and disrupting the twister's ability. A black fog next swirled around, sweeping down to choke out life. I summoned a box, grey and stable, blocking all attempts of the fog to enter yet enabling me to see out. Fast as thought the fog dissipated. The fog was replaced with a giant mountain of darkness, crushing down on the frail, gray magic. A slight twist, changing the box, enabled the box to absorb the mountain of magic. The box strengthened preventing harm.

"Well done, you have clearly learned well, and to defend that well you must also be among the top students." The head priest scrutinized us closely. In normal circumstances that much defense against powerful magic would weaken whoever was doing it. Since I was drawing from the magic summoned against us, there was no energy cost to any of us. We remained standing firm, with no sign of exhaustion. Those casting upon us were beginning to look a little tired.

The head priest smiled grimly and glanced at his companions. "However, that was but midlevel magic. Not too difficult to defend against, if you know the mode to use. But since you seem to have mastered that..." his voice trailed off. He resumed a second later "the highest level of magic has no defense, you may leave the arena, or remain and fall."

I glanced over my shoulder at the other, cocking one eyebrow I asked for their decisions. Frost grinned, and gave a small nod, her jaw tightening. The others imitated her.

"We will remain, since you are directing the magic at the traitor in the center, it is hardly likely to hit us. So we might learn something."

The priest nodded, and stretched his right arm up to begin an incantation. Instantly I cloaked our group, throwing up a mirage of light to imitate our locations. I added a second cloak, of darkness, to hopefully disguise the Light and prevent a flash being seen if the darkness struck the shield.

As bolts of crimson lightening began raining down. They struck the cloak, and ricochet off into the sky. I grimaced, strengthening the darkness, and throwing out a cloaking mirage of Light to cover the others flight from the arena. Crouching low, I threw a third mirage. Watching carefully as a whirling twister of crimson flame descended toward the center of the cloak. I had to time this right or we would be detected.

The others were gone. Jay had brought cutters in to remove the chains. The second I had mirage cloaked them, he had freed John and headed for the stable. I smiled and dashed for the exit, still under cover of Light. Hitting the exit, I turned and strengthened the dark cloaking shield. Drawing from the magic hurled against us, I was surprised as the shield became as crimson as the twister which was now trying to penetrate it. The shield weakened rapidly despite drawing from the twister. I withdrew the Light cloaks from underneath the darkness. Throwing a last strengthening at the dark cloak, I slipped out of the arena.

Throwing caution aside, though remaining covered by the mirage, I dashed for the stables. We had arranged to meet Ian there to train this afternoon, he should also be able to help us get out of here. We had planned an equestrian training session to last all afternoon and he was to bring some provision. Taking horses and some provision would therefore be no surprise to him, though the addition of John would be.

When the twister hit the ground, the shield would dissolve, and the sand blacken. No bodies would be there, for the strength of the magic was enough to destroy the strongest person. I smiled, it would take a few minutes, if not forever, for them to figure out we had escaped. By then we would already be on our way.

I reached the stable out of breath. Running was still not my strongest point. Frost threw herself at me as I entered. "We were worried you wouldn't be able to get out of there." she gasped out. Then began giggling, and stumbled back to the others.

"We have all gotten out of the arena, the question is whether we can get out of the school and to safety before the cavalry realize who is slipping through their fingers." I said grimly.

Ian walked out of the tack room carrying seven bundles. "Jay and Zoe briefed me on what happened today. Well I know nothing of Light vs. Darkness, I like you guys far more than the priests. And as I'm known to be your friend, if something happens and your ploy is detected, Jay thinks I'd be in danger. So I'm going with you, I think we should take the horses for the first bit since it was planned anyway. I'll leave a note saying that I'm taking a few students for horse exercise, as planned yesterday. They won't suspect anything till the horses come back tomorrow. By the time they get to where we ditched the horses we'll have another day, maybe two, head start. If they even bother following, since we can make it look like a brigand attack or something similar."

I mounted a bay mare, and nodded slightly at the others. Nudging the horse forward I approached the door.

The door crashed open, as three of the judgment mages charged through the door. I cloaked the others without thinking, leaving myself in plain view.

"So you are alive, and where do you think you're off to on that horse girl" said one of the priests, his voice thick with suspicion. His eyes narrowed reminding me of a viper prepared to strike.

"I had arranged yesterday to go for horse training for the next week, I thought that was fine."

"Perhaps" one of the priestesses said, glaring at the horse "but not when there's a light mage wandering around, possibly even the cursed prophet. Everyone is ordered to their rooms pending the investigation. You as well, though how you left the arena without anyone seeing you is strange, and how did you survive that twister? Where are your friends?"

"I do not know, and I refuse to return to the room without my ride." I snapped back, something had gone wrong. My back was straight and the horse pranced under me in anticipation.

The priest raised his hand, whispering an incantation. From the first word I recognized a binding spell. I smiled, raising my own hand and said clearly "cast to caster is this day, bind the binder, lose the mage, Light is dark and dark can't light. Blind the day and seize the night."

A black chain shot toward me. Striking the wall of words, in a blaze of light, the chain recoiled. Hurtling back, it bound the caster, and his two priestess companions. Thrown back by the force of the binding, the priest and priestesses were no longer in the way, and were conveniently facing the wall.

"My apologies for this inconvenience" I said calmly "but no one stands in the way of my afternoon training. Even officially canceling training for the day. As for the light mage, I thought the priest you overpowered was the only Light around here." Chuckling at the barb, I renewed the mirage over myself and headed out into the school grounds.

Turning north and west I trotted steadily away. I would not return to this school or to the hands of the priests again. At least as long as I was alive and able to resist, I smiled as the sense of freedom lightened my heart. As soon as we were out of sight and within the cover of trees I dropped the mirage cloak. "Well that was a workable escape. Hopefully they won't suspect that we are the light mages they want. Though I have no clue how they detected the Light, I made sure to drop the shield before leaving the arena." I shook my head.

Zoe spoke suddenly "If we used Light outside of the stable tack room, the upper school room, or your bedroom it could be detected. Even if they did not see the light, they could probably still detect it."

"True" John spoke for the first time, "I did not know there was a safe place to practice, so I just tried to train at unusual times and places. I was a fool to think I would not be detected. Though how you managed to defend me I have no idea, I owe you my life."

"It was Mayim's doing" Jay smiled "all I did was use the bolt cutter. All of the defense and cloaking was from Mayim."

John turned painfully in the saddle, and bowed gravely. "I did not want you to take the risk yet you did so anyway. But how is it that you can wield the dark magic, but are not tainted by it?"

"That is a tale for another time" I replied "for now we need to put as much distance as possible between us and the school, and hide our trail as well."

Chapter 22: Hiding the Trail

Reaching the edge of the stream, I lead the others straight in. Turning I rode downstream, away from the mountains.

"Why are we riding downstream Mayim? Is not our road to the mountains and Brachite Forest?" Jay said, drawing abreast of me.

"It is, but I know there is a rock ledge a short ride down. If we draw out of the stream there the water will evaporate. It will be a less obvious lead. Also if we truly were priests we would head straight, not downstream since that leads to the raiders, and not upstream since that leads to the outlaws of the forest."

Jay nodded, and then dropped back. Taking up the hindermost position, he kept watch. After five minutes of wet riding we arrived at the rock ledge. We drew out on the east side of the stream and headed deeper into the marsh.

The ground was nearly impossible. Deep pools lay hidden within beds of reeds, while ground that appeared solid could just be a mat of moss over water. Despite the unpleasant conditions and traitorous ground we rode on. Skirting shallow pools that teemed with biting insects, and jumping over narrow gullies flowing with water that was slimmed by rotting vegetation. The decaying aroma of the swamp clung to everything, particularly clothing and hair. The going was slow, but at least it was steady.

"When do we plan to halt tonight Mayim?" Ian called "It's deucedly damp and miserable here. And I dinnah know about you but I'm getting tired and I'm sure John is exhausted after his ordeal."

Turning I scanned my tired friends, then said "One of the books mentioned a small island that rises above the swamp. I have been charting our course in that direction. We should be there in about another hour." I nodded toward the others "John, I know you must be in pain and we have done nothing to ease you as we should have. Though this ground is not necessarily the best for tending injuries it does not mitigate our responsibility."

John nodded, his face pallid. "I can hold out for a bit, but not much longer." He sighed, slumping lower over his steed's neck. I nodded and turning again led on. Frost said no word, but urged her horse close alongside John, nodding to Ian who had already taken a supportive position on the opposite side.

It was happily only thirty minutes before the ground rose, and a solid path became clear. Rising out of the mists was a low island, topped with an aged tower. We dismounted wearily at the door. From the time we left the stable till we arrived here was eight hours of riding and the night was now advancing.

"There is a small stable alongside the tower, Ian can you and Jay see if the horses can remain there? I will see if I can open the tower" I said, glancing at my weary party. Jay nodded, and without a word led the horses around. John leaned against the tower, completely worn out.

The tower door was locked, but no keyhole was visible. Running my hands down the door I stared at the heavy planking. There had to be a way to enter. My fingers felt no knob or other means of opening the door. As I stared at it, a cold chill caused a shiver to course through me.

I turned away from the door, scanning the area for some hint as to how to enter. Nothing stood out against the drear background of the swamp. John leaned against Jay, appearing weaker with each passing minute. I bit my cheek and turned back to the door, the misty clouds cast shadows as they flitted over the moon.

After more staring, I shrugged and turned away from the door. At the same moment the clouds broke and the moon cast a dim light over the door. As the moonlight strengthened, the words that were engraved into the stone appeared. I faced the door again, and read:

"Friend of light to enter here, show they friendship, make it clear. Find the lock and smite the dark. Open and rest, heal and be blest."

"Well that sure makes no sense" Zay said, walking slowly up to the door.

"I think it makes perfect sense for a riddle. The book which I found the tower's location in was a book on the Light." I smiled slowly and added, "That particular book taught a net type technique. It is used to cast a net of light over an object. The idea is to immobilize or reveal any darkness."

"Canna we naught get in?" Ian said, intruding into my monologue with his heave brogue. "The stables are cozy enough if the tower's a no go."

I shrugged, and instead of answering, loosed a small quantity of Light to cover the door. Instantly a spot in the very center formed a dark mass.

The dark tendrils spread over the whole door, preventing it from opening. The tendrils were of darkest crimson, tinged with black, an indication of the highest possible level of dark magic, a magic unique in that no other darkness could break it.

The Light I cast changed to a destroying Light, blasting the dark threads apart but not harming the center spot. The door swung silently inward.

"That is the strongest of dark magic, yet even that tiny thread of Light was greater" John said, "I cannot believe it. How could men who knew the Light have fallen so far so as to lose their skills and bow to darkness?"

"They preferred wealth and status to truth and justice" Frost said, her voice quiet as she approached. "Love is greater than hatred, and making things right takes more courage than war. We have lost that gift." She looked at us, with a sad smile. "Well, are we going to stand here all night or go inside?" she added glancing at the now open door.

"I guess we can enter" I smiled, "and perhaps we shall find some useful information before we leave tomorrow. Yes" I continued in response to the groans of the others "we must press on as swiftly as we can. Those at the academy detected my light, and they will pursue."

As I finished speaking I stepped through the entryway. The tower was simple, plain hewn stone. A curved staircase started on the right and went around the whole tower to the top. The first room, or entryway, was carpeted with rushes. A stone fireplace and cooking area were to the left of the door. The door swung shut as soon as Ian, the last in line, entered.

All light was cut off, and the tower entrance was plunged into deep darkness. A small globe of Light bloomed to life in my hand, even as similar lights blossomed in the other's hands.

Ian glanced around, shuffling his feet. "I think I'll stay here and do some cooking. You others can explore this place, it feels like we're being watched." His voice trailed off. Pivoting abruptly he headed to the fireplace and began laying a cooking fire.

"Frost, can you tend to John's injuries?" Jay said, also glancing around though with less nervousness than Ian had exhibited. "Zay and Zoe if you could assist with the meal preparation as well" Jay paused. Short nods greeted the distribution of tasks. Frost guided John to a low bench close to the fire, while Zay and Zoe bustled around gathering food from the packs.

"I suppose that leaves you and me to explore the rest of the tower" I raised an eyebrow at Jay. He grinned back.

"Aye, if this is the tower we read on, there should be sleeping rooms on the floor above this, and an extensive library on the top floor. We may be able to get some more vital information, even if we are here only overnight."

With my light in hand I started up the stairs without replying. They were wooden steps, coated in a thick layer of dust. I stepped lightly, trying to drop as little dust as possible down upon those cooking. Narrow loopholes followed the stairs, providing a mode of defense and permitting whatever outside light there was to filter through. Twenty steps above the first floor, the second floor began. It was indeed a sleeping room.

The open room held a dozen couches set along the wall away from the stairs, were two large wardrobe type cases. Wardrobe? Now that was a second term I had never heard here. I shook my head, pausing to stare again at the wardrobe.

Jay opened the wardrobe doors, "there are blankets and pillows in this one, and sheets and linen pillowcases in this. There is also no dust in this room." He trailed off, glancing sharply at me.

I took a closer look around; the staircase was indeed coated thickly in dust. A decade of dust at least, if not more. But no dust was on the floor in this room. The beds were dustless, as were the wardrobes.

"That is passing strange, how can dust be upon the stairs but not in the room? " I shrugged again and continued "we may as well make up seven beds at least tonight we will rest comfortably, which is more than I can say for the remainder of our journey."

It took half an hour to make up seven beds. The couches were soft, though firm enough to provide a good night's rest. The sheets were of fine linen, finer than I had yet seen in this land. The blankets were of soft wool. At the bottom of one wardrobe were ten thick blankets. Fashioned of courser wool, they were well finished and would be nearly waterproof.

"These would be invaluable on our journey" I said hefting one blanket to catch Jay's eye.

"They would be, but to whom do they belong, to who does this whole tower belong? This makes no sense. If it belongs to no one, why the protection, and if it belongs to someone why aren't they here?"

"I do not know Jay, but I think we should take these blankets tomorrow. We did not pack any of our own, and these will be useful. As for who this tower belongs to, I have a feeling the next floor may hold some answers."

Chapter 23: Revived and Strengthened

Before we could ascend however Ian called us down to supper. Supper was simple. A plain soup made of dried vegetables and dried meat. The highlight was fresh bread, skillfully baked by Zoe.

Ian still seemed nervous, but no longer about the tower. "We grabbed enough supplies for a few days. It will not be enough to get to the forest, let alone the mountains. Our weapons are inadequate since we have but two swords and two bows amongst seven. No blankets for ourselves, and no feed for the horses. I was grateful and surprised to find both hay and grain in the stables, but we can scarcely hope to find provisions, weapons, armour, and blankets in this old tower."

"We have already found blankets, and there is likely either a cellar under the tower. Or a root cellar outside that could contain some provision. As for weapons, there may yet be something on the upper floors, though because of the Light we are never completely defenceless." Jay said, his voice calm but with an edge of impatience.

Ian fell silent and stared moodily into his soup. "Jay, why don't you assist in cleaning up from the meal?" I suggested not sure why he was being impatient with Ian. I expected the questions. We had never used Light skills in actual combat before today, and had never practiced in front of Ian. He only knew our actions, skill with physical weapons, and friendship. It was no wonder he doubted our ability to defend ourselves with Light.

"The meal was delicious. Also, as Mayim mentioned there may be a cellar, I would like to have a search around for it" Frost smiled lightly "I also think that Mayim should explore the remaining floors. I have a feeling that she should be alone" she trailed off, glancing upward.

With a nod to the others I headed up the spiraling staircase a second time. Without pausing on the second floor, I ascended another twenty steps to the third floor. It was a library.

The books were as clear of dust as the floor below had been. Yet the upper stairs were just as thickly covered in dust as the lower stairs. The tower was silent, not even a whisper of sound came from the main floor. Leaving the stairs, I sauntered through the library.

The shelves were ten feet high, with small movable step-ladders in grooves on the floor. The books themselves were a Light wielders' dream come true. The whole library was on Light, without a single writing that covered darkness.

It seemed the library was the pinnacle of the tower for no steps ascended beyond it. A narrow, but proper, window would provide daylight to the lone study desk. I moved slowly, savoring the abundance of information. The sheer quantity of knowledge was euphoric. It was like finding a flowing river hidden within the edge of a forest after traversing a barren desert. Finally I meandered my way to the study desk. In the center of the desk rested a single small volume, another volume rested upright at the back of the desk.

This small volume mesmerized me, pulling me slowly toward it. It was bound in plain brown leather, worn at the edges. Upon the center of the cover a silver lightning bolt blazed diagonally across. No title or name graced the cover. There was no indication of who had written it.

I slid into the chair, resting my globe of light upon a small candle stick type stand. The stand was made of metal, which gleamed white as the globe rested upon it. I glanced around again, of all the thousands of books this one was the only book that seemed to be begging me to read it. Resting my hand on the cover, I picked it up carefully. The scent of leather floated off the cover, the leather was soft, well-tanned and supple. The lightning bolt was smooth, an unknown metal inlaid within the leather.

After staring at the book again, I slowly opened it. The book began:

"To the one who finds and reads this book, greetings. You are in as great a danger now as I had ever faced. If you have indeed found this tower then your doom is drawing rapidly near. I am the sixth in a long line of second-prophets; you will be the eighth. You battle with an unknown past, and a deadly future. This tower is here to aid those fleeing the darkness. Take whatever supplies you require. The topmost tower room, reached by trapdoor, contains arms and armour. Take enough to equip whoever is with you. For hope and strength remember…"

I paused before turning the page, this writer was a prophet before Angusina. Who knows how long before, yet this writing was as to a friend. I glanced again over the words, there was another room. Leaning back I scanned the ceiling. There, just over the stairs was the outline of a trapdoor. To the side inset against the wall was also a ladder. I smiled grimly, if what this prophet said was true it sounded like we were in for a crazy time. I paused fingering the page again, then turned it. As I had suspected what was to be remembered was a prophecy.

"Trust only those who have proved true
Hone the sword and don the mail
Even those you trust may rue
The day the battles fail
Hold hope close, don't let it go
Fight to win and fear no ill
When the darkness overwhelms
Remember what love o'er comes
Cold the steel, dark the fear
Hold fast though your time is here
In the battle, blood, and mire
Facing death, the need is dire"

A chill settled over me. All the prophecies I had yet heard involved death, and sounded like sacrifice. Even on that first night on the cold tor in the darkness, facing the death of a fellow prophetess, prophecy rang. Even now her words echoed in my memory "as the Reaver doth enter his doom enters too."

The book fell to the desk as understanding hit me. I was the Reaver's doom, and he was mine. His power was in darkness and fear, mine in hope, love, and light. Which would prove the stronger? Again I looked over the prophecy that was written by my predecessor. It was becoming clear. Somehow the darkness would be overcome. Subconsciously my hand slid over my heart and I fingered the copper tinged scar. With a scar like that, I should be dead.

I glanced around, fingers resting against the scar. Another book was set on the desk as if whoever had written the prophecy had also left it there to read later. It was a tome of Light healing. Flipping it open, I scanned through the pages. One passage caught my eye, "all wounds inflicted by darkness can be healed by light. Depending on the severity and purpose of the darkness, the scar may heal without a trace, or heal the same colour as the blade that inflicted the wound."

I frowned, since the scar on my chest was copper tinged did that mean that it had been inflicted with a copper blade? If so, what was the purpose that the scar should remain? Unless it was to show me that I was shaped not by what I now knew, but by things that were now forgotten? Lost in thought, I started as Jay and Frost came up the stairs, drawn swords in hand.

"There you are Mayim, we've been worried half out of our minds and Ian's been swearing that you were taken by some dastardly dark magic trap or something. What's going on?" Jay's tirade abruptly stopped as he came to face me.

For answer, I handed him the small book, opened to the prophecy. Frost stepped alongside, reading over Jay's shoulder.

"It's a dark look out indeed Mayim even with the mention of hope. Prophecy is not always accurate though."

"I think this prophecy is accurate" I said, my voice dropping "it echoes the other three prophecies I have heard since my time here began. But it is not the prophecy that puzzles me. It is my inability to remember any life before I awoke on Blood Tor but eight months ago." I faced them fully now studying them. If I could only trust those who had proved true, how would I know they had proved true? I felt I could trust my comrades here, even Ian who had no light skill and John who had been a priest. Yet how would I know if I could trust others?

Jay spoke softly "We will remain alongside you no matter what comes. But the question remains, at least downstairs, what provision we should take and whether we should try and locate weapons here?"

I smiled, and headed to the inset ladder. "There are weapons and armour above here, left for our benefit. It was mentioned in that little book you are holding, written by the prophet before Angusina."

I led the way up the ladder, easing open the trapdoor I crept into a room that was a warriors dream. The circular room was divided into four basic sections. In the nearest section were a number of swords, ten in total, made of the same mysterious metal as the lightning bolt on the book. In the next section were sets of chest armour, again ten in number. Next to the armour was a selection of daggers, and alongside that a section of bows and quivers of arrows. Every section numbered ten. There was enough to outfit ten warriors here.

Jay scrambled through the trapdoor and stopped, his mouth dropping open.

"This is amazing. I've never seen armour or weapons like this." He shook his head and walked cautiously over to the swords. Hefting the nearest weapon he swung it, checking the balance.

Frost joined me then, standing and gazing upon the weapons. After a few moments of silence she spoke softly.

"There are ten of everything, I would guess as sets. There are but seven of us, I think the remaining three sets should be carried with us. Though for what purpose I do not know."

Jay nodded, "These are indeed sets Frost. I would guess this set, placed higher than the others is also the best." He smiled glancing lightly at me. "It is only fitting for the prophetess to have the best. This symbol upon the armour is also the prophet's symbol."

I nodded, studying the armour. The chest piece, sword, dagger and bow all bore the same symbol etched into the grips on the weapons, and blazing brilliant on the chest piece. It was a six pointed star, formed from two overlaid and intertwined triangles. This armour was silver on gold, unlike the other sets which bore gold on sliver. No other mark or sign was upon them. When a Light Prophet's shield became visible this was also the same form that it took, the form of the intertwined triangle star.

Jay carefully lifted the armour, sword, dagger, and bow that were placed above the others and carried them to my side.

"I will brook no protest Mayim, you are the only hope against the Reaver, and you will be the target of his wrath as well." Jay said, sensing that I was about to protest his actions. Before I could step back, Jay had knelt and proceeded to gird the armour and weapons upon me.

The armour was light, far lighter than I had expected. The sword rested easily against my left hip, and the dagger rested against my right. I adjusted the basic sheath for the bow, and the chest belt for the quiver so that they rested easily against the small of my back.

"It is way lighter than I expected, and it feels made for me." I trailed off, drawing the sword and gazing upon the silver blade.

"It is light because it is high quality, I have never seen armour such as this." Jay smiled, carefully collecting the other armour, swords, daggers and bows with Frost's help. "It will be easiest to carry these sets downstairs and gird the others there. They are probably wondering what is taking us so long" Jay chuckled.

Gasps greeted our laden return. If they could have, I am sure some eyes would have popped out. I smiled remaining quiet, still puzzling over the meaning of the prophecy from my predecessor. Whoever he was, he seemed to have had a good idea of what would eventually be facing us. Otherwise why would he have stored up not only all the known Light knowledge, but also normal weapons and armour? I shook my head, and turned my attention to the others.

John was staring at the armour, a look of shock and possible fear on his face. He had backed up to the far wall, as far from the table where Jay had deposited the armour as possible.

"What is wrong John, it is armour, it is not about to bite" I said, raising an eyebrow at his reaction.

He shook his head slightly, and faced me with a sheepish smile.

"There is a legend among the priests, and although I have always sought to embrace the Light yet that legend was recalled to me just now. It is a source of fear, even for the strongest of the priests." He glanced again at the armour and then spoke keeping his voice low.

"In this legend it is said that those who defend the Light wear armour that shines like molten silver and liquid gold. The armour is said to be impenetrable by any mortal weapon, and even the strongest of dark magic cannot avail against it. The only way to defeat a bearer of such armour is to lure their heart to the dark magic, for once the armour is equipped" John paused, glancing pointedly at the armour I already wore. "Once the armour is equipped" he repeated slowly "it can never be taken off except in death."

"That is a rumor easily tested" I smiled, and unfastened the shoulder strap. Although I could untie the leather fastenings, the armour itself would not be removed. "That rumour is right, therefore we must take care on the remaining armour. It's a good thing the armour is so light" I added.

"I ain't touching nor wearing no armour that won't come off" Ian said, stumbling abruptly away from the table where he had been admiring the armour and weapons. "There's something unnatural about that."

"You do not need to fear, Ian, we will not force you to wear anything you do not desire to. However, we are protectors of the Light, carriers of knowledge long lost, and comrades and protectors of the prophet, er prophetess. It is our responsibility to do our best to protect our lives so that we can protect hers." Jay said, glancing sharply at Ian.

"I feel that you should be the one who hands out the armour Jay." I said, glancing around at my friends, now comrades in exile and deadly pursuit.

"If that is your desire" Jay nodded, and carefully scanned the laid out armour and weapons. Selecting one suit, he turned to Frost. Kneeling even as he had with me, he carefully girded on the armour. Moving down the line, Jay carefully selected similar sets and girded them on Zay, Zoe, and John.

"This set is yours Ian, for when you are ready." Jay said, calmly wrapping the fifth to last set of armour and setting it alongside the gathered provisions.

"Which is your set Jay?" I asked, stepping to his side.

"This one" he indicated the simplest set of all.

Lifting it up I turned, and kneeling girded it upon him. "You have acted as armour bearer to us, my friend, it is only right that I should act thus for you. For none of us are greater than the other, and it is only together that we can hope to stand."

Finishing with the armour I rose and turned to face the others. "Friends, until today we were companions in danger of discovery. That discovery has now been made and we are companions in flight and exile. We will be hunted, as a rabid wolf is hunted, until we are either killed or we kill our greatest foe. This tower will not remain safe past this night, and indeed we should draw attention away from it to preserve the knowledge within its walls. This knowledge will be essential when our battles are won. Yes" I continued in response to their surprised glances. "I believe we can survive and triumph against this darkness. In the day of triumph the knowledge contained on the third floor will restore the lost Light understanding."

I sighed, a sense of foreboding slowly settling over me. "In the morning we must retrace our steps halfway to the stream, and then head north to the mountains. Our goal will be to reach them without conflict. If we are attacked we will defend ourselves. Full strength will be needed to reach our journey's end in safety. Let us rest in peace tonight, and for a few hours forget our struggles."

Chapter 24: Through the Swamps

The morning was cold and drizzly, a gray mist hung low over the encroaching swamp. Dragging our feet, since no one wanted to be first into the dampness; our little band began to move. Ian still refused to don the armour, though he bundled it and tied it upon his horse. As we were leaving the stable, Zoe came running up her armour gleaming brilliant even in the dim light.

"I found ten long black cloaks in the tack room Mayim" she said, her arms full of the cloaks. "I think they would cover the armour so we were not shining beacons to anyone trying to find us."

"Good thought" I said, accepting one of the black cloaks. Like the blankets we had found the night before. The cloaks were fashioned with travel and protection from the elements in mind. Thickly woven and tightly finished, the cloaks would keep off rain and even ground moisture. I smiled as a sarcastic thought flitted through my mind. The cloaks were invaluable, unless we fell in a pool. Then the cloaks would be useless.

The path was worse today due to the increased moisture, and progress was slow. The horses' hooves sank into the mud, each step accompanied by a sucking release.

The day dragged past, John was silent and still in pain. Ian seemed morose, riding watchfully in the center of the company. Jay rode in the rear, always alert to every sound. Though what could be heard over the sloshing plodding of the horses I do not know. It took over four hours to cover half the distance back toward the stream. I turned off, leading north on a slightly firmer path than we had hitherto followed. As the ground was less sticky the horses also perked up and began moving faster.

Despite the better trail the day still dragged by, and it was with some trepidation that we settled on a willow covered knoll about ten miles north of our first line of direction.

"Mayim are you sure we should stop for the night? Would it not be better to press onward and get as much distance as possible?" Jay said. Drawing me aside as the others began setting up camp.

"We are all tired and cold Jay, it is best to get some rest while we may and keep the horses fresh as long as possible. If necessary the horses will provide an alternate trail to turn trackers off our proper route. If for no other reason than that, it is still worth keeping the horses as fresh as possible. I feel nervous in this dim swamp myself, but we have run into no peril."

"Just because peril has not found us does not mean it does not exist. Places that are safe are different from places that seem safe. As it is, I am more concerned about Ian's reluctance to don the armour. It offers more protection than his leathern jerkin."

"It is more the thought of having it bound to him, not the armour itself. If it was normal steel armour there would be no issue. It is because it is unique and that makes it dangerous. He also has no skill in the Light and the armour is bound to those who protect the Light." I smiled, and began setting up a basic tent from two of the blankets as Jay shrugged and walked away.

A rough tent would help keep off the wind and rain, even if we could not have a proper roof. A little later, Jay reappeared with a selection of sturdy branches and soon had fashioned some basic stools close to the spluttering fire.

After a warm meal, we settled on swiftly constructed raised mats, and soon the others dozed off. I remained on guard. The hours went by slowly, and I alternated between dozing and being watchful. The night was dark and as misty as the previous day. No sound stirred in the still air. Even the mud seemed to be holding its breath. I started as a low purring growl sounded close at hand. Turning my head I saw three Tigri stretched out by our guttering fire.

Catlike, with mottled gray and brown fur, these animals are creatures of the swamps. Held in terror by most priests they are classed as ruthless slayers. Yet these cats made no move, seeming to be on guard. I paused, glancing around. The others slept soundly, none of them having heard the soft purring growls that had alerted me. Still cautious, I sat up on my makeshift pallet.

The middle, and largest of the Tigri, sat up mirroring my position. Meeting my eyes, the Tigri's green and gold pupils stared into my own. After a few moments of silent starting, a low purr rolled over the Tigri. I rose and walked carefully to the fire, keeping the low embers between myself and the three. Not that the fire's feeble coals would be a deterrent. If they did decide to attack only the armour would keep me safe, if even it could stand against their four inch claws. Though, John had indicated that no mortal weapon or darkness could pierce the armour unless the heart had already fallen, though that would be a normal priest or high priests' darkness, not the darkness of the Reaver.

The lead Tigri purred again, low and rumbling, this time looking back along our trail. Suddenly the left Tigri sprang up and dashed off along our old trail. The Tigri's movements were low and swift.

A sudden thought crossed my mind. The Tigri's running reminded me of a greyhound. But what in the world was a greyhound? My sigh was audible. Here was yet another strange term to add to 'compass points' 'wardrobe' and the strange copper scar over my heart.

The lead Tigri had also risen, and now stalked around the fire toward me. Now I remembered what I had read of the Tigri. I froze fear creeping over me. The Tigri were dreaded by practitioners of dark magic. If anyone who was tainted with the Darkness entered Tigri territory, they would not make it out alive. Their mutilated body would be found the next morning, at the marked edge of Tigri territory. Now, a Tigri nearly the size of a pony was walking around the fire toward me.

A slight movement caught my eye, and turning my head I stared at our horses. They did not care that giant cats were within fifty feet of them. Instead the horses were browsing contentedly on the marsh rushes. I looked back at the Tigri. It had paused, and seemed to be waiting for me to make up my mind.

"So I know those who use darkness fear your kind, so why are you here?" I said, keeping my tone low and non-threatening. The Tigri stepped up to me, and leaning slowly forward nudged the necklace I was wearing. The cat's wild scent flowed around me, a mixture of crushed grass and woodsy overtones. There was no swamp scent clinging to it. It nudged the necklace again, breaking me out of my revere.

I touched the necklace slowly, and stared at the cat with a wry smile.

"Of course, we are no longer in the school so there is no longer a reason to hide the mantle." Carefully I unfastened the necklace, moving it to bind about my waist. Instantly the mantle expanded to full size, the leathern part on the necklace changed back to a belt, and the dagger and brooch expanded to become sword and shield. Now however I had another conundrum, I had two swords.

After I had donned the mantle, under the black cloak, and adjusted the brooch back to brooch size, the Tigri lay down at my side, waiting. I moved the Prophet's sword to my leg, to become a hidden dagger. Glancing around now that I had adjusted my weapons I observed the area. The dawn was breaking. In the distance birds sang, but slowly they fell silent. As the silence deepened, the Tigri became alert.

Suddenly the sound of slogging hooves fell on my ears, and the Tigri that had left earlier returned. Following it docilely was a horse, with an injured man upon its back. The lead Tigri looked at me calmly, then nodded toward the horse. I rose and stepped to the side of the man. And bit back a scream.

Chapter 25: A New Light

Bound to the horse's back was Brenan. His back was covered in open wounds, many of which were still bleeding. His arms and legs were covered in bruises, and his left leg was broken.

"Ian, Jay!" I called. Not caring if everyone woke up "I need assistance now." As I called the others, the Tigri slid out of sight behind the horses.

Jay stumbled out of the shelter. "Help me get him off this blasted horse" I snapped, already cutting through the bonds that held Brenan to the animal. "I don't know how long he's been like this, but whoever did this probably thought it was a death sentence." My hands were shaking and it was an effort not to add to Brenan's wounds as I sliced the ropes.

Jay said nothing, still looking more asleep than awake, and stumbled to support Brenan's limp form. Ian also assisted, and soon Brenan was placed on one of the raised beds under the shelter.

"I need boiled water, and some clean strips of cloth." I directed, moving to inspect the broken leg, which seemed worse than when I had first seen it.

"I hate to say this Mayim" Ian said, "but he already seems fairly far gone" his voice trailed off as I glared at him.

"He became an adopted father to me. I do not know why he is in this condition, but if I can save him I will" I said, my voice sharp with fear. John's hand rested on my shoulder, stilling my tirade. He said nothing, merely stood alongside as we waited for the water to boil.

I glanced up, making eye contact again with the largest of the Tigri, now watching me from the edge of the bushes. I stilled as the realization hit. They had guided Brenan's horse here for a purpose, and I was sure that their purpose was not to let Brenan die, but live. The Tigri had insisted that I don again my prophet's mantle, but for what purpose. I gazed silent now, on Brenan's still features. His skin was pale, and his chest barely moved with each breath. Indeed his breathing seemed harder now than it had been. Even as I watched his arm twisted unnaturally, breaking as he moaned in pain. Something was actively torturing him.

I leapt back to his side. Light blazed. A cocoon of protective light blossomed around myself and Brenan. Tearing back the bloodstained and tattered shirt, I found a chilling device. A small stone on a fine steel chain, a stone filled with black malice. Under the Light I could see the darkness slowly killing him. It was preventing his body from responding to the attack, having immobilized him to prevent his Light from fighting back.

I leaned forward, placing my right hand upon his head, and my left hand over his heart. I paused, slowly gathering and focusing the Light as I remembered what I had read in the book of Light healing. My vision blurred, as Light, whiter if possible than any I had yet summoned blazed over his body. At the same time I spoke "As love is stronger than hatred, so reconciliation is mightier than war, as light overcomes the darkness, so can mercy triumph over cruelty. By the One whose Light we bear do I break these bonds of darkness, and by the One who brought us life do I claim healing."

As I finished speaking, the Light blazed up even brighter. I waited a few seconds with my head bowed and eyes closed. Suddenly a hand closed over my wrist. I opened my eyes to find Brenan staring at me. I smiled, glancing at his chest. The amulet was gone, completely destroyed by the Light. Sighing, I dropped the protective shield, and glanced around at the shocked stares of the rest of my party. Who I suspected were now fully awake because of the Light show.

"Friends, I would like you to meet my adoptive father, Brenan Donague" I smiled feeling tired again after the stress and watchfulness. "Brenan, these are my friends and companions in Light. Frost is on the far right, Zay and Zoe look alike but Zoe's shorter, Jay is the tall guy on the left, Ian is the redhead, and John has the partially healed bruises."

"I am pleased to make all of your acquaintance" Brenan nodded, looking confused. "But isn't it dangerous to do such a blatant display of Light Mayim? Aren't we close to the school or something, I can't remember what happened" he shook his head, gazing around in bewilderment.

"We are in the swamp to the east of the school Brenan, I doubt we are in danger from darkness at this point. If we are" I exchanged meaningful glances with Jay, Frost, Zay and Zoe "I think we can take them."

Zoe shrieked, jumping back toward the fire. "What?" Jay said, spinning and half drawing his sword.

"I thought I saw something moving in the bushes" Zoe said, shaking slightly "but I didn't see what it was."

"It is not a threat to us" I said, smiling softly "What you just glimpsed I saw in greater detail just before they led Brenan's horse here." I glanced over at the horse, now recognizing it as the younger horse from the farm. "There are at least three, if not more Tigri in the area. I doubt we have to worry about any but a very strong body of darkness wielders trying to come to this camp site."

Brenan's jaw dropped, "We're in the Tigri swamps? I thought..." he trailed off, staring at the low bushes and the misty haze that obscured the sky.

"I do not know how you got here, but we are headed for the Brachite forest and then the mountains. Two days ago John was detected and sentenced to death so we got him out. However" I grimaced suddenly as a memory kicked in "I had placed an invisible Prophet's shield in place, and I forgot to remove it when I left the arena. That is why we were found out at the stable and they know that one of us is the Prophet, their biggest threat."

The others stared grimly back at me. "That was unfortunate" Jay said slowly "I am surprised they have not caught up to us, unless our little detour was enough to throw them off."

"Once the Reaver hears" I said raising my eyebrows "we can expect hard and fast pursuit. We'll likely have multiple skirmishes until we are cornered, or manage to draw the Reaver into a full on battle." I sighed, then shook myself and straightened up. "We had better be moving out then, unless we want to be caught. We should be fairly safe until we pass beyond the Tigri territory, wherever that ends."

We moved steadily but rapidly through dismantling the camp. Brenan still seemed tired, despite the potency of the Light healing. Light healing, I hadn't even known it was possible for me to do, until I had acted. The book had said it was a trait of the first prophet, not the second prophet who was a warrior more than a nurturer. Sometimes I longed to understand more of my calling, it almost made me regret leaving the tower and the knowledge it contained.

It was after breakfast, that Brenan declared himself strong enough to mount and ride. Looking around as we started Brenan paused; catching my eye he mouthed a single word. Worry lines forming as he did so "Finan?"

I smiled reigning back alongside him. I did not have to lead as the largest of the Tigri was now visible and doing a fine job of leading, and on solid paths no less.

"Last I knew Finan was doing well. He never entered the school but found a different vocation. He took over the leadership of a band of Plains Raiders who had tried to take the students captive. It was a rather interesting diversion en route to the school." I smiled remembering the shock and terror evidenced when the Varat spell struck my first Prophet's shield.

"En route" Brenan said, puzzlement evident in his tone.

"It means, on the way" I said, a frown flickering over my brow.

"Where did you learn that term?" Brenan glanced sidewise at me.

"I do not know, it is just another of a number of different terms that I do not know how I know them. Perhaps it is from previous memories, or learning, though Finan only found the Tor in my mind on that first night." I sighed and continued "I have a feeling if Finan did a check now there might be more, these terms and thoughts have to come from somewhere. I hate feeling like I have no roots, no anchor, no memory..." I trailed off.

Around the same time the way narrowed and for a time we were forced to ride single file. As we rode my mind wandered again. Words and phrases that were unfamiliar sprang out of my mouth at random times. They fit the context, but did not fit the time it seemed. Rising up in the saddle I scanned the dripping treeline. Crushed grass mingled with mud under the horse's hooves giving off a pungent, swampy scent. Damp branches swept across my face, and I smiled, the trees seemed to be making up for my lack of personal care this morning. At least my face would be clean. I glanced down at my mud covered robes and paused. Mud besmirched the main robe, and the black cloak was heavy with gathered moisture, but the Prophet's mantle was as white and shining as ever, perfectly dry too. Yet another puzzle to ponder I sighed.

As the way widened I drew alongside Brenan. We did not ride much longer, as the Tigri lead us to a low hill rising above the mire. A stand of thick trees crowned the small rise, providing much needed shelter from the drizzling rain. Seriously I was not sure if it was rain or mist, and the weather itself did not seem to want to make up its mind.

As we rested, Jay quietly approached Brenan. "At the tower were we spent the night before last there was armour. It is such that once equipped it cannot be removed except in death, not even betrayal or changing sides can remove it. I feel that this set is to be yours." Jay hesitated, and then carefully unwrapped the armour.

Brenan stared, his jaw dropping open in slow motion. "I have heard of the armour of the Prophet's protectors, but I had not thought to see it" he paused shaking his head. "Let alone be offered the chance to wear it" He suddenly smiled.

Brenan leaned forward, placing his hand lightly on my knee. I blushed slightly as the others glanced over, noticing what was going on. Brenan ignored them, speaking only to me but loudly enough for all to hear. "Donning such armour is no small or light decision, and I do not make it lightly." He smiled acutely aware of the low snickers at his pun. "I love you as a daughter, and respect you as a prophetess. It will be my pleasure to wear this armour in your service and if needs be to die for the one who saved not only my own life but the lives of both my sons." He paused, blinking back tears.

"I am not worthy of your loyalty or commitment Brenan, Foster Father" I said blinking back tears of my own as I spoke. "Yet because of my position I accept your words and your service. But if in any way I can save you, or any of this party, I will do so." I looked around making eye contact with the others. Grim and sincere smiles greeted my gaze. Zoe looked a tad scared, but still game for a good fight.

These were my friends and companions; hitherto we had trained alongside each other. Now if needs be we would fight and die for each other. My smile widened, two had become five. Five had become seven, and seven had changed to eight. There were yet two armour sets un-given, and one un-donned. Battle could not be far off.

Chapter 26: An Ambuscade

The Tigri appeared again when it was time to move on. Our stop had been short, and though we had eaten, little rest or dryness had been achieved. As we continued, the Tigri leading seemed more uptight. Frequently pausing to sniff the air, and often glancing back. When I had started to drop back to speak with Frost, the Tigri had looked me in the eye and growled. It wanted me to stay close, though I did not know why.

We traveled through variegated swamp. As dusk fell, we came to a small open glade seated deep within the swamp. As the bushes failed, the Tigri slid away leaving no sign of their presence.

"I guess we may as well camp here for the night" Ian said, yawning loudly. "I for one am ready to stop and if this ground is firm all the better."

Tired nods came from the others, and we rode forward. I stiffened, alarm coursing through me. We were being watched, targeted. Scanning I saw nothing obvious, but my internal alarm was ringing overtime.

"Stop" I said, "and draw in." Rising in the saddle I scanned the low treeline at the far side of the glade.

"There is nothing here Mayim, have you ever seen a quieter and safer location?" Ian said, spurring his horse forward.

Words, a quote perhaps from another time filtered through my mind. "Things that seem safe, and that are safe, are often two different things." Even as the thought finished, I made my decision. Without gesture or sign I cast a Prophet's shield over everyone, then spurred on to follow Ian across the glade. The closer we came to the far side, the louder my alarms rang. Suddenly drawing to a halt, Ian turned to face me a cocky smile on his face. "See, there is nothing except mist here. We have nothing to worry about."

Mist? I froze, I saw and felt no mist. But Ian suddenly fell asleep on his steed. The others nodded off as they neared the point where Ian had fallen asleep. I dropped my hand to my sword's hilt and yelped from pain and surprise. The sword was hot enough to burn. Without thinking, I drew it despite the heat, holding it above my head as I advanced toward the forest.

A bolt of dark purple lighting struck strait at the group, mostly aimed for Ian. The Prophet's shield became visible in a blinding flash as the darkness impacted and fizzled out upon it.

"Come out" I called, forcing my voice to be calm "I know you are there."

"I was hoping you'd expose your hand girl" a familiar voice called, not bothering to hide the sneering tone I knew so well. "I always knew you were trouble."

"And I knew better than to trust a viper, Evean of the house of Brachide" I responded. "If you think to take us prisoner, I must inquire what reinforcements you have. If it is to kill us, I will inquire what army you have brought to back you."

"Always the overconfident one aren't you," he replied. "I think your friends are quite asleep, though why it did not work on you I don't know." His voice trailed off, as if in thought.

A very slight motion to my right caught my attention. Brenan was gripping his sword so tight that his knuckles were white. Other than the death grip on the sword however, there was no sign of alertness. A grim smile flickered over my face the others were in similar postures. Ready for action, their stillness a deception. Except for Ian who was snoring loud enough to shake leaves off the nearby trees.

"Even alone I doubt you'd find me an easy capture, or kill" I said, studying Evean's stance. "Though why you seem to hate me I have no idea, we never spoke after arriving at the school, unless you were shouting insults at my friends and I."

"You usurped my place of leadership" he said, his eyes narrowing as he prepared to attack. "The others at the school looked up to you, and if it wasn't for you..." his voice trailed off. The continued with more venom "that Finan would be dead, I hate that family and I am glad his father died at my hand yesterday"

Before I could respond, Brenan spoke, casting off the semblance of sleep and also the black cloak so that his armour blazed. "I'm worth a good many dead men yet Evean, thanks to my adopted daughter. I would suggest you leave now, otherwise it would be my pleasure to slay you."

Evean staggered back two steps, his face paling as if he saw a ghost, "Attack them, kill them all" he shouted. Before turning and fleeing into the forest.

Twenty acolytes stepped from the treeline. Raising their hands, palms facing us, they began an incantation. My eyes narrowed. On each of their necks hung a red stone set in a steel collar. The stones pulsated with a rhythm of their own. The stones were identical matches to the one the Light had removed from Brenan, though in collars not on a chain.

I acted fast to beat the incantation. Light flowed from me, expanding over the glade. Reaching over, it first surrounded the acolytes, and then encased them. Some fingers reaching out into the forest behind them. Choked cries of surprise came from the acolytes and one cry of terror from the forest, then silence. The light diminished, and twenty acolytes stared at their surroundings. There was only one expression on their faces, deep shock.

Chapter 27: The Party Grows

I rode forward and dismounted alongside the acolytes.

"Where are we?" one who seemed to be the eldest finally said. "The last place I remember was the temple with the priests, darkness, and a ceremony" his voice trailed off.

"You are with friends" I said struggling to calm my anger against the Reaver and his exploitations "and we will take you to safety within the Brachite forest, we are in the swamps to the south of the forest."

Their eyes widened and terror gripped the eldest, before he managed to whisper. "But what of the Tigri?"

Before I could respond, the three Tigri stalked regally into the clearing and walked up to the acolytes. Look at the acolytes now, I could see they were little more than children, young pawns in dark hands. The lead Tigri walked up to the eldest of the children, then nudged up the lad's hand while purring.

"I think they are saying that you do not need to fear them. They fight against the darkness, even as the eight of us do."

He stared into my eyes and gave a slight nod, "I am called Janis, let me speak with my companions for a while."

I nodded as he turned away biting his lip. The other nineteen joined him, gathering close they whispered together. I moved back to my seven companions, Ian was still asleep.

I shook my head "dump a bucket of water or something over him so that he wakes up. I can't figure out why the rest of us were not knocked out by whatever that 'mist' was."

"I suspect that the armour might have something to do with it" Zoe said, glancing with a wry grin at Ian. "He was the only one of us to not don the armour, and was the only one who fell asleep like a log."

"Which would indicate some element of protection on the armour which prevents the darkness from taking hold" I finished, nodding. "But what are we to do with these twenty young'uns, they cannot fight or survive alone." I shot a quick glance in their direction.

The youngsters seemed to have calmed down. They were watching us, and had sat down together under the relative shelter of the treeline.

"If they are willing to come I would say we had a responsibility to take them with us. They are still innocent, and it is not right that that evil which was controlling them should continue its exploitation." Brenan said, looking among the others.

Zay nodded, "I agree, though I hesitate for I do not know what skills they could use against us. What happened to Evean anyway?"

John turned from whispering to Frost and Zoe. He smiled with a look of sadness and said "Having already passed through the acolyte stage myself" he hesitated then continued "I know they do not learn dark skills until the third level. By which time there is considered to be no escape. As for Evean, from the yell in the forest he is probably out cold for a bit, we should be safe to travel on."

I nodded, struggling to remain calm. Not only did I have eight friends who could be killed just for being with me. I now had the added responsibility of protecting twenty children who we had now officially stolen from the darkness.

Taking a deep breath I said "then if the twenty are agreeable we will head out, though someone should probably tie Ian onto his horse before we leave, since the water didn't wake him. Otherwise he could fall and break his thick red headed skull."

Zoe laughed and headed over to secure Ian, while I walked over to the, now former, acolytes. "We have agreed to have you travel with us, if you yourselves are agreeable. Possible the foresters within Brachite forest will agree to take you in."

Janis, who had acted as spokesman before rose and stepped forward. "We are willing to go with you." The lad bowed slightly "we trust your word, you are the prophetess." He smiled, seeming calmer and happier than hitherto. He glanced at the others and then added with a broad grin. "Can you teach us Light so that we can defend ourselves?"

I nodded, rising to head back to the others. "We will begin your training tonight" I smiled, "however wielding the Light requires knowledge of the Light Giver. We'll have to cover that first."

With Ian secured to his horse, and two lads mounted on each of the other seven steeds, our much larger party of walkers headed north again. The Tigri appeared as before, leading us by firm and clear paths through the night. Every few hours those on the horses were switched with those walking. Four of us remaining on foot at all times in different locations in the procession.

It was not till the next afternoon, after we had covered nearly thirty miles and the edge of the forest was within a few miles that Ian woke.

Yawning Ian struggled to sit up, pausing in consternation as he realized that ropes bound him to the saddle. Looking around he relaxed as he noticed me, and then Zoe.

"Mayim! Why am I tied to this saddle like a sack of goods or something?" Ian said, glaring at me and tugging on the ropes.

"Because we didn't want you to fall off and break your thick skull" I said, glaring right back at him. "You've slept through some interesting developments, including an ambush, and our taking charge of twenty former acolytes. We've also traveled around thirty miles since you fell asleep, so be happy you have not been walking."

Zoe meanwhile had been unfastening the ropes, and now stepped back with a giggle. "Good thing I tied those ropes tight Mayim" she winked, "otherwise this lump would have fallen off, one of the knots was cut half through by the friction."

Ian shook his head, and glanced around over the whole procession. John and Zay were in deep conversation at the rear with eight of the youth in front of them. Next were Jay and Frost leading two horses with four kids on them, and following six more. Walking alongside Ian's horse was one carrying the other two sleeping youth. Ian dismounted lightly, and began talking with Zoe as I sauntered ahead, closer to the Tigri. Brenan acting as the rearguard.

Our procession remained unchanged, except for the number of youth on or off the horses, until nearly nightfall. Then the Tigri lead us to a stream, where a large hollow provided protection from the wind and a way to hide our cooking fire. Another of the Tigri came in hauling the half of a freshly killed deer to provide us with sustenance. I smiled. At least as long as the Tigri remained we would have plenty of food, otherwise what we had in the saddlebags would not last two days with the expanded crew.

Dinner consisted of roasted venison, and some roasted water-plant roots. The plant from which we harvested the roots was similar to a giant grass, but with broader and longer leaves than most rushes. It also had a central spike that towered above us, and the lower half of the top part of the spike was thicker than the tip and brown in color. The thick roots first had to be peeled, and then the inner core could be roasted. They tasted good with venison.

Chapter 28: Stories of the Former Time

As we relaxed after dinner, the first time we had rested since leaving the tower, I turned and said "Brenan, how about you tell us of the Light Giver? I think the acolytes would enjoy learning about Him."

"Gladly Mayim, if the others are interested" Brenan said, glancing around at the circle of faces. The former acolytes nodded, and even Ian leaned forward with interest.

Brenan began, his voice rising and falling melodically in the manner of storytellers.

"The Light Giver is also known as the Creator, and The One, for there is no other like Him nor above Him in power and glory. As you may have been taught, after the One created man a deception happened. Now those with the Reaver and the darkness he represents taught that the serpent offered knowledge and wisdom to mankind and freed them from bondage to the One."

Slight nods came from John, Ian, and the former acolytes. Brenan sighed and continued.

"That is not the truth. Aye" he smiled in response to some shocked glances "the knowledge and wisdom the serpent deceived mankind into taking was the knowledge of evil, of pain, and of sorrow and suffering. The knowledge that the One would have imparted was the knowledge of good, of what is pure, just, true, and loving. After the deception some of mankind remained with the One, while other's embraced the serpent's teaching. You know who those sides are now, do you not?" Brenan said, glancing keenly at the acolytes.

Janis nodded, and spoke up "we know what darkness and pain are, but what of the things the One offered knowledge of, love, justice, truth...?"

Brenan continued his tale, smiling at the acolytes. "The One always had followers, sometimes more and sometimes less. Among these the One gave some the gifts of Light, to counter the darkness being practiced. These Light gifts include the simple forms which provide physical light to an area, the medium forms which enable something to be infused with light to counter darkness, and the complex like the Prophet's Shield which protect and defend or heal. One thing about Light is that it cannot be used to attack darkness directly, only to defend and protect against it. However, Light and Darkness are such that while Light can permeate Darkness, the Darkness cannot enter the Light."

"There is one other gift that the Light giver gave, and that is the prophets. There have always been two prophets since the time of the division, one of highest rank who is said to speak directly with the One. The first prophet also has the gift of healing wounds caused by darkness. The other is a prophet of second rank who is said to be the most powerful warrior protector of all, and is given the gift of fighting and of defense."

Brenan looked directly in my eyes as he spoke of the second prophet. Pausing, Brenan continued.

"The Reaver is only one of many servants of darkness who have infiltrated this world, and other worlds. His goal is domination, to wipe out the Light and to plunge the land into darkness."

"Why does the darkness hate the light or desire domination?" Ian asked, glancing around at the night surrounding us.

"Power and hatred are the only reasons for the darkness, and hatred is simply because of what darkness is. Darkness is the absence of light, everything that defines Light has its opposite to define darkness. Who can reason with unreasoning hatred? Anyone who is against those heading for ultimate power is considered an enemy as well. 'Why do we fight?' could be another question to ask. Would you like to answer it Mayim?" Brenan gave a sad smile.

"War is sad" I said slowly "it causes great loss of life, sorrow, and pain. Yet war must be, not because of our own choices but because of 'The Enemy' whose goal is to devour our land, people, and families." I paused, giving my head a shake and added. "Some glory in war. The warrior can glory in his strength, enjoying the swiftness of the arrow, and the sharpness of the sword. But these things I do not love, I love only that which they can defend. Family, freedom, friends," I leaned forward to join hands with the others, "and fellowship."

One of the other acolytes spoke, his voice low. "So the Light Giver is also our creator, and the darkness is controlled by those who hate the Creator?"

I nodded, watching as the acolytes exchanged glances. Then Janis spoke "we would rather follow the Light than the Darkness. What happened in the Darkness was horrible, and I would rather fight it than serve it."

The others nodded, and even Ian joined their nod. Ian then spoke, "I would also like to learn some light skills. I know nothing and think it would be best to know something, and I should don that armour once I know a bit. I dinna want to fall asleep on the battle field as I did today. Good thing Mayim didn't let it become a full blown battle, I'd never ha' forgiven her."

He winked at me, his grin and humor finally restored. The others joined the laugh. As soon as some semblance of sobriety was established we began training. First we trained the simple light skills, sensing the Light, forming a ball to give normal light and coating a weapon with Light.

At the very start of training, each of the acolytes renounced any bond they had with the Darkness, any claim that the Darkness had, and any use of Dark powers. After the renunciation they turned and walked through a veil of Light. The Light from the veil was formed by their words, through the renunciations, and through the declaration of determination to follow the Light no matter what. As the acolytes passed, I smiled, remembering my own choice.

Even though I was the prophetess, I had still had to make the choice to embrace the Light. Otherwise I would never have learned a single light skill. No one who had not fully embraced the Light could wield it, and any attempt or fake would fail. The veil felt tingly, like walking through the mist of a mountain waterfall. It also felt hot, searing and purifying as the Light sought out any darkness and cleansed it. Darkness could still be embraced later on, but as of passing through the veil no Darkness remained.

As we completed the light training and renunciations, Ian headed over to his belongings. Pulling out his armour, he flashed a shy smile to the others as he donned it, helm, breastplate, and sword. Jay and John exchanged winks while Frost high-fived Brenan, as Ian finished fastening the armour.

"Well, looks like I'm ready for trouble now" Ian said, with a wry grin. "Teach me to listen next time."

Morning came too soon for the newly trained youth. A quick Light practice accompanied breakfast and breaking camp. There were more smiles and chatter today than before, and indeed we were noisy enough to be heard a mile away. As the miles wore on however, silence fell. Nearly five hours after starting only the sucking plod of the horses and the shuffle of tired feet broke the silence.

The silence was broken by the clash of arms. Sword banged against shield. Men shouted, and horses neighed. The sound was close, only a clearing or so away. I turned to the others, casting back my black cloak and exposing the silver armour. The emblem upon the chest-piece blazed a brilliant gold and silver.

"Let us see what this fight is about. Ian and John, do you remain back with the acolytes. Brenan, you are still recovering. Do you desire to remain behind as well?" I shot him a questioning glance as I spoke. He shot me a grim smile.

"I will remain behind, there are eight of us. A third held back is a good number. But take care, only show yourself if it is friends who are fighting."

I nodded, reining my horse around and urging it toward the sounds.

Men screamed in pain, and the shouts that were rising louder and louder stopped. Silence fell. I dismounted, leaving the horse and sliding through the underbrush on foot. The other five following close on my heels. Jay, ever conscientious, paused only long enough to secure our horses to trees before following.

Belly down I crept to the edge of a bloodstained clearing.

Chapter 29: Friends in Need

A score of raiders crouched on the far side of the clearing. At least ten, if not more, raiders were strewn around the clearing, either wounded or dead. Their leader was held between two high ranked priests, being forced to kneel before another priest.

Two score priests stood around, sneering at the defeated raiders. None of the priests had serious injuries. The raiders that were injured had been injured by darkness. The raider's leader spoke, and I froze.

"I will never bow to you, carrion" he spat, glaring daggers at the priest before him, his voice somehow familiar to me. He was refusing to bow his head, despite being forced to kneel.

"It is too bad that your courage is misplaced. Do you think perhaps that anyone will rescue you? There is no Light in these swamps" The priest laughed harshly, and continued. "Indeed, there is nothing better to break the spirit of new captives that to see their leader executed in agony. Perhaps being turned into a Varat will cure you of your insolence?"

My heart was pounding, and I scanned the clearing to pick up the other's positions. Jay was closest and I waved him over.

"We have to rescue the raiders at all costs" I said, keeping my voice low but not whispering. "I can shield and turn the spell, but it will reveal me, so we will have to act fast. The armour should help" my smile was grim, as the eagerness to fight filled me.

Jay nodded and slipped away to carry the message to the others. I turned my attention back to the clearing. Two of the priests had brought a steel cage, setting it up alongside the Raider captain. A wagon was near, I realized, now seeing it outlined through the bushes. It had more than one cage.

"Perhaps" the raider said, still oozing defiance "you could inform me of why you interfere with travelers at the edges of the swamp and forest? These are areas you, cowards, would never travel."

"You may ask, and since you will never escape us alive I do not mind informing you. We seek a dangerous Light Wielder, and also weapons to fight against her. You will become one of our weapons, a twisted Varat." He laughed again, as the raider struggled against the priests holding him.

"I will never serve you, even as such an abomination." The raider said, passion flushing his face and lending strength to his struggles.

The priest backhanded him across the face "Silence, clod, you will serve and have no choice. And when all your precious comrades are turned, you will enter this forest and destroy all the accursed ones, holding to the old way, that shelter in it. Then once those foresters are destroyed you will hunt and destroy that paltry light wielder."

The raider smiled "If you think that Light wielder is paltry than I doubt you've ever encountered her. But I have."

"Really, I did not know the raiders dealt in Light." The priest said, his voice dripping malice.

"They do not, but my band has" The raider smiled, seeming calm and enjoying taunting the priest.

"Do you think then that that Light Wielder will help you? She doesn't even know you're in trouble. Besides, no one can reverse a Varat spell, not even our most skilled mages." The priest shifted position, his back toward the tree line. A shadow seemed to pass over the clearing, and a dark presence filled the area. The raiders stiffened, frozen in place. Even their bold captain could no longer move.

I hoped that Brenan had used wisdom and gotten the acolytes under shelter, for though the armour protected us from the aura of evil, the lads would be vulnerable. I glanced around, keeping low as I waited.

The Reaver materialized in the center of the clearing, his back to me and his face to the raiders. It was the first time I had seen or sensed him since the night on the Blood Tor. His evil was stronger, if that were possible. He leered at the captured raiders and then turned to the priests.

"When blood is shed it increases our strength, when innocence is lost it does likewise. This paltry raider boasts in light that he does not know." An eerie chuckle came from the Reaver "turn him to our servant, and we shall stamp out the paltry prophetess. Then this world will be ours forever. First the prophetess, then the foresters, then the plains peoples, and we will have complete domination. We will not fail. You have done well priest and will be rewarded on your return." He laughed, a chilling rippling sound.

A black whirlwind surrounded the Reaver, and he disappeared from the area. The taint of evil lingered for a few seconds, before dissipating. The Reaver had spoken his plans in plain hearing. Either he was confident that the raiders would be turned and the priests would remain faithful or... I hesitated, glancing around again. Either the Reaver was overconfident, or he was dropping misinformation hoping it would get back to us.

My attention jerked back to the clearing as the priest began his incantation. The raider had been forced into the steel cage, and was now trying to remain calm.

I smiled, and dropped an invisible Prophet's shield over the raider captain, and also over the other captives. Glancing around I saw that Jay and the others were in position. Inhaling, I stepped out of the bushes, cloaking the others as I moved and drawing my black cloak around me to hide the armour.

"Hail priests of the Reaver, who or what do you have captive here?"

The head priest jumped, dropping his incantation and spinning around to face me.

"Light wielding raiders, who think they'll be rescued. Who are you and what are you doing here." He said, suspicion sharpening his glance as he took in the black hooded cloak.

"I could ask you the same question, were it not obvious that you are trespassing in the Tigri swamps" I said. Observing the fearful glances, that the other priests exchanged, at the mention of the Tigri.

The head priest sneered "we are strong enough to face down any force, Tigri or Light. I ask again, who are you? What are you doing here? If you refuse to respond I will turn you into a Varat, since that is the incantation you interrupted."

"Who I am matters not. And if you desire to turn one who is not restrained into a Varat, do so at your peril. As for my business, it is no concern of yours" I smiled now, the priest struggling to maintain a straight face as his anger neared the boiling point.

"Then your fate is sealed, brash woman" he said, hissing in his anger.

"Sealed?" I said, permitting a hint of scepticism to lace my tone. "I doubt you could turn anyone, even yonder captive, into a Varat. Let alone a freeborn woman."

The priest did not bother responding, instead beginning his incantation anew. A few seconds later a bolt of darkness, tinged with crimson hurtled toward my chest.

Striking the center of the breastplate, I felt the darkness surround me. Tearing around like a whirlwind, seeking an opening. The Light flared and the Darkness subsided. I had not moved.

"Was that the best a dreaded priest of Darkness could do?" I taunted, breaking the shocked silence that greeted the failure of the spell.

"How?" The priest said, spluttering as he stumbled backward, stumbling over a low hillock. "Not even the strongest can turn that spell, and no one can resist it without..." The priest's voice trailed off and fear sparked into his eyes.

"Yonder prisoners are mine" I said, a cold calm infusing my tone "leave now, or die here. The choice is yours."

The other four stepped out of the forests edge, black robed and silent. The five of us stood unmoving staring at the priests.

"Who in the Reaver's name are you" the lead priest said, shaking with fear and anger. The prisoner was staring at me, tense and excited, hope blazing from his eyes.

"Who I am does not matter. What I am might" I said, fixing my gaze upon the priest. "Leave now, or die here. The choice is still yours."

Two Tigri now stalked out of the forest, radiating majesty and power. The priests stepped back again, their fear now palpable in the air.

The head priest's eyes narrowed, glaring at us. Then he spoke "There are only five of you, and two cats. Can you truly stand against the priests? We outnumber you more than five to one, if you hadn't noticed"

"Believe me, I noticed and I do not care" I said, my body tensing in anticipation of the thrill of battle.

"Cloaks" I said, and the four dropped their black cloaks onto the ground. Brilliant light streamed from the armour, blinding in its brilliance. I walked forward, now flanked by the Tigri and by my four armoured protectors.

The priest turned away from us and sent a wall of blackness hurling toward the prisoners. A wall meant to destroy. Without breaking stride I released the Prophet's shield around them and it became visible. The blackness broke upon the shield as a wave upon thirsty sand. The darkness was absorbed and dissipated in an instant.

The priest spun around to face me, a look of pure fear on his face. A wall of crimson now swept toward us, blocked without effort by a second shield of Light. With a shriek, the priests drew swords and hurled themselves upon us. Our weapons flashed white as we drew them and sprang forward to engage our foes.

The battle raged. The Tigri yowled each taking down a priest in an instant. The head priest engaged me. His sword swept at my head, then back at my feet. It was with difficulty that I parried his attacks. His blade flashed crimson with black power. Mine blazed white with the Light. Back and forth we battled. From the center to the side of the clearing and back again we went. Parrying and blocking, jumping and dodging we wove around the clearing, our skills an equal match.

Parrying a blow to my head, I leapt to the side. Evading a sword thrust from behind. Spinning, I jerked the dagger from its hidden sheath, and it swelled to sword size as I parried my second opponent's attacks. I stumbled backwards, fighting to keep two hungry swords from finding a mark. Taking advantage of the ground, I threw myself behind a tree. Leaping a few yards to the side, I wove around the trunks. Dashing back out of the forest's edge, I re-engaged the two priests with rapid strokes.

As the fight continued, I took a chance and glanced around. Four of the priests were heading toward the caged leader, swords in their hands. Ten others were heading for the captive raiders, crouching against the treeline. My four companions were engaging four foes apiece, while the Tigri had their paws full with a group of priests casting spells.

Spinning, I dropped both swords, and then dove between my attackers. Regaining my footing I spun to face them unarmed. Both priests paused, exchanging uncertain glances.

I dropped to a crouch, placing my hands flat on the ground. Light filled me, as I focused on the One. Closing my eyes I sensed the clearing in variations of light and dark. Close to me were dark spots, and surrounding were gleams of white and taints of black.

As the scene solidified, I saw the closest two sources of darkness getting nearer. As those closest to the caged light, drew closer. Dark shadows drew toward the captive gray to near white lights, closing the distance.

The light surrounding me rose, until it seemed I was cradled within it. A Presence drew near, and a form like that of a man became clear.

"I do not want to slay them" I said, my voice a whisper. "For that is not what Light is supposed to do"

"They have chosen darkness, and rejected light." the figure replied "if they embrace the light as it rises they will live, but if they hold fast to the darkness. Then the darkness will take their life as it flees." Sadness tinted the figure's tone as it turned away. The light blazed outward from me, expanding like a super nova. A moment later, no darkness remained within the clearing, and the gray had become white.

Chapter 30: Friends Rediscovered

Opening my eyes, I smiled at the shocked stares of the raiders and my four comrades. Ignoring their glances I scooped up my blades, sheathing them as I headed for the still locked cage. Arriving I met the gaze of the raider captain.

"Impressive" he said as his smile broadened, "I see you've gotten deeper Light training than I have. Nice sword play too Mayim"

Pausing, I stared in shock. Struggling to reconcile the dashing raider captain with the lad to who the voice belonged. "Finan?" I said, shock tingeing my tone. Though I had suspected it when I heard his voice, the reality was still a surprise.

"Aye" his grin broadened more as he realized I had not recognized him. "Finan it is, now are you going to let me sit in this cage all day or get me out?"

Shaking my head, I smiled as I drew my Prophet's sword again. "Stand back then" I said, and clove the lock from the door with an easy swipe. No material given to darkness could stand against the Prophet's sword. It clove the iron as if it were softened butter. No effort at all.

Finan gave a low whistle "Nice sword, I do not think I've seen that one before. And" he glanced at me keenly "how did you mitigate that spell without giving a sign?" he chuckled suddenly "I guess I have more questions than answers right now."

"I did not have to worry about mitigating it." I smiled slightly, brushing my hand over the armour. "The armour did the mitigating for me, without sign. It is the armour of a prophet and the other suits" I nodded to those worn by Jay, Frost, Zay and Zoe, "are the sets of the prophet's companions. Now what I want to know is how you managed to get tangled up with that band of priests?"

"The tangled part was easy" Finan rolled his eyes and sighed as he gazed around at those of his company who had fallen. "After some unsuccessful raids against Priest-led caravans, we decided to join up with the Brachite Foresters, if they would have us, so that we could learn light. We have lost a few too many men to being turned into Verats in combat while the others watched. On the way we were seen, and followed by this band of priests." His face turned grim and he faced me fully. "Mayim, before you arrived, for I sensed your Light approaching, the priest boasted that the Reaver is forming an army of the souls of men."

"An undead army?" I said surprise tingling through me. "Are you sure that is what they meant?"

Finan nodded his jaw set in a grim line, "He told us that the souls of all who had been sacrificed in preparation for the Reaver's coming belong to him, and he has summoned them as his army. If you had not intervened" Finan paused his tone softening, "Calanan's soul would have been taken that night, since he had been dedicated to the Reaver."

"The Reaver mentioned that after me and those with me, the next target would be the foresters. We may as well make it a simultaneous target." I said, turning to face the forest.

"Jay, get the wounded tended. Zay and Zoe head back and bring the others forward. Frost help those who are unwounded prepare to march. We need to get to the forest's edge tonight. Then we must take counsel," I called.

Orders were obeyed, and soon the wounded were cared for, the dead buried, and the living gathered together and enjoying a meal. As stillness settled over us, a thought occurred to me. I had compared the Light blazing around me to a super nova, but I had no idea what a super nova was. "Brenan, have you ever heard of a super nova?" I asked, glancing around those closest to me.

"Can't say I have, Mayim," Brenan said. "Have any of you?"

Shaking their heads, the others looked curious. "Why do you ask?" Finan said, leaning forward.

"Because when that Light blast happened I thought it was like a super nova, but I have no idea where that comparison came from" I shook my head. "Yet another of my unexplained sayings that are not familiar here, but make sense in my head. Though I do not know why they make sense."

The other's laughed at my chagrined look. And even I could not help a faint smile at how silly I sounded, complaining about unknown words with battles and foes to face. But, they did not know what it was like to have no memories.

We traveled a short distance further toward the forest that night, less than three miles but it was some distance between the place of the battle and where we rested. The Raiders set watch fires and watchmen and soon most of the camp was asleep. I, however, could not rest. Restless and wakeful I soon rose from where I had lain down and walked to one of the watch fires.

The night was still, no sound of insects or even of the breeze. Gazing into the fire I listened and waited. I scanned over the sentries, most of whom seemed uptight and over watchful, though I sensed nothing in the vicinity that was a threat. I smiled as a glint of green eyes showed at the edge of the firelight, and then faded away. The Tigri were still keeping watch. It would be impossible to surprise us with them as guards.

The night passed slowly as I sat staring into the flames. As the new day dawned, I busied myself preparing a meal to break our fast. The raiders and others woke up over time, last of all being Finan and Brenan who had talked far into the night. Jay nodded to me as I served the food, and said "we need to have a meeting, but who should attend?"

"Whoever is perceived as a leader and all the prophetess' guardians" I said, dishing up Frost and the others, as they came by. Ian gave me a slight smile, his armour looking quite bright this morning. It seemed like the armour was happy to be worn and used.

Finally having served everyone I stretched, loosening the muscles in my shoulders and arms. Porridge may be an easy meal to prepare, but it was a hard meal to serve. Grabbing my own bowl of, now thick and lumpy porridge, I settled down to eat. I had just finished when two of the raiders sauntered over, and began to clean the pot and the dishes.

One of them winked at me, though he seemed nervous, and said "Finan sent us over, said ye should not be doing all the work no matter how used to it you are. Brenan also said ye should head over to them, sounds like they want to take council"

"Thank you" I smiled, making eye contact with both the men. "I appreciate the assistance, and the message." Nodding to them, I jogged across the camp to where the others were. The bright gleam of armour made their location obvious.

"Remind me not to order a night attack" I said, smiling as I settled down alongside them. "The armour shines bright enough to blind, even without other light hitting it."

"We won't be doing sneak attacks that's for sure, lassie" Ian said, also smiling easily "It was amazing how the spell didna impact you yesterday."

"Aye," I said, looking around at the others. Brenan and Finan seemed grim despite the light banter. Zay and Zoe were calm, while Frost was staring at Jay who was watching me. John seemed relaxed, though alert.

"My friends" I said, sensing that this meeting would not begin without me officially starting it. "The priest indicated yesterday that the Reaver has not only achieved an army of souls to fight for him without hope of redemption. But also intends to first hunt me down, and then eradicate the remaining pockets of Light wielders. Undead army or not, we cannot permit the Reaver's goal to succeed."

Nods ran around the circle. Agreeing that foiling the Reaver's plans were our first priority.

"Second," I continued "we have twenty former acolytes who are too young to fight, though they were already partially trained for that work. They will need somewhere to be protected and raised in safety, where the Reaver cannot get his hands on them."

Nods again, and John spoke "The priest yesterday mentioned the Brachite foresters, might they have the ability to take the lads in, and perhaps a safe location where non-combatants can hide while those able to fight do so?"

"They might" Brenan said, glancing toward the forest wall only a few miles distant. "My wife and youngest son are with them, and if we can connect it is likely we can co-ordinate shelter for the young'uns. However we ourselves might be viewed as bringing trouble, or war to their boarders. They may be bandits, but they prefer not to have open confrontations."

"It seems open confrontation will come to them, whether or not they prefer it" I sighed. "It is right that we should not bring war to their borders, at least not without first speaking with them."

Jay and Finan exchanged glances, then we all looked to Brenan as the oldest of the party.

"Why are you all looking at me?" Brenan said, glancing around. "To discourse we must first send a messenger and it is up to our leader to choose who will go." He nodded to me.

"How many would you recommend go, Brenan?" I asked, glancing over the others as I spoke.

"I would say three is a prime number for such a mission. One is too few, and five could be a threat. Three will not be seen as a threat, and will be large enough to beat off an attack if necessary."

I nodded, "Brenan, you are known to the Foresters and I trust you to accurately construe the situation. Zay and Zoe will accompany you. They are strong in the Light and have proved alert and active."

Brenan nodded, then said hesitatingly "are you sure I couldn't take Ian and Finan with me instead? Three guys would have more chance of fighting if it came to that."

Zay glared at Brenan, and if looks could injure he would be bleeding from a dozen wounds. "Nay Brenan, Ian needs more training, and I have plans to discuss with Finan as well as training to accomplish with his raiders and the former acolytes. Zay and Zoe are well able to hold their own in a scrimmage, but if you are still uncertain you could always spar them." I smiled, winking at Zoe who began smiling while mischief twinkled in her eyes.

"Bah" Brenan grumbled "I suppose I can take the lasses though I hope we do not encounter trouble on the road. What message do you want to be conveyed?"

"Simply that news of the Reavers plans have come to our attention, and the Reaver plans to exterminate the Foresters using an army of undead. However, they are not his first target, rather the prophetess is his initial target and she requests permission to enter the safety of the forests, first to hide, and then to choose her own battleground. The Reaver plans to exterminate all Light, to prevent any challenge to his kingdom of darkness. It would be well for us to ally if possible." I nodded, then added "and of course you can add any relevant information necessary to further explain. I am not skilled in diplomatic measures or in convincing people."

"I hope the evidence will be enough" Brenan said, "Where will I find you when my mission is done?"

"Return to the same point you entered the forest, a Tigri will meet you there and guide you to where we are. We will be moving camp every day so as to prevent being surprised." I sighed, and then gave a broad grin. "Of course if the Reaver does a small attack, he may be the one surprised." I winked at Jay and Frost who winked back, their grins as broad as mine.

After packing provisions on one horse, the three set off. A Tigri led them to the start of the forest, and then returned to its brethren in the swamp.

Chapter 31: Visions in the Night

As soon as Brenan had left I called the camp to assemble around a small knoll. My friends, and guards, gleaming bright in their armour, flanked the knoll. The raiders were to my right, and the youth to my left.

"I'll make this short, friends, but it is important" I scanned the faces before me, over fifty in number. The raiders looked grim, while the youths looked nervous and kept glancing at shadows. "As was openly proclaimed yesterday, the Reaver plans to exterminate us with an army of captured souls, an undead army. Because you are with me" I touched my prophetess garb meaningfully "you will be the first to be attacked and hunted. The second will be the foresters, and third any scattered Light wielders they can find and track down. The Reaver desires complete and utter control, and the darkness he serves desires our destruction and annihilation. If we do not fight we will die. If we fight we may live or at least weaken the enemy before we die. But, to fight we must all be trained and know the Light, otherwise the darkness can and will overwhelm us. Are you willing to first remain with us, secondly to train with us, and thirdly to fight and maybe die alongside us?"

I paused, looking slowly over the raiders and youth. Janis stepped forward from among the others. "We have no desire to return to the darkness, nor to serve the Reaver and what he embodies." The youth shuddered "we will remain, train, and fight with you. We will never go back." The other youth murmured their agreement.

Some of the raiders were nodding in agreement with the youth, a few were smiling openly at the hesitant yet bold declaration.

Finan stepped forward from his place in front of the raiders. "For myself I will remain, train, and fight. I already know and trust Mayim and will stand alongside her till the end, whether it is bitter or sweet. I do not speak for my men however, for this choice must be made individually. I will hold it against no man who decides to leave what seems to be a hopeless fight."

Low chuckles greeted Finan's statement and one of the men, who I recognized as the second in command before Finan took over, called out, his voice rising through his declaration. "Well said commander, and if ye trust the prophetess then we'll trust you. Who said we looked for fights that we're sure to win? If it's for what is right and the Light, which ye've demonstrated as a powerful but gentle thing unlike that destroying darkness, then I dinna see why we shouldn't stand and fight."

Brisk nods and low calls of "aye" and "I'm in" greeted the conclusion of that little banter. I smiled now, more relaxed than I had been for a while and stepped down to be at eye level with the others.

"Then it's time to start training" I said, "Jay, Ian, John, and Frost will come through and see what you are good at. Then they will split you into four training parties and begin training. At noon today we'll move camp to another location, and continue training there for a day, and then move again."

I watched silent as the training split began. Those proficient in different normal weapons were divided amongst the parties, while light skill was also measured and shifted among the four parties.

Finan was moving around, as agile as ever despite the bruising he'd received the day before, speaking with and encouraging his men and the youths. It was easy to see why the men followed him willingly, even into this hopeless situation. He engaged with them where they were, speaking as an equal neither toning down or up his natural actions. Being from the land and not nobility or raised to position, he put on no airs and remained natural, despite the respect and honor they gave to him.

I slipped away from the noise and bustle of training, going a short distance into the woods. As I walked, two Tigri slipped from the shadows to flank me. Guarding, protecting, and leading me, it seemed. The trees dripped moisture from the swampy air. Though it was not as bad here as in other locations. The rich scent of damp and disturbed earth tickled my nose, no longer mucky or swampy but a rich earthy fragrance.

About half a mile from our encampment I came to a small glade, empty except for a single large tree stump perfectly shaped for a seat. A thick cushion of light green moss covered the lower part of the stump, while the other half rose in a semicircle at the perfect height and incline for a comfortable chair.

Even as I settled down to enjoy the quiet setting, my mind became busy. Conflicting thoughts whirled through my head, nearly making me dizzy.

How could I hope to train and lead men and youth into a war we were hardly likely to win? With the forester's help we might stand a chance at winning a few isolated skirmishes, indeed we had won some isolated instances but we had never faced the full might of the Reaver, nor his undead army. Even choosing our own battleground and having a prime defensive location would be no guarantee of success, even temporarily.

I shook my head, focusing on the ground near the stump. A small white flower blossomed there. The flower was a bare three inches in height, rooted in a tiny crack on the stump's side. It was a tri-petal and was also tri-leaved. The flower rested exactly upon the rich green leaf, with the flower petals being slightly offset to the plant's single tri-whorled leaf. Delicate, fragile, yet also adaptable and determined enough to survive in a tiny crack. The flower seemed almost to turn to face me, growing and thriving in a near impossible location.

Leaning back, feeling reassured by the presence of the flower, I drifted into a light slumber.

Light swirled around me, comforting and assuring. To the right side, out of my line of sight, I heard voices talking one hard and cruel sounding and the other softer, with a hint of kindness.

"You've hauled her out of her time to this, and now you expect her to continue guided by nebulous prophecies" said voice one, hard cruelty shimmering through the tone.

"If she remains faithful she can topple your plan, it only requires standing firm." The second, softer and gentler voice responded.

"Bah" snapped the first voice "you always bring your servants to this point, and then abandon them to my blades. She will fall as the others fell and my servants will rule this world forever. You will fail, you and your wimpy light." The voice laughed a harsh grating laugh. Then a cold wind whirled around me for an instant, and it was gone.

The second voice spoke, now close to me but still out of sight. "Remain strong. Child, you will return and remember what has taken place here.

You will need the skills of the now for your future. Do not doubt child." The light grew brighter, then dimmed again.

Now I was gazing down into an audience hall of some type. A large throne, crafted from black stone, dominated the end of the hall. Kneeling before the throne, in an attitude of submission were four figures. Two were children, a boy and a girl, and the other two were adults, a man and a woman. The wrists of all four were bound with chains, nearly as black as the throne. Tapestries covered the walls behind the throne, crafted in dark colours with a predominance of crimson; they depicted scenes of violence and bloodshed. The single carpet before the throne was in crimson and black.

The central curtain lifted, and the Reaver swept into the room. Before him the four captives cringed, trembling. The girl child began sobbing, and all crouched closer to the floor. Two men now stepped from the shadows, or at least they appeared to be men. Dressed in black armour, and black helms with only a narrow slit to see through, they looked like animated armour.

The Reaver's hand jerked, indicating the woman. One of the armoured figures grabbed her. Pulling her to her feet, the armour clad figure thrust her before the Reaver.

"So woman," the Reaver said, his tone expressionless. "What do you know of the escaped party, they rode through your farm."

"I know nothing of them, sir" the woman said, breathless and gasping. "We saw the tracks in the field of five horsemen and that was it. Twas only the next day when your men arrived we suspected something was off and by then we could learn naught."

"What pray did my men do while they were on your farm, and why did only one of my men return from the swamp?"

"I dunno sir" The woman's trembling was violent. "Believe me I do not know." She collapsed sobbing on the floor.

The man stepped forward without being bidden "We only know that horsemen cut through our property and entered the swamp. They did not return over our land. Your men entered our land and then the swamp, and one returned. Then we were hauled here. Why?"

The Reaver snapped his fingers, and the four captives were hustled to the side of the audience chamber. Evean now strode slowly forward. A fresh scar ran down his neck, from his chin to his collarbone, marking a line straight through the collar he still wore.

"Tell me, servant" The Reaver said, leaning languidly back on the throne. "What happened to those twenty acolytes you took? Their souls have not come to be restored to my army, which is what should happen within a few hours considering their bondage. Tell me again of your experience."

Evean gulped noticeable, then spoke, the confidant swagger gone from his manner and voice. "On finding the one we pursued we found a location and set a trap. The trap was detected due to the presence of Tigri. On the encounter unfolding I used my power against her and was hurled back. I then commanded the acolytes to step out, figuring she'd attack them while I tried a different tactic. Instead of attacking them, as the darkness built around them, she sent some type of Light. It hurled me to the ground and left this scar. When I awoke, none were near but my horse was at my side. The party I encountered was eight strong."

Leaning forward the Reaver touched the collar with a finger of darkness, and then snatched it from Evean's neck. "Fool," He said, spittle flying as he glared at Evean. "She broke your collar, and likely the collar of every acolyte present. Without the collars they are no longer bound. Twenty souls lost thanks to your foolishness."

Evean staggered backward, cringing, the whites of his eyes shining pale against his tanned skin. "I live only to serve you" he said, tumbling onto his butt from the bottom step.

"And in death you can serve me just as well. Tell me," the Reaver paused, measuring his words and watching Evean squirm. "Why should I let you live?"

"I hate that girl and all who stand with her" fire crept back into Evean's voice, anger and malice dripping through tone and action. "She humiliated me the day we met, and never ceased to show me up at the school. Now she is a traitor and has humiliated and made me nothing again. I will never stop till she falls."

"Good" the Reaver smiled "then we have work to do and souls to summon." As he turned to leave, the Reaver paused glancing again at the four trembling captives. "Guards, send these four to the slave pens. I have no other use for the fools." As the captives were dragged away, the men in a different direction from the women, the guards laughed. Even the Reaver laughed.

Chapter 32: Training in the Swamp

The vision, if such it was, faded slowly. The clearing was dusk and I could barely make out the trees. The army we would face would not be men or even flesh and blood. Rather, I realized with a chill, it would be souls with no choice but to fight. Gazing at the sky I whispered, "How can flesh and blood stand against spirit animated by malice and rage?" I shook my head, rising I leapt down from the stump. A Tigri slide to my side, and proceeded to guide me back to camp. The camp was quiet, tired out from the day of training, all except the guards were sound asleep.

Funny, none of the guards challenged me as I entered the camp. Sliding as quiet as a shadowy Tigri, I crept past them, and to my tent. Not much of a tent, I realized with a wry smile, merely some cloth stretched over some poles and a pile of fir branches. The central fire was nearby, but not so near as to disturb slumber. Alongside my shelter were those of my friends, Frost was alone since Zoe and Zay were off with Brenan. Ian, John, and Jay were sharing a shelter. Finan was farther away, with his two raider sub-commanders. Lying down on the branches, I stared up at the stars. My mind continued to whirl as I contemplated the Reaver's actions.

The vileness of the darkness was palpable. Only darkness took delight in terrorizing commoners who may or may not know anything. Consigning them to be slaves and captives for who knows how long, if not forever. And then summoning the souls of those he has bound, yet died in his service, so they can continue in servitude forever. Not to mention that the Reaver himself had been summoned into this world through the blood of the innocent.

I drifted into slumber, my thoughts troubled. The morning dawned clear and bright, brighter than any previous morning in the swamps. After breakfast and packing up camp, we headed out. Following the lead of a Tigri, though the raiders grumbled at trusting their safety to a cat, particularly when their horses were led away by a different Tigri. Finan laughed off most of the grumbling, but could not silence the growing unease that crept through the group as we penetrated deeper into the swamps. After a good four hour hike through increasingly mucky, stinky, and unpleasant landscape, we ascended an abrupt hill and found ourselves gazing on a four mile long, and one mile wide dry grassy knoll. The raiders instantly became happier seeing the horses waiting and grazing at the far end of the knoll.

After a swift meal, the traveling party broke into training groups. Every group included people more experienced in certain weapons, who shifted from learning to aiding in instructing those less experienced. Finan soon sauntered over. "The men wonder why we are dividing the skill sets, why not have the groups specialized? One of swordsmen, archers, spearmen, and horsemen, it would be simpler to train."

"It would be simpler perhaps, but would not give the desired impact on the battle field. Having everyone skilled with the bow means that anyone can fire shafts, it is the same with sword, spear, and horse. If one party is defeated we will not have lost our entire body of cavalry, or our entire group of archers. With a blend of skills each party can act in complete independence if needed. At this point we do not know our battle plan, but whatever it is we must still be prepared for all contingencies and all adaptations that may be needed" I said, watching the training around us.

"That makes sense Mayim, and I do not gainsay you. It is that the men were curious, and indeed I wondered as well. Though sometimes I do wonder, you seem to have more battle smarts than 'a lassie ever should' as Ian would say" Finan smiled as he sat down alongside me.

I nodded, leaning back into the grass. "I took advantage of the libraries at the school. Most students did not care for history, only for power and magic. So I was rarely disturbed if they thought I was reading a history book. The history books were also thick enough to hide the thin books on Light, and so enabled me to study Light and battle tactics, while everyone thought I was studying history."

Finan chuckled, leaning back alongside me. As I watched the training, I noticed Jay staring over at where we were. The intensity of his stare was surprising and it seemed to be directed at Finan. Glancing sidewise I saw that Finan was gazing back just as hard at Jay, almost glaring.

"What is it with you two?" I said, turning to face Finan. "Ever since your rescue Jay has been glaring at you like, well, like a foe not a friend. What is it?"

"I do not really know, but he does not seem to like my being near you, particularly alone. Perhaps he does not remember that you are like an adopted sister to me? Though that is not the relation I would have personally chosen, now that I know you."

Finan rose as he finished, and made a rapid scramble down the hill and back to training. Leaving me to ponder what he meant by "you are like an adopted sister to me, though that is not the relation I would have chosen." What other relation could there be in such a situation? Even if he meant a closer or further relation, like a cousin or wife, my thoughts trailed off. If indeed Finan meant wife, then Jay and he were engaged in invisible battle for the sole reason that each was interested in my hand...

I stopped the thought before its completion. There was no time or place for such thoughts when approaching the battle field. And indeed, there was little hope for such a future anyway. The prophecies had promised that I should hold fast, trust in the light, and remain firm to the end. Yet all the prophecies were dark, and none promised a day for me, only evening with a battle to fight.

I stilled as understanding came. It was a battle that I would not leave alive. That was what the prophecies meant, I ran through them again in my head in order, their similar messages resounding as a death knell to myself and the Reaver.

"Ninth to fall, yet first of all.
A doom is nigh so heed it well.
In darkest hour light draws near,
 remember now your time is here."

I focused on the message. I did not know what the first part meant, ninth to fall yet first. Doom was either mine or the Reavers, or both, the light drew near in my darkness for now I could wield the Light. I focused on the next two prophecies, given at the same time.

"In the time between times the veil grows thin. Between world and world the twining doth dim. From dark unto light the colors do weave. As the one enters in, who this world would reave. Yet even in darkness the light shineth still, as Reaver doth enter, his doom enters too. To face unafraid mid darkness and blood, a maiden of valor, of shield and sword, of courage and light like never before. Enters she now this world of death."

"By these signs you shall know her:
 Faith is her shield when all seems lost,
 Truth is her sword in which she trusts.
Light is her garment, mercy her belt.

When all seems lost she never despairs, and the darkest storm her friend shall bear.
Of her deeds all will speak, from greatest to least. But to you who so ask, she shall never be revealed for this very night her doom is unveiled.
When the Reaver falls her own doom will come. "

I gave a slight smile as I reflected on these prophecies. In Light I had indeed gone beyond any of my predecessors being able to turn the strongest darkness against itself. Yet, the last line of the second confirmed my fears "when the Reaver falls her own doom will come." My heart calmed from its nervous pounding. It was when the Reaver falls that my doom would come. The Reaver would fall, and if his fall meant my death... I let the thought trail off, fingering the clasp of my brooch and scanning the youth. I had promised them that I would protect them even if it cost my life.

My resolve hardened, if I could defeat the Reaver but it cost my life, so be it. Even so, the Light had promised some type of hope "in your own time" and that copper scar was an enigma that I did not understand.

I sighed, shaking off the sadness that had arisen with contemplating the prophecies. My jaw tightened as I surveyed the men and lads, my army, an army fifty strong. And we had to face an enemy with an undead army of unknown strength. It was unfortunate that none of the resources I had studied mentioned how to deal with undead souls singly, let alone an army of them wanting to destroy you.

As the army reconvened after training, I headed down to meet them. Nodding to Frost and Ian, I beckoned those leading the training over.

"Any difficulties or concerns come forward in today's training?" I said.

Frost shook her head, her face red and sweaty. "Sword training went well, Ian's a good teacher and most of them are quick learners."

Similar statements filtered in from the other trainers. "I have one question" Jay said, glaring openly at Finan who had just walked up. "When are we going to give them light training?"

I nodded, smiling broadly now. "That is next on our agenda, and it's going to be interesting."

It was indeed an interesting time. Most showed an aptitude that surprised all of us, Finan particularly. While Ian and John were near prodigies in the speed at which they learned all that I could verbalize of the Light skills. After hours of training and summoning small walls, coating weapons, and sending bolts of pure shimmering light which are perfect for deflecting dark spells from a distance, the army returned to camp. Tired, hungry, and feeling confidant of their skills, the little army was also noisy.

Settling down with a plate of unidentified-fish soup and a small roll of bread I chatted easily with Frost, Ian, John, and Jay. Jay looked concerned, and as he finished his soup he blurted out. "Who is that Finan guy to you Mayim, err I probably shouldn't have said that" he said, turning aside and staring into his empty soup bowl.

"I do not mind Jay, Finan is as a brother to me. His family took me in and trained me when I first arrived in this land. However, if you are thinking of a different type of relationship, I think there is a war to fight first. Personal feelings have little place on the battle field, particularly jealousy" I gave a slight smile.

Jay's face fell, and the blush deepened. Finally after many moments of awkward silence he said. "I guess I should have thought of that. This does seem a rather hopeless battle, but somewhere there has to be hope."

"There is hope, hope in the light, in friends, in fellowship, and in what is right. I am not perfect, and am struggling right now with seeing hope in any of this, let alone a desire to keep fighting." I sighed, and shook my hair out of my eyes. Brushing it back and quickly braiding it to keep it contained. "I am young to lead, and book knowledge of war does not translate into being able to lead a real battle. However, lack of the knowledge of battle does not justify a lack of preparedness. It is time to sharpen our skills as a group."

Frost winked at Jay as she scrambled to her feet. "First spar sword and then light?" she said, doing a slow and deliberate full body stretch.

"I would say swords and then swords and light and then just light" Ian said, joining in the stretching session as the rest of us scrambled to our feet.

I nodded, and after finishing a good stretch we jogged to the sparring field.

As we formed up, facing partners in preparation to spar, Ian suddenly laughed. "We seem to be back down to five, meself, John, Frost, Jay, and Mayim. Who can we get to spar Mayim?"

"Finan would be willing" I said, "He and I trained together daily before heading for the school. You four start and I will be back."

I headed back up the short slope to camp, weaving between simple branch arbours in which the youth and raiders were resting. The normal raider tents were not set up, as they would be too noticeable in the low swamp, and keeping a low profile was the priority. I soon located Finan, who was sparring Light with his two second-in commands. Light gleamed over their swords as they cut and hacked at each other. Finan easily held his own against both attackers. Leaping between their charges, spinning out of the way of their strikes and parrying their lunges and jabs. Finally, breathing heavily the three separated and stopped. Leaning on their blades, the two captains had broad grins plastered on their faces. Finan turned, as one of them gave a slight nod in my direction.

"Mayim, what brings you here?" Finan said, sheathing his sword and rolling his shoulders.

"I was wondering if you wanted to spar, though it looks like you have already had a good practice today" I smiled, "Ian, Jay, Frost, and John are down sparring and as I did not have a partner I thought you might be interested."

"I would be happy to, and these two can take each other on. Today's spar was the closest they've come to beating me and that was still a mile away. I need to keep on my toes to stay ahead of them" Finan laughed.

When we got back within sight of the other four's sparring I paused, watching them. Frost relied greatly on light shields, though her attacks were swift and skilled. Ian fought as before, swift and cunning with the sword. John had gained greatly in sword skill, though his blocking needed work. Jay's use of sword and light was almost flawless. The only flaw was that his light would flicker and dim if his concentration wavered.

Turning to Finan I raised my eyebrows, laying my hand on the hilt of my sword. The armour I wore gleaming with its own light, bright even in daylight. Finan return my smile, and drew his sword.

"Just like when we'd train together before leaving, eh Mayim."

"Aye, now let's see if you can still beat me" I laughed, dropping into a ready stance. Sword up, legs spread, knees slightly bent and with a slight lean forward.

Finan nodded, dropping into the same stance, though slightly off since we were still on the hill. A moment later, he attacked. Feinting at my head, he dropped the blade swinging a sharp cut toward my legs. Jumping over his blade, I caught the side swipe, and pulled back into a thrust at his chest. Leaping back, he tried a quick combination of feints and slices, each of which I parried rapidly. Spinning aside, I leapt over a low log, and dogged to the right.

On the attack now, I charged in. Throwing a quick left thrust, I spun and followed it with a right slice and center feint. Evading his counter I continued throwing a barrage of cuts and slices. Suddenly a bolt of light shot sidewise at me, I rolled under it. I responded with a web of Light, which Finan narrowly evaded. With the addition of Light the heat of our spar rapidly increased. Each of us narrowly dodging what the other threw. Light blossomed over my blade and my armour, causing Finan to wince as the brilliance increased to blinding brightness.

Chapter 33: Undead Encounter

I froze, dropping the Light and raising my left hand to pause Finan before he tried to continue sparring. "Everyone to their positions, as we discussed this morning" I said, my voice low but carrying clearing to those who had gathered to watch our heated spar.

I ran back toward camp, dropping into my position in the center of the hill, behind a low clump of prickly bushes. Swift bustle had greeted my order, and as my little army slide silent to their positions, stillness fell.

I could barely breathe. Oppression had approached and was thick around us. Dead silence hung over the swamp. No sound of bird or insect anywhere nearby made me nervous. Silent and lethal, a Tigri slide alongside me, turning its head it stared into my eyes. A picture flashed in my mind, a small scouting party of priests. The party consisted of two high ranked priests with twenty non-dead, or un-dead, soldiers following them. The priests had detected the Light being used in our spars and were advancing to investigate.

I beckoned Frost to me from her position nearby, "It is a party twenty two strong, scouting for us, two priests and twenty un-dead. They are coming up from the south, where the animals are silent. Tell Jay to be prepared for anything, and to have his command coat their weapons in Light as soon as they engage. Then carry the same message to Finan if the foe have not yet arrived."

Frost nodded then said in a low tone, "we don't really know how to fight the un-dead do we? I guess this is our chance to figure it out on a small party instead of in a giant battle." As she slipped away to the left to speak with Jay, I gave a humorless smile. If we survived this small battle we would have an advantage. But, first we had to survive.

Today we would face, with half trained men and lads, a group of fighters the Reaver considered undefeatable. I inhaled deeply, a light breeze caressing my face. We would see. Life has more power than death even as Light has more power than Darkness.

A few minutes passed, and soon hints of movement could be seen on the swampland. Hidden among the bushes, and behind the larger rocks, not one member of my command moved. Keeping my breathing light, I watched focusing on the slight movement I could see in the swampland. The movement drew steadily nearer, until I could see individual uniforms. One dark blue and a medium blue robe were leading the band of twenty muddy, green clad figures. The figures moved slower than the priests, and seemed to jerk and pause at random times.

The priests were together ahead of their men, and seemed to be in deep conversation. Paying no attention to their surroundings and being a good thirty meters ahead of their men, the priests walked right into the arms of Finan and Jay. With no time to respond, and less time to register what happened, the priests were our prisoners. But the green clad figures marched on. Seeming to follow a pre-set trail, they veered abruptly around the hill, skirting our position.

Moving soft and silent, we followed the figures from the dry ground. The figures marched clear around the hill, and then began marching back the way they had come. All would have been well, except that Brenan, Zay and Zoe walked straight into their path.

The three froze, staring at the figures which also froze. Then an eerie howl broke from the foe. Transformed in an instant from mindless walkers to savage hunters, the figures charged for the three. Whipping out my sword, I charged down. "Protectors to me, all others stay hid" I shouted, throwing out a Prophet's shield around Brenan and company, who still seemed frozen in shock.

The first figure reached the shield, and plunged through without being harmed or delayed. I grimaced, the shield would only stop spells, not souls it seemed. Zay, now responding to the danger, pulled out her sword and kindled it with Light. The figures were now all plunging through the shield without being impacted. I ran faster, leaping down the hill. My sword kindling with light, even as Zay spun to parry the attack of the first foe.

Slicing sidewise she hewed off the figure's arm, but it kept coming. Stumbling back a step, Zay plunged the glowing sword through its chest, striking the heart then slicing up to split the head. As her blade struck the heart of the figure, a stream of blackness shot into the sky and it collapsed defeated.

"Light your weapons" Zay shouted, slapping Zoe and Brenan as they recovered from the shock of the attack. "Strike for the heart. That is where the darkness resides in them" she added, spinning and thrusting her way into the center of the attackers.

As Brenan and Zoe engaged their charging foes, I reached the rear. Dropping the useless Prophet's Shield, I hurtled forward and began slicing through the chests of the figures. Brenan and Zoe were now fully engaged. Leaping, slashing, and dodging the grasping hands. The four of us fought our way back to back. We paused facing the remaining ten foes.

The foes paused. Waiting it seemed for some signal. Frost and Jay had slid into position to the right of the foe. To the left of the foe, Ian and John crouched hidden in a low gully. A rush of wind whirled around us, and a low howl broke from the surroundings. The foe straitened, each one thrusting out their right arm to take hold of a scarlet sword of pulsating darkness.

"Ignite" I called, dropping into a ready stance and kindling renewed Light upon my blade. The Light was near brilliant enough to blind as Brenan, Zay, and Zoe also kindled their weapons. As the foe prepared to charge I also kindled my armour and stepped forward.

"By what right do you attack servants of the Light Giver?" I said, challenging the force behind these foes. Adjusting my mantle so that the Prophet's brooch could be clearly seen, I paused ready yet waiting. The wind whirled around us again, and one of the foes jerked forward speaking without moving his lips.

"I am the Reaver, fool of a prophetess to challenge me. I shall crush you for none can stand against my weapons."

"Since half of your weapons are extinguished, I don't see how you can truly claim we cannot stand. There is more power in life than in death" I said, glancing at the fallen foes with a sense of nervousness, despite my confidant words.

The foe laughed, a shrill nerve grating sound. Wind blew again, swirling around the bodies of the fallen foe. These twitched, and I froze watching. Darkness, thick enough to sense without trying, swirled around the fallen. Darting through the bodies, the darkness melded the flesh together solidifying twisted bodies, not healed completely, but whole enough to fight.

Un-dead, and rapidly becoming reanimated our foes were bathed in swirling scarlet light. I noticed then that Jay was trying to get my attention, waving and gesturing. He pointed to the scarlet swords and made as if disarming the weapon then catching and using it. I nodded to signal Jay that I understood. If necessary I could twist the Reaver's magic against him, forcing the darkness to fight against itself. But would it be necessary was the real question. Wielding such powerful darkness even against darkness itself was still an unknown risk, one that could prove fatal.

Facing again the twenty foes, Zoe whispered in my ear "This doesn't look too good, what are we going to do?"

I shrugged, and then grinned back at them. "Leave them to me?" I quipped, before charging into the middle of the reanimated foe. Sword and armour both blazed with light as I bulled forward. No war cry heralded my charge, only the firm knowledge that I had to strike before the darkness could finish its work. I glimpsed a surprised look on the faces of my friends as they scrambled to join the charge.

Hurtling forward, well ahead of the others, I struck the swirling darkness around the foe. Dodging the scarlet blades and whirling between the grasping arms. I focused on the cohesiveness in the dark cloud, striking and destroying those spots with the Light. The others had figured out what I was doing and charging into the foe, struck at the darkness.

As I dropped deeper into seeing, and could again see Light and Dark together I detected familiar strings attached to those who had been attacking us. Strings of Darkness like that which had sought to enslave Calanan before I left for the school. Understanding blazed, I knew how to defeat the foe, and how to free them.

Sheathing my sword, I snatched out my Prophet's dagger dodging a blow from one of the foe. Seeing clearly now, I sensed a tiny spark of light in each of the foe attacking us. Light smothered and disguised by the darkness surrounding them, but the light was there.

I screamed as a scarlet blade sliced my shoulder, just stopped by my armour. Spinning sidewise, I lashed out, kicking the foe hard enough to knock him over. Lunging under a head-swipe I slashed through the string that bound the man I had kicked. His sword fizzled out, disappearing as his eyes cleared. Leaping again, I attacked the strings with a vengeance, ignoring the pain in my shoulder. Zoe and Zay reached me a moment later, fighting alongside me as protectors and distraction. Jay and Frost hurtled through the thinning foes to join Zoe and Zay on my flank.

Barely dodging an onrushing foe I shouted "Protect those who have been freed." For as I freed the captives the priests, who had gotten free from their ropes, hurtled darkness to destroy them. Ian, John, and Finan turned to engage the priests and moved away from the center. They needn't have worried, as four of the raiders charged down on the priests with kindled blades.

Tripping over a low hummock of ground and tumbling head over heels, I managed to cut the string binding a foe who had rushed past me to attack Frost. The last two foes standing charged forward, blades pointed at my chest.

The earlier sword strike had damaged my armour, cutting a short distance into the upper edge. I had no place to dodge to evade the onrushing foe. Grabbing the darkness of the swords with my mind, I wrenched them to the side, directing the raw power against the last of the controlling darkness. The two blades dissipated into the air, and I dove between the two foes. As they stumbled, I slashed both strings. They parted with a flash of blinding light.

Silence filled the clearing. On the ground were six dead, two women and four men who had attacked us under control. Sprawled on the ground, or standing staring at us in bewilderment were the other fourteen victims

I swayed and would have collapsed had Finan not come up at that moment. "Frost, we need herbs here Mayim has a serious cut" he called, worry tingeing his tone. I pushed myself up, weakening from blood loss and now hard pressed to stand as the adrenaline faded.

"Some of those freed also need tending" I protested.

"Aye" Frost agreed, busying herself with cleaning and stitching my wound. I winced as the needle pricked my skin, thankful that the wound was partially numb. After Frost had smeared a paste of yarrow, hawthorn, and cottonwood balsam over my wound, she applied a light bandage to prevent fresh bleeding, and moved on to tend the others who were injured. Two of the raiders had also come to join in the healing efforts.

Four of the remaining freed individuals were those who had sustained severe injuries earlier. The makeshift binding the darkness had done had unravelled, though free they now lay dying near where I was. Ignoring the pain in my shoulder, I inched over to the dying, and took the hand of one, a lad near my own age.

Gazing at me for a moment, the lad gave a faint smile. "Thank you" he said, his voice just above a whisper. "You have given us freedom." He paused, his breathing growing more laboured. "And freed our souls from captivity to darkness" his head dropped back against the ground. Gasping now and labouring for every breath he said again "given as sacrifices our souls were bound, though pure, you have freed us from this bondage and for that I thank you Prophetess and bid you farewell." He exhaled again, and never inhaled. At the same moment the other three alongside him also exhaled and did not inhale.

I sat back, stunned. Souls, stolen at birth, resurrected to serve the Reaver without choice. Yet these souls were still able to be freed. I started as I realized that I was still resting where my sight was able to view Light and Dark simultaneously, I looked over to the remaining ten who had been freed. Light was blazing around them, from within their own souls. The darkness had not managed to corrupt those involuntarily bound, it was only those who voluntarily bound themselves to darkness whom it could corrupt and destroy.

The remaining ten were surrounded by the strongest Light I had yet seen. Light that blazed and wove around them, while they lay or sat on the ground. Slowly the light dimmed, shifting into swirls of color with splashes of gold, and then dimming out to plain internal light. The ten straightened up, looking around as they did so.

Chapter 34: Decisions in the Making

Finan came to me and knelt at my side. "Mayim, what is going on? How were they freed?"

"Remember what happened to Calanan the night before he and Calawen left? It was the same thread with these captives. I had dropped deep, deeper than before, into the realm where Light and Dark rage against each other. Each of the souls had a gleam of light remaining. But that Light was bound around by the darkness enslaving them. However darkness could not destroy the Light, because they had been bound involuntarily to its service. When the strings of darkness were cut, their Light was freed and they will no longer fight against us."

"Is there a way other light wielders could free them as well?" Finan said, helping me to scramble to my feet. "If the darkness can always reanimate the captives we will fight a losing battle. If we can steal the captives" he paused, a grim smile flickering on his face "then, we just might win."

I nodded, heading over toward where Brenan was seated on a stump, getting his shoulder bandaged by Zay and Zoe. I hadn't seen the two priests since the raiders charged upon them, they were either dead or fled. Either way, with the Tigri still near, they would not make it back to report our location.

Brenan grimaced as we drew up. "I thought I was hardy enough in a fight, but this was like no fight I had ever witnessed. It seems our injuries match. Though I have a more important question, what did you do to change the tide?"

"This bondage was the same as what they tried to do with Calanan" I responded, leaning forward to have a look at the injury. "That's a nasty slash, Zoe is doing a fair job of stitching though." I smiled at Zoe before continuing. "It was the darkness in a threadlike form that was binding them. The darkness could not hold when struck with the Light."

Brenan nodded, wincing as Zoe tied off her stitching. "There, shoulder patched and should heal as good as it was before. Twill scar, but that is to be expected. The underlying cut was not that deep, so should heal without an issue. There are others wounded, so we will attend them and leave you to your report Brenan." Zoe chuckled at Brenan's amazed look, as Zoe led the others off to tend to the newly freed people.

"My report" Brenan grumbled, "After fighting a crazy battle and being wounded those young whips go off and tell me to make my report. Though they are good fighters, two of the best Light wielders I have seen" He added, turning to face me again.

"It took a bit of convincing to get through to the leader of the Brachite Foresters. We had an easy time of it, when found. Some of the foresters recognized me and knew that Calanan and Calawen were among the forester's families. Getting an audience with Taug, their leader, was much more difficult. For the first, no one really knew where he was, and second of all, due to the hatred the priests have for Taug he grants audiences only to those whom he knows. Thankfully, at least as far as we were concerned, our patrol got attacked by a small band of soldiers and two priests. The priests immobilized everyone, except Zay and Zoe who were able to somehow prevent the immobilization. The two of them proceeded to take on the entire patrol single handily, and it was a light-show of an experience." He smiled and shook his head. "I am glad I accepted those two lassies now, they're nearly as good as you Mayim."

"What happened?" Finan said, leaning in close to his father. I leaned forward as well. Zay and Zoe were skilled in the light and able to identify and twist the darkness. It sounded like their training had paid off and that I was right to send them with Brenan on a diplomatic mission.

"Well, first they drew and coated their weapons with Light. At the same time their armour began to blaze, and even mine lit up and burned off the darkness, so that I could join in the fight. But by the time I'd oriented myself those two gals had disarmed and disabled the soldiers and slain the priests. The priests stood no chance. As their darkness recoiled from the light it coiled around them and ended up destroying them in an effort to spend its strength."

Brenan shook his head and looked me in the eye "The darkness devoured its own when they did not fulfill its desire."

"What happened to the soldiers?" I said, "and how did Zay and Zoe's little demonstration assist you in gaining an audience?"

Brenan smiled again, leaning back and then wincing as his shoulder came in contact with wood. "The soldiers were taken captive, quite bewildered at the turn of events I think. I learned after the attack that every previous one had been successful and destroyed the Foresters captured by the immobilization. This time it was the soldiers who were defeated, and that with only three people able to fight." Brenan chuckled again.

"Taug, sent for us to meet with him as soon as he heard of the attack and positive outcome. He had many questions about how we had the power to resist, and the skills to fight. I explained about you, the Prophetess, and the Light that we bore. He was interested and wanted us to come and train them. I explained to him of the danger facing both you and him. At that point he refused to listen, and so we left and had an amazing supper. It was like we were heroes, which I guess we seemed to be since we had been the first to successfully stand against the priests without falling victim to the immobilization."

"That is an impressive tale" I smiled, "Yet the news of the hour would be Taug's final response, if indeed he gave any."

Brenan nodded and continued. "Taug summoned us the next morning and requested that we bring you for an audience, with all your followers. He gave no other words, except that he would have men waiting to guide us at the edge of the forest."

I nodded, rising and looking over the field where we had battled. Zay and Zoe were just finishing with the last of our former foes. Our own companions had returned to training at Jay's orders. Ian and John were in an argument over sword forms.

I beckoned one of the youth over. "Call those bearing the armour of the Prophet's guards and Finan; we need to have a council. Also, give orders for the men to break camp and prepare to march. While the council assembles I'll need to talk with the freed."

The youth nodded, and jogged off to assemble the council before heading for the training ground, to initiate the breaking of the camp. I headed over to where Zay and Zoe were stretching after working with the wounded of the freed.

A man, gravely scarred but no longer seriously injured, stared at me without speaking. His gaze was steady, not challenging but also not giving any indication of what he was thinking or feeling. Finally he broke the silence. "Greetings prophetess, breaker of bonds, it seems thou hast a question for me."

"Aye a few questions actually. First, how I was the only one able to see and break the darkness, and second is possible for others to break the darkness in some way? Thirdly, what is your name? I would like to know who I am addressing."

"I have no name. I and my companions were the infants that were cast into the flames as being unsuitable for life. We were considered deformed or defective in some way" he sighed "as we were given to death our parents never named us, and we were bound to the service of darkness. We are the unnamed, and on the day the Reaver falls we shall go to where we truly belong. Until that time our souls are bound to this plain and to the Reaver's fate."

"Then I name you as my friend," I said, sadness creeping over me.

"I thank you," he said, maintaining the annoying formal tone to his voice. "As for the darkness, those of us who were bound are able to see it and now to break it. Our lives here cannot last beyond the Reaver's doom for reasons I cannot explain. Unless we act now we'll never have a chance of acting on the mortal plain, or making a difference to others. If it is in your mind to infiltrate the enemy encampment and ranks and free others, we would be pleased to have that duty."

"I would be grateful for you to take that service as well" I said, as Janis came running up. "The others are assembled, and camp is nearly half down." He saluted and turned to scamper off. "Make sure Finan is there for the council as well" I added, before he could leave. He saluted again and dashed off.

As I headed back to where Brenan had regained his seat on the stump, I glanced back. The one I had named my friend rose to his feet and headed to where the other freed nameless had gathered. After a few moments they gathered into ranks and slid into the fog of the swamp. A chill breeze swirled around me as they departed. I shivered, and hurried to join the others for council.

I nodded for Brenan to begin as we settled into a circle.

Chapter 35: March to the Forest

"Taug has asked us to journey to his land so that he can confer with the Prophetess. When Zay, Zoe, and I were there, the only reason we received an audience was due to our defeat of a priest patrol. Normally the priests were successful in wiping out whatever bodies of foresters they encountered, except for this time."

Brenan paused and nodded to Zay to continue for him.

"The fight was weird" Zay began glancing at Zoe for confirmation. "Only Zoe and I retained the ability to move, even Brenan was frozen in place until the light began having an impact on their magic. After the initial attack the fight was easy because the priests didn't expect any resistance. Brenan was summoned to speak with Taug that same evening" she concluded.

"Taug appears protective of his people and unlikely to desire us to remain once he learns of how hard the Reaver is hunting us. However, he may be willing to tell us of a defensible location where we can lure the Reaver.

Though how we can hope to win is beyond me" Brenan shook his head, glancing at me as he finished.

"We will meet and speak with Taug. However, I suspect the reason the spell did not affect Zay and Zoe was because the foresters' patrols are normally male. Thus the spell would target men particularly, and with the benefit of Light endowed armour, Zay and Zoe were unaffected. Brenan might have been affected since he has not used light in battle since gaining his armour, as such it may not have been able to disengage a spell that powerful. The sleep spell we encountered was very weak darkness, while an immobilization spell is medium to powerful depending on the one who casts it."

Slight nods greeted my conclusion. I hesitated and then nodded to Jay.

"We have two suits of armour that are yet un-given and unbound" I said slowly making eye contact with my assembled friends and councillors. "I would that Finan were given one set, as he is one of us and I suspect will end up in the thick of the battle."

Jay nodded, as he went and retrieved the armour. This suit was the most spectacular suit next only to the Prophet's. Kneeling deliberately, Jay girded the armour upon Finan. Rising he placed the sword, dagger, and bow into Finan's hands and said. "We are sworn to protect the Prophetess at all costs, do you accept this charge and will you keep it with your life?"

"I do" Finan said, a determined look on his face. "I will protect her as I would have protected my own sister." The vehemence in Finan's statement caused Jay to draw back in surprise. He did not know of Angusina's fate I realized, I would need to speak with him on the march.

Janis ran up at that point. "Camp is broken and we are ready to march. The Tigri have also come to the edge of the camp, I think they mean to lead us again."

"Then we march" I said, shooting a smile at Janis as I rose and assisted Brenan to his feet.

The Tigri lead us through the swamp, retracing our earlier path and then leading us toward the forest. As we marched, I fell back until I found Jay marching on guard at the rear. As I drew abreast of him I nodded and gave a slight smile.

"Why was Finan so vehement? Do you know?" Jay said, glancing at me as I ducked under a low hanging branch. "I am afraid he is angry at me, though I did not mean to offend."

"It is not you, but the past at which he is angry" I said. Sidestepping a thorn bush and nearly slipping off the trail. After I caught my balance I continued. "On the night I and the Reaver arrived, Finan's sister Angusina, was sacrificed as part of the Reaver's summons. She was a prophetess in her own right, also a second in command, and it was her prophecy that informed the Reaver he would not have everything his own way. Finan beat himself up over her fate for many months, and it seems this stress is reminding him of it. Particularly since he already pledged himself to protect me, and now it seems that the protection will be needed soon."

Jay nodded, glancing ahead to where Finan marched among his men. Those around Finan laughed and chuckled despite the dreary road, and even Finan seemed to have cheered up. From the sounds of it they were cheering up over the thought of battle.

"I am glad he is not mad at me" Jay said finally. "You should be near the front. I will continue to watch the rear." I responded to his concern with a nod, and doubled my pace to regain the front.

After three hours of steady marching, at first through dripping swamp and then slowly into drier territory, we arrived at the edge of the forest. The tree towered over us forming a clear barrier between the marshy scrubland and the forest.

The trees were huge, easily dwarfing any tower we had encountered. The undergrowth was dense, reminiscent of the nearby swamp. However, unlike the swamp the undergrowth was dry and covered in thorns. Brambles flourished, growing up and across the trees. These brambles made it impossible to travel anywhere except on established game trails, and resigned daylight to a dim green haze.

After skirting the edge of the forest for a few miles, we encountered a broad game trail. At this point the Tigri turned, and with low growls darted back to their swamps. We were alone now, waiting at the forest's edge for foresters to appear. At this point the ground was open, leaving us exposed and vulnerable to attack.

"Finan" I called, not caring if my voice would carry. "Have some of your men take sentry positions and get the others to help us set up some type of defensible position."

Finan nodded, and with his two raider sub-captains at his side, got to work. Zay and Zoe got the youth to begin preparing a meal, using the driest wood possible for the fire. Brenan stood watch alone at the entrance to the forest. Any foresters waiting for us would recognize him at least. Ian and John had joined in the cooking endeavours and were teaching the youth more about cooking over open fires. I began moving around the encampment, flexing my injured shoulder and working the travel stiffness out.

Thirty raiders, twenty youth, and nine bearing prophetic armour, with a grand total of barely fifty uninjured men. We are too few to go against the Reaver openly. Yet what hope did we really have? If we sat and did nothing the Raider would grow in strength and increase his undead army. The land would be reduced to slaves and the pockets of Light would be snuffed out. As impossible as a battle would be today, it would be even more impossible tomorrow I realized. Our only hope lay in finding a defensible position and luring the Reaver into attacking it. I sighed, hope indeed. Such a move was little better than suicide.

The evening passed slowly as we waited outside the forest. After a meal the raiders engaged the youth in spars, recommencing their training in sword, bow, and dagger. Due to our exposed position Finan and Jay both negated the suggestion of training with Light as it could draw foes down on us.

After sparring for some time with my friends, I headed to the forest's edge where Brenan still waited, leaving Frost, Zay, and Zoe sparring with Ian, Jay, and John. Finan went back to sparring with his two captains after I left the field.

"Any sign Brenan?" I said, as I approached where he stood guard.

"No sign, nor sound of anything that I can recognize. I know the sounds of my own wood well enough, but this section of the Brachite had sounds that are unknown to me." Brenan shook his head, and continued staring into the forest.

I waited, standing alongside of him. Slowly I tensed. The night sounds faded away. Not even the crickets were chirping. Keeping my voice low and calm I said "Go, get everyone to battle stations we're about to have company. Make sure the fire is banked. In this dark they will be unable to see us. And tell them to keep their heads down."

Brenan nodded, and crouching low headed into the camp. We had set up camp in a slight depression, so if everyone stayed low we would not give our presence away by silhouettes against the night sky. I crouched low, still tense, and laid my ear to the ground. A faint thrumming sounded deep within the earth. It was a large body of cavalry by the sound, coming along the forest's edge. They would be here in five minutes flat. I sighed, woods are more defensible than the plain even if they felt ominous.

Rising I ran low into the camp. "Grab what you can carry, and send the horses off, we're entering the woods now" I called, keeping my voice low.

"What is it" Finan said, running up in a crouch.

"Horsemen, a large body of them" I said, scooping up the deconstructed remains of my tent. "They'll be here in three minutes flat."

Finan slid away, signalling his raiders to draw into the path. We tripped and stumbled as we scurried into the forest. Gritting my teeth I made a snap decision. Extending invisible light I felt for weaknesses in the surrounding brambles, and soon found them. Still moving forward I guided groups of ten through the weaker sections, until we were all in hidden positions along the trail.

After laying down my burden in the position farthest from the forest's edge, I crept back. Ignoring Finan's questions, and the worried whispers of the others as I left. I slipped through the trees and brambles to make my way close to the forest's edge. An oak tree was handy, and I climbed its branches to get a view of our former campsite.

Fourscore horsemen had surrounded the bowl. Three of them had dismounted and were inspecting the ground with torches. One of them straitened and called out "There were fifty or so of 'em, with horses it seems. Some of them are warriors it looks like they had a practice area down here. I don't sense that cursed Light, but that doesn't mean that they aren't the ones we're looking for. The horses were sent back toward the swamp it seems."

"Bah" growled a larger horseman in black armour, "Foresters or that cursed prophetess, they cannot get far. No one, not even foresters braves this section of the Brachite forest at night and survives." His laugh was harsh. He continued "I'd wager when the vines waken they'll be nice and dead ere morning. We've only to wait to hear their screams."

As if cued by his voice, a vine moved. The vine trailed slowly, caressingly over my leg. A thin golden mist began spreading, falling from the vines to the forest's floor. As it touched my nose I felt the urge to sleep nearly overwhelm me. It would have overwhelmed me had my dagger not dug into my thigh of its own accord, breaking the sleepiness with a burst of Light.

Sliding sidewise I jumped to the ground. All around me my companions were succumbing to the pollen. And we were spread out into six parties. I formed a shield of solid light around the group, covering the ground as well as causing the light to arc over them. The active vines draped over it, hiding the light from sight but were unable to penetrate it. They were darkness rather than soul, so the shield would hold until I returned. Leaving them, I ran.

Dashing through the forest, I slashed at the groping vines with my prophet's sword. As soon as I drew the dagger it enlarged to sword-size. As if it knew it was needed. The second group was just falling asleep and the vines had not yet moved. I cast the shield and kept running. The next four groups were the same. The pollen was just causing them to sleep when I arrived and the shield would keep them protected from the vines for the night.

Staggering from exertion, I sprinted to the final group, my side aching from the forest running. As I drew into the clearing I froze. The vines had begun here and there were no people in sight. All I could see was a writhing mass of vines. The Light blasted out from me like a wave of fire, burning through the vines and the darkness controlling them, faster than fire burns through chaff.

As the Light dimmed I winced. It was a fine way to announce to the enemy that I was within the forest and that the vines were not doing their job. I hurried to the nearest body, afraid of what I would find.

It was Finan. The vines had twisted tight around him, cutting off his air supply and preventing him from struggling. A slight touch of Light confirmed that he was alive, and would recover. The others were in better condition than Finan. Possibly because whatever had controlled the vines had targeted Finan first as the senior Light bearer and the only one who could effectually fight them. I formed another shield to protect them and headed back to the roadway.

With my companions deep in slumber, only I could keep watch on the foe. Keeping low I ran back to the forest's edge. Not bothering with climbing trees I waited in the underbrush watching the encamping enemy, the vines avoiding the light pulsing within me. The men were relaxing around a low fire. The sentries were lax on the forest side, probably assuming that no one would brave the vines to attack from the forest's edge. As the night deepened their leader made his appearance.

"The vines will have triumphed and our foes are naught but fertilizer for them" he chuckled darkly. "In the morning we will adventure to find their remains and remove their weapons as proof of their death. When we return with the trophies, we will be richly rewarded." He laughed again and my blood boiled.

Chapter 36: A Challenging Encounter

The pollen was still thick, even close to the forest's edge, and I soon filled my mantle and gathered an extra pile for later. After all, if it works as an air-born sleeping potion, who knows when it could be useful? Lying flat I belly-crawled into their encampment. Taking careful advantage of every inequality of ground I crept close to the campfire. Keeping just out of the light, I waited.

Men tromped around me, careless. They joked and laughed about our supposed demise. It seems they forgot I was a prophetess. Maybe not a prophetess with history and memory, but that did not change what I was now. I realized with a start that the past no longer mattered, what mattered was not who I had been but who I now was.

The camp stilled as the evening progressed. Except for the steady tromp of the sentries' feet, silence and slumber reigned. Their leader slept near the fire, wrapped in his gray cloak. He was a warrior, not a priest, but that changed nothing. Creeping into the dim light of the dying fire, I rose. A vessel of liquid simmered gently over the low flame. It smelled like stew.

Into the stew pot I emptied the contents of my mantle. Every grain of pollen slid into the hot liquid and dissolved. A stick snapped. Dropping down I slid back into the shadows. A sentry stumbled into the low light, glancing around.

"I thought I saw something" he muttered softly before taking a swift taste of stew. He did not make it back to his post. Taking only two steps from the fire he tumbled face first onto the ground, snoring.

My plan was perfect. The pollen was indeed a sleeping agent, and would work when heated. The men would be unlikely to realize it was the stew putting them to sleep. At least they wouldn't realize it before most of them were out of comission. That would leave me only a handful to deal with instead of 80. I smiled grimly and chuckled. They would learn not to take the servants of Light so lightly.

I waited, staying hidden in a low inequality in the ground that was screened by a pile of saddles. As the sentries were changed, those freshly relieved were grabbing bowls of stew. They did not realize that the stew would provide them with a much sounder sleep than normal.

As the dawn broke the leader of the pursuers stirred and woke. Glancing around he beheld his entire company, except the current sentries, stretched out in slumber. "Sentries, wake the men and get them ready to move" he shouted, shooting a nervous glance at the forest.

The sentries could not wake a single man. I nearly laughed as the leader began stalking around kicking the slumbering men, but not a single one woke. One of the awake men headed for the stew and grabbed a bowl for breakfast.

"Funny, the stew is almost gone" he called, before guzzling his portion. Unfortunately he was standing over the fire and his suddenly sleeping form knocked the remaining stew over the fire. It was a good thing the fire had burned itself out. That left four members of the pursuing party awake.

"What is going on?" The leader growled, "One would think we were attacked by the vines" He snapped, turning to face the remaining three sentries. "Bah, search the camp and if you want to eat, you'll have to wait, the stew spilled."

The men scampered around searching the encampment. After a few seconds, one of the men dipped his hand into the stew and snuck away to lick it clean. Another sleeper joined the ranks. Soon the other two sentries had also succumbed to the lure of stew, spilled though it was, leaving only the leader awake and standing.

He was staring at the forest and suddenly turned to address his men. Confounded he stared at the encampment, bathed in sleep. "What in the world is going on" he said "Its witchcraft it is. Now I'm alone and who knows what else is out there."

"Perhaps a prophet?" I said, stepping into full view.

"Who are you? And what have you done with my men?"

"I have done nothing with your men, perhaps you'd like to explain the carnivorous vines to my comrades?"

He stepped back slightly, worry lining his face. "I know nothing of er, carnivorous vines. What does carnivorous mean anyway?"

"Carnivorous means meat eating, like the Tigri. I know you know something of the vines for you and your men were laughing about it last night, for over two hours."

He paused, and then spoke clearly and distinctly. "I don't know who you are, and you don't know who I am. So that means I'd better tell you, before I kill you. I am Chief General of the Priestly Defense Forces. It is my duty to hunt down and kill all who my master deems a threat to society."

I nodded "I expect you wanted me to be impressed sir Chief General of the Priestly Defense Forces, but I am not. I have no intention of letting you defeat me, but I did want to tell you who I am. I am the one you are hunting, the second Prophetess bearing the armour of the Prophet." I dropped my black cloak to expose the emblem emblazoned on my armour.

"Your men should wake around noon from what I gathered from your talk, and how this pollen works in large doses." I added.

The general drew his sword, dropping into a ready stance. "I guess it is time for you to die, woman. I cannot let you escape."

"I doubt it" I said as I drew my own blade and also my dagger. Dropping the cloak to the ground I slid into a ready stance.

 One thing Brenan had mentioned during our last spar was to always attack first. I was not sure if it was the first attacker who was at a disadvantage by showing their hand, or the responder who was put on the defensive from the start.

Taking Brenan's advice, despite my misgivings, I attacked with a swift lung and parry. Dodging his counterstrike, I adapted and struck at his unprotected side with my dagger. He twisted away, swinging a backhanded blow at my head. Dodging the strike, I jumped back on guard. The blows fell swift, and I had little time to parry let alone attack. Falling back across the encampment I suddenly stumbled over a sleeping soldier.

The General swept forward, striking a killing blow at my head. The fight slowed as my thoughts crystalized. If I moved the solder under me would die, if I didn't I would die. Unless…

I acted without thought blasting a ball of Light strait into the general's face. Temporarily blinded he staggered back. Tripping over one of his men, he landed flat on his backside. His sword tumbled out of his grasp on impact. I rose, grasping my sword firmly and advanced to face the unarmed general.

"I guess my fight is over then" he spat, "go ahead and kill me. That's all you Light wielders do anyway. That or torture."

I faced him, my anger building under his accusing glare. "Your accusations are unfounded. When was the last time you were at the mercy of a light wielder, excepting myself? When was a captive in the hands of the priests treated with respect or decency, even if the suspicion they were arrested on was unfounded?" I paused struggling to control my anger and the urge to slap him.

"I came to talk, and this was the only way I could think of to speak with you one on one. The Light is not given for destruction but for building up and defending. I could not harm you with the Light if I wanted to" I shook my head before continuing.

"You were sent to make sure we died at the forest's edge, in the vines or by your hand, correct?"

He nodded, confusion flickering over his face.

"Return to your master and inform them that we were indeed driven within the forest's edge in the evening glooming. When you adventured in you found we had taken stations along the trail, divided into groups of ten. All were slain. If you are asked for greater proof"

I carefully unfastened the dagger that came with my armour and tossed it on the ground. "Take that dagger and say it was born by one bearing the sign of the prophet's shield, but no other part of the equipage around could be taken, including a brooch and short sword."

Interrupting me, he said "So you are releasing me, expecting me to carry a lie to my superiors and tell them you are all dead. Why? And how do you know that I will carry the message true and not tell them that you live?"

"To tell them that I live would be to slay yourself and your men" I said, glancing around the camp. "You do not strike me as the kind of man who would do such a deed, even if you would carry out your orders without question. Also, I have a simple plan which needs the Reaver to believe I am slain."

He hesitated and then nodded. "You read men well prophetess. I would not have my men harmed, and if it will protect them I will assist you for their sake." He paused again before adding, "What you say rings true. If you were a priest you'd have placed poison in the stew not turned it into a sleeping potion" He smiled now, relaxing as he realized that I did not mean him harm.

"The Reaver's next target will be the foresters. I had a vision when watching your encampment, of a location in the mountains. It is a narrow and highly defensible valley with a small village at the end. In this village are all the forester's women and children. The valley itself" I stared into his eyes for a second, "contains two armies. A blue clad army of priests takes the lower end, far from the village. Close to the village lies a smaller army of green and brown clad foresters. In the front of the forester's ranks are nine figures clad in black. In the intervening ground between armies are two combatants, the Reaver and myself."

The general stiffened, "are you saying that you will face the Reaver in single combat?"

I nodded, "It is the only way to prevent more bloodshed and to ease the suffering from the people. At this point the valley is unknown to the foresters. I need you to instigate the invasion and prepare for it."

"That will only take two weeks, plus a day or two of travel time" the general hesitated.

"Two weeks will be enough time. I ask for no more. However, if the Reaver has any idea that I am alive, he will push for it to be sooner rather than later. That is why he must think I am dead." I was turning away when another thought occurred to me. "One more thing, when I reveal myself you must not be near the Reaver or any of his intimate minions. Otherwise you could well be slain as a traitor."

He nodded, "that is astute reasoning, and I should desert the night before. Though that is not behaviour fit for a general." He rose and gave a graceful bow. "Our spar was insightful and our conversation more so. I will support you in this small matter, because you intrigue me. I know you as the prophetess. My name is Todd McKirk and as I have mentioned, general of the priestly forces in Phire."

"I am known as Mayim Donoghue. What is Phire?" I was curious since I'd never heard the name.

"It is the name of the world we live in, Mayim, how do you not know it?"

"That must remain a story for another day. If I succeed in my goal, perhaps one of my friends will recount the tale or a bard will sing of my life here. It is a strange narrative. Suffice to say that I have no memory beyond the day the Reaver arrived which was the same day that I myself awoke in this land. Now I bid you farewell, Todd." I gave a slight bow before turning and walking into the forest.

Chapter 37: Into the Forest

Once out of Todd's sight, I hurried back to where I had shielded the others, leaving Todd unwatched. I trusted that he would be honest. It would do him little good to admit letting me escape. Hopefully the questions I had raised would be enough to encourage him to go with my little plot. Even if that plot had less chance of success than the chance of Todd himself would remaining faithful.

As I passed the mound of pollen, I scooped it into my cloak and fastened it shut. Dropping the Light shield as I approached, I found that the first group was just waking up. "Mayim," Frost called, struggling to her feet, "what happened, what is the time?"

"It is about an hour after dawn, we should be moving deeper into the forest today. I must go wake the others. Get your group onto their feet and have a drink. It will help your head clear."

"I have one crazy headache" Frost replied, beginning to help the others awaken. I smiled and headed off to wake the others. Each group had a similar situation. Pounding headaches and aching limbs, all except Finan.

"I feel like I got squeezed between a rock and a hard place" Finan grumbled. "How in the world did I get all these bruises? What happened last night Mayim?"

"I'll explain once everyone is together" I said, heading off to see how the earlier groups were recovering. It was funny. As the dew dried it dissolved the pollen. Within an hour and a half of dawn there was no trace of the sleep pollen, except for what I had collected.

Hardly had we marched for thirty minutes when a band of Foresters stepped onto our path. The lead forester looked relieved as he recognized Brenan.

"I'm glad you did not reach the forest till dawn" the forester said, bowing to us as he approached. "There is a strange phenomenon in the forest, we have lost men without a trace on this edge."

"Actually" Brenan hesitated and I stepped forward, interrupting him. "We camped outside the forest last night and entered at dawn. I am Mayim, called the Prophetess."

The forester bowed again, "If you will follow, we will lead you to Taug's current location."

I nodded, and we headed off. The foresters wasted no time with talking. Alert as any soldier, they slid through the narrow trails without a sound. Trees towered over us, draped with lichen and moss. Cool and shady, it lacked the dampness of the swamp.

The foresters led us to a small encampment, built among the tree branches. It took two hours from the time we met the foresters, and our pace was swift.

"Brenan will you and the prophetess accompany me?" The forester asked, looking nervous again. "Taug fell ill last night. I only hope he is well enough to see you."

Brenan and I exchanged a quick glance, before following the man into the largest hut in the village. The darkness was palpable. Without thinking I reached out and twisted the darkness against itself, forcing it to withdraw as I advanced. Lying on a low pallet was a man in his mid-fifties. His hair and beard were graying around the edges, and his face was worn and pale from care and sickness.

I glanced around. Darkness had to have a source. My eye fell on a small ornate dagger. "Where did that dagger come from?" I whispered to the forester, still standing alongside me.

"We claimed it from one of the priests your friends slew." The man whispered back.

I nodded. It figures that a priest's weapon would be tainted. It looked like a ceremonial dagger, which would make the darkness stronger.

Taug barely turned his head as we approached. Moaning softly, he said "no visitors, let me rest" his voice degrading into a hoarse cough.

"I can help if you would let me" I said, stepping closer and bending the darkness away so that its hold on him weakened. He tried to shake his head.

My jaw tightened. I had had enough of the stealing ways of darkness. Turning, I walked straight to the dagger. Placing my hand on the hilt, I sent a wave of light washing over it. The darkness retreated, withdrawing its hold on Taug faster than snow melts in boiling water. Within seconds the hut was free of the taint of darkness, and the dagger was cleansed.

Facing Taug, I grimly said "taking the weapons of darkness without proper precaution is dangerous."

He stared at me, shock written over his face. Finally he spoke "The pain is gone, what did you do? How could a mere dagger cause harm to me?"

"It is not the dagger that was the problem, but the darkness that it served and carried. Darkness seeks only to destroy, but the Light enables things to grow and flourish."

Taug nodded, glancing at the forester. "Bring the captains to me, and any of the Prophetess' men that she desires. We must hold council." After the man left, Taug added "any doubts I had concerning you, you have put to rest. I bid you welcome and name you a friend of the Brachite Foresters."

I nodded, and then winked at Brenan. "The other Prophet's guards should be part of our council, Brenan and I can fetch them if you do not mind?" Taug nodded, and I headed to fetch the others.

Taug soon joined the assembled council in the center of the village. The huts, built in trees, were located around a small but grassy meadow. Within this meadow, far enough from the trees to avoid eavesdroppers we held council.

The foresters had twelve captains, each responsible for one section of forest. Alongside Taug, myself, and my eight guards it was a crowded meeting. At first the twelve captains argued about whether we should be permitted to remain in the forest. After Taug shared how he was rescued from the bonds of darkness, some of that resistance dissipated. Finally, tired of their arguing I stood and stepped into the middle of the council.

"I am sure you gentlemen find this debate quite invigorating. However, we have not the time to waste in frivolous debate. At this point the Reaver believes that I am dead. He also believes that you are the last strong bastion of resistance left in this land. For this reason, I believe, he is currently arming an army to destroy you utterly. That army will be here in less than two weeks. What will you do about it?"

Silence fell, the argumentative men staring at me in shock. After a few moments of silence, Taug spoke. "What would you have us do? I feel that you have a plan and it is probably a good one. Any objections to the Prophetess speaking?" Taug asked, glaring at his men. None of them dared say a word. Taug nodded for me to begin.

"My plan is simple. North of us, at the edge of the mountains is a narrow valley. It ends in a wide open meadow with plenty of fodder and clean water, there is also a route out of the valley deeper into the mountains. In this valley we must move all non-combatants, women with children, children, and the elderly. Those who can fight must be trained and drilled to fight as an army, not as skirmishers or guerrilla fighters."

I paused glancing around the council. My own friends listened with rapt attention, while the twelve captains seemed bored though Taug was watching me intently. "Our army will wait at the mouth of the valley, where we have prepared traps and defenses, for the Reaver's forces to arrive. When they do, I have one final trick up my sleeve that should win us a nearly bloodless victory." I nodded and returned to my seat.

"That is all well and good, at least in theory. But what happens if the Reaver burns the forest? Or if your final trick fails?" snapped one of the twelve, a blond haired woman.

Taug spoke "The prophetess speaks well, and you would do well to listen. If the Reaver burns the forest, our scattered people would have no hope anyway. This way there is some hope for the non-combatants, and even those in the army if the day turns ill. I know the valley of which Mayim speaks, and it is well disguised. Those who do not know it would think it simply a waterfall from the heights. They do not know that the waterfall hides the entrance to the valley."

I rose again, waiting till I had everyone's attention. "We can train all the foresters in Light skills, which will help us against any Verat or other twisted creation they throw at us. I have infiltrators in the enemies encampment, so hopefully we shall face none of the undead."

"Undead?" one of the male captains asked, "I thought those were simply a legend from the past"

"A legend no longer" Finan said, "Brenan, Zay, and Zoe nearly fell before their attack on their return from visiting you the first time. It was Mayim who figured out how to break the darkness that bound the undead and free them."

Chapter 38: Preparing for Battle

The next days' went by in a whirl of preparation, training, and taking council. Patrols continued throughout the forest, with greater caution than before. One of my guards accompanied every patrol, just in case the priests decided they needed information and tried to pull a kidnapping.

Three days after our arrival the scouts reported movement on the forest's borders. Slowly the Reaver assembled his army in plain sight of the trees. With scouts constantly patrolling and watching, it was easy to see the numbers we would face. Around forty Verats constantly patrolled the enemy encampment, preventing men from deserting and us from infiltrating.

After four days the makeshift village was set up and ready for occupants. My small band pitched in to help the forester families' move, along with the few animals that they had. During the moving process I ran into Calawen and Calanan again.

"Mayim, I'm so glad you are safe and well. Finan and Brenan stopped in yesterday to help us pack up, it is crazy how much foresters have to move." Calanan babbled, talking nearly incessantly as I assisted Calawen with her unpacking. Finally Calawen spoke.

"I hear from Brenan and Finan that you have a plan for facing the enemy, what is it?"

"I cannot tell" I said, placing a vase gently on the tiny mantle. "It is a chance, and it relies on the enemy general not revealing that I still live. Even if all goes according to plan, I doubt that I shall outlive the battle."

"Don't' say that" Calawen said, staring at me in shock. "You will survive, otherwise how can we learn and grow if you are not here to lead us?"

"My friends know as much as I do," I said, continuing to put items in their places. "They know where to find the knowledge of Light that was lost for generations. They also know how to fight. As for myself, you know that the prophecies spoken when I arrived indicated but one thing"

Calawen paused, and then whispered "when the Reaver falls her own doom will come. What doom is that? I want to stand alongside of you in the battle. There may be nothing that I can do, but I want to stand with you."

"You can stand, if Brenan is willing. I have room for one more guard" I smiled, then headed back to the training field.

Choosing a young forester I squared off for a spar. The youth was swift, but lacked finesse. "Blocking and parrying are as useful as attacking. You must be prepared for both on the field of battle" I said, deftly blocking his attacks. "Do not be afraid to move when fighting, if you cannot win here move the battle to your preferred ground."

Taking my advice he managed to shift the battle to a low hummock of ground, where he would have a height advantage. I smiled, the higher someone climbs the harder they can fall, and the easier it is to knock them down. Charging in and feinting an upward thrust, I deftly swept his legs out from under him. "Well fought, but remember, what you do not expect in battle is deadlier than what you do." I smiled gently before headed over to continue Light training with my friends and guards.

Shortly after I joined them, Calawen approached. Drawing Brenan aside she whispered to him for a while, until Brenan beckoned Jay over. Jay and Calawen disappeared, and soon returned with Calawen decked in the final suit of armor of the Prophet's guards.

I waved Finan over, "Someone should check and see how the traps and other preparations are progressing. We have only another day before the army arrives."

"Should we go together? The other eight can train without us, and we can spar on the way."

I nodded, and we headed through the valley to the place selected for a battle field. Parties of foresters were hard at work, digging, shaping and preparing a multitude of traps and defenses. Across the mouth of the valley, in front of the waterfall, there was a simple breastwork of interlaced trees. The work had added depth, since a large ditch had been constructed in front of it. The front of the breastwork and the ditch were lined with sharpened stakes. Other similar works had also been created before this one. Breastworks of movable branches covered with prickly branches and prickly vines.

Staring at the vines, my distraction idea crystalized. Calling a small group of children to me, and beckoning over a few adults, I began. "If we are attacked before I can get the Reaver's attention, we'll need something to slow them down. Something more than the defenses we currently have, since they can only be held through bloodshed. I think we can set a trap for the foe, that will cause havoc, but not death and I need your assistance to accomplish this."

The children looked interested, while the adults looked exhausted. Inhaling deeply I explained my plan. Slowly smiles grew, and soon we were busy setting the trap. We set the trap at the edge of the forest, and slightly into the field. Hopefully the enemy would attack, spring the trap, and be out of commission for the next twelve hours. A time frame plenty long enough for what was going to happen to happen.

Suddenly a scout sprinted into camp. "They're coming, the army has arrived on the forest's edge." He panted, coming to a stop alongside me.

Taug came hurrying up, "our time is arrived, are you sure your plan will work Prophetess?"

"I have no doubt if that is what you mean Taug. The defenses are well set up, and when I have set the illusion the non-combatants will be safe."

"What happens to the non-combatants if you die or the illusion breaks?" Taug said, worry tinged his tone as he glanced at his wife and infant daughter.

"My friends and guards will hold the illusion, and even without them the Light would not fail for it is not as the dark magic that requires constant effort. For what is right, it needs only to be set in place to endure."

Taug shrugged, heading off to finish securing combatants and non-combatants.

I sighed, everything I had done, all I had learned, was coming to a head. Within two days the Reaver and his army would fill the valley floor, triggering the traps and facing our defenses. Provided Todd had remained faithful the Reaver would not expect me to be alive. And hopefully would accept my challenge, this battle was really between the two of us, the representatives of Light and Darkness.

Chapter 39: The Calm Before The Storm

The night came, quiet and still. No wind stirred the trees. No birds whistled in the dusk. The stillness was complete and oppressive. The scouts were on high alert, watching and waiting near the edge of the forest.

Accompanied by Jay and Finan I moved through the encampment. Finalizing preparation, and hoping we had accounted for all contingencies and possible foes. Light wielders were stationed at every barricade, to protect those who had not yet learned the Light, or who were not yet proficient enough to wield it as protection in battle.

A low exclamation came from the edge of the forest. A few moments later, two scouts approached us dragging with them a man. His uniform was tattered, and blood and bruises marred his face.

"He says he has info for the Prophetess" one of the scouts said, saluting Finan. I was behind one of the barricades, out of the scout's sight."

"However," the other scout added "I don't trust him. I've seen him kill our men. He's the main general of the Reaver's forces. His word cannot be trusted."

I glanced through the barricade. It was indeed Todd and he looked terrible, swaying on his feet, and barely able to stand. I stepped out from behind the barricade, "I am here" walking forward I faced Todd.

He spoke without hesitating. "I've been blamed. The Reaver's plans are failing." He paused, coughing heavily. It looked as if he had been wounded in the chest, or had sustained a severe beating.

"Let him go men, Finan, Jay, and I can handle anything he could throw at us."

The two men hesitated, then released him and hurried back to their scouting. Todd would have fallen, had I not stepped forward and caught him. Darkness threatened to overwhelm me and I suddenly saw the necklace on his neck. A red stone set in silver, exactly the same as the one used to torture and almost slay Brenan. I let go, stepping back before the darkness could touch me.

"Finan, you must remove the necklace with Light. The Reaver is watching through it, and will detect whoever does the removal."

Finan looked surprised, but took Todd's hand in his. Looking at the red stone, his jaw tightened. The light welled within him, and flashed out. Light raced up Todd's arm, through his body, and into the necklace with vengeance. Darkness flashed in return, seeing for a moment Finan's face then disappearing. The necklace shattered, and Todd gasped as the pain released him and his body was restored.

"Crikey" he exclaimed, "I had no idea Light could do that. I thought my life was over and all I could hope for was to carry you word before death won." Straitening up, Todd faced me.

"As I mentioned, I've been blamed for some fortunate delays. These include the undead being freed and disappearing out of the Reaver's reach, many of the Verats being killed or transformed back to men and over half the slaves escaping completely. All that is left for the Reaver to attack with is twenty five Verats, all his priests, and two hundred captives."

"All the undead are gone?" Finan questioned, clearly doubting his own ears.

Todd nodded, smiling as he watched me.

"Remember the undead that attacked us in the swamp when Brenan returned?" I said, glancing at Finan. "Those who were freed went to free those still captive. From the sound of things, they were successful. We may have a chance of success tomorrow. I wonder what the Reaver thinks of your being freed by someone he did not know of, Todd?" I asked, unable to resist the broad smile spreading over my face.

Todd broke in before Finan could reply, "I suspect the Reaver is furious, and probably beating up whoever my successor is. He taunted me that, since the Prophetess was "dead" then no one could hope to free me. One thing it will do is make him more cautious in his attack tomorrow. It may make him more likely to accept a challenge, since he will want to crush any strong Light wielder before an all-out attack happens."

"If he attacks head on, he will find himself in an efficient trap. We've positioned pollen sacks throughout the forest's edge and the first part of the field. They will cause a cloud of sleepiness to descend on whoever breaks them."

Todd nodded as we turned and started heading back up the valley to the encampment. "That reminds me of a question I had" Todd said, glancing at me. "How was it that you were unaffected by the vine's pollen? It is supposed to be impossible to resist."

"I am not sure, maybe I suspected something? The Light may have enabled me to resist as well, my dagger did hit me in the leg and gave me a blast of Light that drove out the sleepiness."

"If it was the Light than Frost, and myself, to say nothing of the other's bearing the armour should have resisted as well" Finan said, as Jay nodded his agreement. "It is more likely to be something to do with you personally. After all, you still have no memory of what happened before the Blood Tor. Maybe it doesn't affect you because you are not of this land?"

I shrugged, conjecture gives spice in life but has little place on the night before a battle. As we entered the valley, I drew ahead, Jay and Finan flanking Todd. He would be recognized, that was certain, and it was best to protect him until we had explained the whole circumstance.

I paused, before we reached the houses. "Todd will be recognized, it were better that we remain out here until the situation can be explained. Jay, would you go and get the rest of the guardians. I would like to discuss our position, before revealing Todd to Taug."

Jay nodded, and sprinted into the encampment. I settled down on the logs that had been set up as a council ring. Todd collapsed on the ground. His ordeal had drained him as much as Brenan's had, though his military training made it harder for Todd to show fatigue.

Soon the others arrived. "Why the meeting Mayim?" Brenan asked as he and Calawen led the others up.

"Just a quick meeting to decide what we must do. You may notice I have not invited Taug since the meeting involves one of his former foes. I would like you all to meet Todd McKirck, earstwhile general of the opposing forces now banished and looking for something constructive to do. Finan did for him what I did for Brenan, namely removing the death collar and reversing the injuries inflicted by the darkness."

"You'd trust the enemy's general?" Frost said, raising her eyebrows, I nodded.

Todd spoke, "I do not ask you to trust me, rather let me prove that I am worthy to be trusted. Mayim demonstrated to me that the Light is different than the Darkness. If that was not enough, that the Reaver desired my death should be. He had bound me to a tree within the forest, but the scouts found me and at my request brought me to the edge of the glade. I did not ask for the Prophetess but rather the Light Wielders, as I did not want my duplicity to be detected. Mayim did well in not freeing me herself, but rather letting Finan do the deed. Finan was seen by the Reaver, Mayim however remains undetected."

Zay spoke "Your story seems plausible, since if it were not true Finan, Mayim, or Jay could discredit you. I think it were best if he were placed in the front line. Let him stand alongside us and prove himself as he has requested." The others nodded their agreement.

"We must remain outside of the village tonight then" Zoe added, "Otherwise we'd have plenty of convincing to do, and there's little enough time for rest."

We settled down to rest at the entrance to the village valley. Lying in the soft grass, alongside the pool with the soothing thunder of the waterfall filling our ears we slept, or attempted to sleep. I could find no rest.

Every potential failure played through my mind. What if the pollen did not incapacitate the enemy army? What if the Verats detected the pollen, or worse were immune to it as I was? What would happen if we were attacked from behind? But my worst fear circled through my head like a vulture. What if the Reaver did not accept my challenge and if he did accept it, what if I failed?

Near dawn I fell into a restless slumber. Voices called in my dream. A women's voice was pleading for her daughter, asking where she was. Dawn's first light silvered the valley, turning the waterfall into a silver veil. The women's voice, from my dream, was so familiar. It caused an ache in my chest. I longed to see that woman, though my mind could not place her.

Chapter 40: The Battle

Drums sounded deep within the forest, drawing slowly nearer. My men, foresters, raiders, and freed acolytes alike, assembled rapidly. Raiders took the first line, spread out with the freed youth and foresters. We had staggered skill sets, so that every barricade had men skilled in a multitude of areas including the Light. Thus no matter what happened, our little army would never be without certain skills. There was no way all our Light wielders could be wiped out in a single attack, since they were too spread out. Hopefully it would also serve to confuse the enemy.

A rustle of wind flowed around us. I took my station close to the waterfall. I had to remain out of sight until the trap took effect. The wind whirled, and through the wind came the first attack. Verats, twenty five in number hurtled down upon us. Bows twanged and spears flashed. The first eight attackers fell, but the rest dropped among our men. Swords, coated in Light, flashed to life and sharp skirmishes soon wiped out the enemy. Only one Verat made it close to the water fall, but it was taken out by a well hurled spear. None of the Verat's got close enough to engage one of the Prophet's guards, or to see that the Prophetess lived.

I gave a grim smile, the Reaver would see that the Light was yet strong. For well we had not utilized shields, the Darkness would have communicated the widespread presence of Light coated weapons. The Reaver would now utilize force, hopefully coming himself.

Stillness came again. I sent out no scouts. It was not worth risking lives to find out about the enemy. We knew they were coming, and there was only one possible way to attack us. The sheer cliffs at our back and sides, and the now dead Verats, made sure of that.

Faint and growing steadily louder, drums sounded in the forest. The army was marching toward us. The only question remaining was, did the Reaver march with them?

"Do you think it will work?" Todd asked, stepping up to my side. The foresters had been hesitant about his change of sides, but they permitted him to remain with us.

"I can only pray to the Light Giver that it does" I said. "It is the only chance we have, at least the only chance that will preserve lives."

"It is a good plan, except that your guards are unaware of your plan once the enemy is sleeping" Finan said. He walked up behind me, and I saw that all my guards were now assembled. Zoe and Zay stood alongside Ian and Jay, Frost had her hand on John's arm. All were in full battle gear, and all looked grim. Brenan and Calawen walked up to flank Finan and myself.

"Whatever happens" Brenan said, "We know the Light Giver has guided you thus far, and will guide you to victory. We trust your leadership."

I nodded, "you are aware of the prophecies that have been spoken, as well as my own strange appearance in this land. Last night I dreamed of a woman's voice, she was calling for her daughter. I am drawn to her, and I do not understand why. I want to go to her, yet am bound here to fight. I may die in the battle today and I want you to understand something." I turned and faced them, staring into the eyes of my friends, comrades and protectors.

"I already bear one scar that should have brought death. I feel today's battle will not end in death, though the life it brings may not be visible to you. I feel there is hope if single combat works" I hesitated, unsure of how to express my feelings.

The others smiled, still nervous. A shout arose, the enemy had been sighted.

The enemy, from what I could see was composed of priests and acolytes. Many of them were lads that should not have to fight. Faint, in the rear of the army, I could feel the encroaching darkness. The very forest seemed to shrivel at its presence. The Reaver had accompanied his army, cloaked in Darkness, hidden by fear. Even at this distance the Darkness was palpable, causing the foresters and raiders alike to tremble.

A shout rang from the foe, and they charged into the field. As they rushed toward the barricades, a yellow cloud rose around them. The shouts dissipated and feet stumbled. Within minutes the entire army of the Reaver was sprawled unconscious and sleeping.

"Fall back, and carry back the barricades" I called. With precision my tiny army fell back, carrying their spiked barricades with them. Soon, a wide space, unencumbered by sleeping foes or barricades stretched from the forest's edge nearly to the edge of the valley.

A slight wind dissipated the pollen, and shortly the Reaver himself stepped out of the forest. A handful of priests, of the most powerful kind, stood alongside him. One lesser priest also stood alongside him. I grimaced as I recognized Evean.

I swallowed. The Reaver had nine priests with him, and I had nine guardians. It looked like this battle would be decided between the best of both armies. "Are you prepared to challenge the Darkness my friends?" I said, looking at Finan and the others who flanked me. "The Reaver's remaining force equals our own. Guardians of the Light are we ready for battle?"

"I am ready" Brenan said, smiling grimly "and may the Light triumph over Darkness as it has since the foundation of the world."

We moved to the front, keeping behind the barricades and out of sight. The Reaver was surveying the field where all his men had fallen asleep. Finally he said, his voice a roar, "Show yourself sorcerer, and tell me how you felled an army without bloodshed or engagement."

I nodded to Finan, who stepped out from behind the lead barricade, perfectly calm. "You should ask, but I cannot answer for no power or might of ours felled your army."

"Fight me" The Reaver roared, striding forward into the battle field, his priest's flanking him.

"We would be happy to oblige you in that matter," Finan said. As Finan spoke the others, well cloaked, stepped from behind the other barricades. Only one spot in our line was unfilled, the central most position flanked by Finan and Brenan. "Single combats perhaps? One of our men to each one of yours?"

"We will crush you like insects," the Reaver said, his face twisting into a sneer as he paused his advance. "There are nine of you, so who then will face me, you Little Man?"

Finan's smile crept into his words, "Our leader will face you, Enemy of Light."

I stepped from behind the barricade, and stood a little ahead of Brenan and Finan. "Do you accept the challenge foe of the Light Giver? Or are you a coward as well as a murderer and enslaver of souls?"

The Reaver almost charged forward at my address, but managed to contain himself. "You have no hope against me without the prophetess" he said, "I know she is dead."

"If she were dead" Finan replied, "Then why would we be here?"

As one, the Guardians dropped their cloaks. Their armour blazed like white fire in the sun that had just risen above the hills. Stepping forward another pace, I dropped my own cloak, exposing the Prophet's star and mantle that I bore. "I am the Prophetess of the Light Giver. As His representative and a wielder of His light, I challenge you to battle."

"That pitiful excuse of a General lied to me" the Reaver said, his voice loud enough to shake the trees. "I will destroy you and all your puny Light wielders. Darkness shall rule the world."

The Reaver charged, followed by his priests. I dashed forward, drawing my main sword. I left my Prophet's dagger sheathed against my hip. It is always good to have a surprise weapon. The Guardians broke off, each heading for an individual target. Streaks of darkness filled the air. The Guardians did not bother with shields, knowing that the Light blazing in and through their armour would prevent any Darkness from harming them.

Hardly had these thoughts crossed my mind when I was engaged with the Reaver. Swift as I moved, he was swifter. Fast as I parried, he was faster. I back pedalled, struggling to parry his blows. Retaliation was the farthest thing from my mind.

He smiled, "You can never beat me" he said, his voice sowing doubts within me. I barely dodged an overhand strike. Leaping to the side, I tried to put some distance between us. Darkness swirled around me, blocking out the sight and sound of the other battles.

"My men shall destroy your guardians and your precious friends. They will fall before me as wheat falls before a scythe."

"The Light Giver is greater" I spat back, barely dodging a head strike. A moment later I managed to parry a chest strike as I stumbled backward. Leaping back to regain my footing, I parried and dodged as his attack intensified. I began circling, struggling to keep from going too far back. I did not want the Reaver to get among the foresters. Though with this darkness it was hard to tell which direction was which.

"Your Lord can do nothing against me, you have too many weaknesses. You are unsure, and hesitant. You know you are weak." The Reavers face darkened and the fury of his attacks increased.

Suddenly he spun, the darkness ripping and light shining through for a moment. As abruptly as it had torn, the darkness reasserted itself, enclosing Finan within its shroud.

"Your guardians may have defeated my priests" The Reaver said, enclosing his arm around Finan's throat. "But you will not defeat me." He hurled Finan to the ground and raised his sword for the kill. I was ten feet away.

The Light blazed through me, and I hurled myself forward drawing speed and strength from the Light. I slid across Finan just as the blade plunged down. The sword of darkness ripped into my shoulder, sliding against the inside of the armour before plunging into my chest.

Pain seared through me, and I grasped drawing the Prophet's Dagger from its sheath.

"You are wrong Reaver, the Light Giver's strength is made perfect in weakness. It is no weakness to love." Light blazed through me, hurtling up through the Reaver's sword and consuming it. Freed for a moment, with blood streaming down my chest, I lunged. My dagger changing to a sword, as it plunged into the Reaver's belly. Brighter than the sun, brighter even than a super nova the Light blazed. The darkness was consumed in an instant.

With the destruction of his darkness, the Reaver fell.

I collapsed back as normal daylight appeared. Burning pain consuming me. I couldn't breathe. Finan's face appeared blurry as he leaned over me, his hand pressing at my chest. Barely able to speak, I whispered "I love you Finan, remain in the Light."

Darkness flickered at the edge of my vision and I closed my eyes. Gray surrounded me, shifting to yellow with tinges of green.

Chapter 41: Endings

The pain dissipated and the ground was cool beneath my back. Confused, I opened my eyes. Forest, pine and spruce, met my gaze. I was in a tiny meadow, surrounded by fir, pine, and spruce trees. There was no sign of the battle field, no sign of darkness or the Reaver. I looked down. I no longer wore any armour, no mantle, or dagger. Shifting the neckline of the T-shirt I was wearing I stared at my chest. There, plain as day was a sliver scar less than an inch above the copper toned scar I already had. Clear evidence of two mortal wounds, my brow furrowed. What had happened?

Speaking of mortal wounds, the T-shirt had a long gash in it right where a knife would have to go to create the copper scar. Nearby, a low alter of rough wood caught my eye. I scrambled to my feet, pausing as nearby voices caught my attention.

"Where is she?" came a woman's voice, a man's replied. "I don't know, Mara has been gone for six hours. She's never gone that long."

I started, Mara, not Mayim, was my name? The voices, I realized, were my parents searching for me.

Moving with skill I slid through the forest to where my parents were searching. Embracing them, I shrugged off their concerns, not mentioning the altar or the rip in my shirt. I led the way back to the house to avoid talking as my mind spun with questions. Feeling exhausted, I headed to my room and collapsed on the bed, dropping into instant slumber.

Finan knelt on the battle field, staring at a bare patch of ground. On the ground lay a suit of armour, a mantle, and a dagger. The mantle was stained with blood, as was the armour. Finan's face was expressionless.

He turned to face the other guardians. Brenan and Calawen looked stricken, while the others looked confused. A short distance from them lay the corpse of the Reaver, reduced to a smoldering husk from the force and power of the Light. Finan turned to the others, his voice breaking as he whispered "she said she loved me" he managed to say before he collapsed weeping.

Jay knelt alongside him. "We do not know if she is dead or not, she came from another world or land and could be returned there again. With the Light Giver anything is possible. Do not blame yourself" he paused, and then fell silent at loss for words.

Zay approached, kneeling alongside Finan and sliding her arm around his shoulder. "Finan" she said, "I do not really know you or the relationship you had with Mayim. But there is one thing I know. When you were in danger Mayim changed. She no longer feared the Reaver. She realized and embodied something different. Fear doesn't have to dominate or win, because love casts out fear and there is no room for a spirit of fear within those to whom The Light Giver has given His Light. Her act of love and sacrifice completely removed the bondage of fear upon her, and that enabled the Light to go through her to the Reaver, slaying him."

Finan smiled slightly, "Thank you Zay, your words bring a measure of comfort. Greater comfort perhaps that the last prophecy Mayim encountered that she shared with me." Finan's voice changed, and he chanted the last lines of the last prophecy I had found.

"When the darkness overwhelms
Remember what love o'er comes
Cold the steel, dark the fear
Hold fast though your time is here
In the battle, blood, and mire
Facing death, the need is dire"
Finan continued, "It was through love she overcame, and cast off the fear. We can do no less."

Finan inhaled and rose, "There is much to do to repair the damage the Reaver and his priests have wrought. We do not know when the next prophet will arise. For now, we must do what we can to heal our land."

The guardians exchanged determined glances. Then Jay and Ian smiled, Zay and Zoe nodded, Frost and John began bouncing in place, while Brenan, Calawen, and Finan stepped forward and joined hands with the others.

Together the Guardians headed back to the foresters. After training the captive army in Light they would spread through the land to eradicate darkness wherever they found it. After they restored the Light to common usage, it would be possible to train young and old in the advanced techniques that the tower in the swamp contained.

A faint light hovered over the mantle and armour, cleansing it of the stain and damage of battle. Slowly the armour twisted in the air, shrinking down into a statue that rested on a marble slab that rose from the ground.

In my sleep I smiled, I would miss my friends and guardians. At least I knew they were safe and were not mourning for me without cause.

My alarm blared, jerking me out of the most beautiful dream ever. Rolling out of bed I stretched, grabbing the jeans and sweater I had set out the night before. I had the gift of remembering my life in Phire, and the warning that I would need to remember it. A grim smile flickered across my face, who knew what would happen next?

The End

If you enjoyed this book, please remember to review it on Amazon. Authors, particularly indie authors, rely on your reviews. Feel free to let me know what you think and your honest opinion of this book.

If you would like to connect with the author personally, please visit

http://sarahdalzielmedia.com/inner-circle/

Coming Soon

The Prophet's Trilogy: Book Two

The Prophet's Fire

Home with memory intact, Mara seeks to understand her experiences. In the wilderness with foes hunting for her life, she must decide who to help and which way to run.

Having rescued fugitives, and become one herself Mara is pursued no matter which way she leads them. There is hope for her friends across the sea, but first they have to make it to the shore. With everything seeming hopeless, Mara can only cling to the Light she knew before and follow the instincts of a Prophetess, particularly when her arch enemy from Phire shows up on the scene.

Society is collapsing, and the world ruler no one expects has arisen. Europe is in chaos, the USA is in rebellion, and no one knows what Canada is preparing for. Israel alone has hope, because her ruler has appeared. But according to everyone else he is a deception. Is the Freedom And Equality Lobby (F.A.E.L.) all that it claims to be, and is the One who came to Israel really the enemy that everyone thinks he is?

In the end, who is right can only be decided through war and no one wants to be caught on the front line.

Coming Soon

The Prophet's Trilogy: Book Three

The Prophet's Recompense

After going safely through the dangers recounted in The Prophet's Fire and learning the truth about the Ruler of Israel, Mara finds herself facing a choice. Continue the path she has selected, or attend to a more dangerous path back in the wilds of Canada.

With one friend at her side, Mara leaves the safety of Israel to chart a new path in yet uncharted waters. Language, culture, and other barriers aside, her chances of success are zero. Uncharted waters are ever dangerous. Who is the man she picked up at the side of the road, and why is he so familiar? In a network of hundreds, are all equally faithful or will a traitor ruin everything?

With her biggest challenge yet to be faced, Mara must turn again to her Prophet's instinct and trust even those who society says should not be trusted. With the forces of darkness seeking to array themselves against the One in Israel, His servants in other lands are always in danger. Mobs, demons, and kidnapping are only some of the dangers to which Mara's friends are exposed.

The battle is accelerating, and the end is closer than anyone realizes. When the critical time comes, will Mara flee or remain to face the fire sweeping the nations?

Other Books By Sarah Dalziel

Scottish Kelpie Tales: Book One

The Kelpie and The Fugitive

Robin, a lad just reaching the age of majority, must flee for his life. With his father murdered, no friends, and his life in jeopardy if his laird catches him, Robin must find his own way. After taking service with a neighboring laird, Robin works as a stable hand while training to become a guardsman.

Making both friends and enemies in the castle, thanks to a mysterious black mare who is determined to choose her own master, he must remain alert, and aware.

Insulted men may think that vengeance is sweet, but they know not vengeance's cost. Whether the slight is perceived or real, some men will not halt until their honor is avenged, or they are dead.

There are foes both without and within, and battle could be at the gates before they know it.

A Note on Scottish Kelpies:

The Scottish Kelpie is an animal of traditional myth and legend. Traditionally a Kelpie is a black horse, which dwells within the depths of certain lochs. It is a magical, if threatening creature. The kelpies of Scottish Kelpie Tales also draw on the Celtic legends of the Pookha, a trickster who goes about in the form of a black horse, and can be tamed if bridled by three hairs from his own tail.

Coming Soon

Scottish Kelpie Tales: Book Two

The Kelpie and The Lady

Within the darkened depths of The Kelpie Pool, Aqay stirs restlessly. A call, sounding in the night, has disturbed her slumber and a familiar voice cries out in anger, fear, and helplessness.

Robin's soon to be betrothed bride, the fair daughter of Laird Etheliel, has been kidnapped on her way to the betrothal feast at Robin's castle. By the time the news is known, the robbers are deep within the hills and only Aqay can possibly overtake their swift steeds.

United in desperate enterprise, yet again, Aqay and Robin must follow the robber band alone. But is the band really just robbers, and will Aqay and Robin succeed in their desperate quest?

About "Scottish Kelpie Tales"

Scottish Kelpie Tales follows the adventures, of Aqay the kelpie and Robin, the lad she has chosen for her master. Initially the tales cover Robin's adventures as a lad, and as a young laird.

Later episodes of the tales will follow the lives and adventures of his descendants. From hiding from the invading English, to defending the Kelpies from capture and death, the descendants of Robin face, and survive, many challenges and adventures thanks to Aqay and her loyalty.

But, what will happen when there are no sons to carry the memory, the kelpies are forgotten, and the highlands are being harried?

Made in the USA
San Bernardino, CA
14 January 2016